CHOCTAW CREEK KIDS

MYSTERY OF THE OLD SHACK

MARILYN RATZLAFF
CHRISTOPHER JORDAN, M.D.

OraGen Books

Mystery of the Old Shack
OraGen, LLC
6616 NW 130th
Oklahoma City, OK 73142
(405) 659-0737
OraGenBooks@gmail.com

ISBN: 978-0-9973437-2-4
ISBN: 0-997-3437-2-9

Library of Congress Control Number: 2017914365

ABOUT THIS BOOK

Mystery of the Old Shack is the second book in the R.E.A.L. Book series. The first book *Mystery of the Old Skull* was released in 2016.

R.E.A.L. Books give readers an opportunity to Read and Enjoy the story while learning valuable information at the same time.

Mystery of the Old Shack, is written with a nod to the old Nancy Drew / Hardy Boys books. Embedded within the text are words appearing in **bold print**. These highlighted words refer to topics that are explained in depth by Christopher Jordan, M.D. at the end of the book in the section titled, "Dr. Jordan's Science Notes."

Dr. Jordan's explanations not only make the story more realistic, but also gives the reader solid information and skills to use in their own real life experiences.

PREFACE

The Choctaw Creek Kids are back! Only weeks after Luis Jorge Garcia Morales known as "Louie" to friends and family was rescued from robbers (*in Mystery of the Old Skull*), he and his twin cousins, Jenny and Mac Joulian, find themselves up to their necks in trouble again.

Once more, the past reaches out to touch the lives of the cousins in ways they did not foresee. Louie and his friend, Joe save their classmate Allison Canary's life. Mac's injury threatens his future as a football star and Jenny helps Joe find common ground with his absentee father. Along the way, Jenny finds new love from two unexpected directions and a young woman with a troubled past discovers her family and starts a new life.

The Choctaw Creek Kids are Oklahoma's new answer to the Hardy Boys, Nancy Drew, and the Boy Scout Handbook, all rolled into one! They are today's teens who go to high school, play soccer and football, text their family and friends, and search the Internet for clues to solve the scrapes they find themselves entangled in. Their ill-considered adventures are also the means to introduce real-life skills needed in emergency situations. Words in bold type in the body of the story lead to real medical and scientific information in Dr. Jordan's Science Notes.

Mystery of the Old Shack is the second in the R.E.A.L. Book (Read. Enjoy. And. Learn.) series, a new concept in fiction that pairs exciting adventures of modern-day teens with how-to instruction in dealing with real-life emergencies. A R.E.A.L. Book promises to keep readers entertained while learning important life skills.

CHAPTER ONE

It was nearly 10:00 p.m. when Jennifer Joulian's cell phone rang. She had just changed her ringtone to "Morning Flower" and found it so pleasant that she didn't want it to stop ringing. As a result, she was a little slow to answer. A quick glance at the caller ID told her that it was her cousin Louie calling. Knowing that it would probably be an extended conversation, she closed her laptop and moved from her desk chair to stretch out on her bed which was still made up with the yellow-flowered comforter.

"What took you so long? Were you asleep?" he asked when she finally answered the phone.

"No, you know better than that," she said laughing. "Anyway, why are you calling so late? What do you want?"

"This is so exciting Jen, you've got to hear this. It's just too awesome!"

Jenny sighed and plumped one of the pillows a bit

higher. She was well aware that awesome to a 15-year-old boy didn't always mean awesome to a 16-year-old girl.

"Okay, what's so awesome?"

"Yesterday I saw Joe in the cafeteria. He doesn't usually talk to me since he's a senior and I'm only a sophomore, but he came over and actually sat down at my table. Can you believe it?"

Before Louie could continue, Jenny interrupted. "Joe who? Are you talking about Mac's friend Joe?"

"Yeah, Joe Stillman. You know, the big football player that helped find me when Danny Collie kidnapped me a couple of months ago and locked me in that old shack. Joe's awesome! He told me that he wanted to get together with me maybe this weekend to show me his new . . ."

At the mention of his name, without realizing it, Jenny subconsciously blocked out everything that Louie was saying and turned her thoughts to Joe, the only boy in school who had captured her attention.

"Awesome, huh?" Louie said enthusiastically. "I can't wait! This is just going to be amazing!"

Suddenly Jenny was back in the moment and realized that she hadn't a clue as to what Louie had been talking about. The last word she remembered hearing was "new."

"So Joe has a new one?" she ventured hoping that Louie would say something that would help her put the missing pieces back together.

"Oh yeah, and it's really awesome! I can't even imagine how much that thing cost. Probably a lot."

Jenny was afraid that she would have to admit that she had no idea what Louie had been talking about but decided to try one more time. She rearranged the pillow for the second time, took a deep breath, and calmly asked, "What exactly is Joe planning to do with it?"

"What do you think he's going to do with it?" Louie said not bothering to mask his annoyance at Jenny's lack of enthusiasm. "He's going to look for stuff!"

Jenny was about to lamely ask "What kind of stuff?" but before she could get the words out of her mouth, Louie filled in the blanks.

"He can find tons of cool stuff with a metal detector like that!"

Suddenly Jenny was back on the right page.

"Wow!" she said trying to sound enthusiastic. "Joe has a new metal detector? That's awesome!"

"You should see it, Jen! That thing can locate anything even if it's buried deep in dirt, under rocks, behind walls, anywhere. I can't wait for him to show me how it works. I'll let you know what we find, okay?"

Instead of continuing, his tone and subject abruptly changed. "Well, I guess I'd better shut up. It's getting late and we've got school tomorrow. See you in the morning."

Before she could respond, the call ended. For a moment Jenny's body didn't move, but her mind started to race. 'A metal detector! What are they going to do with that?'

Almost instantly a troubling thought surfaced. 'Oh no! They're going to use that thing to try to find the gold that was supposed to be lost in Choctaw Creek! Why else would super jock Joe Stillman want to hang out with a real nerd like Luis Jorge Garcia Morales! That's got to be it! Joe wants Louie to show him exactly where I found that old skull. That stupid old story almost cost Louie his life. There's zero evidence that Indians carrying gold to start a mission in Texas were hijacked and killed by robbers at Choctaw Creek. Why won't that horrible old legend just die? I can't believe Louie would agree to go back down there.'

Jenny rolled over and sat up on the edge of her bed. The thought of her hero taking advantage of her best friend infuriated her. She bent over, untied her colorful neon pink and lime green athletic shoes, and hurled one shoe at her closet door. As it crashed to the floor, she yelled, "How could you?" at the top of her voice to the absent Joe Stillman before she hurled the other shoe.

The commotion coming from Jenny's room could be heard clearly throughout the house and especially in her twin brother, Mac's room next door.

Almost before the second shoe hit the floor, he was pounding on her door.

"Jenny! What's going on, Jenny?" her tall, athletic twin shouted with obvious concern in his voice. "Are you okay?"

"Yeah, I'm fine," his sister said as she slowly opened her bedroom door. Clearly embarrassed at her outburst, she motioned for him to step inside. "I'm sorry, Mac. I hope I didn't wake you."

"No, you didn't wake me. I was trying to finish my homework before I went to bed. What's with all the yelling and banging?"

Jenny sank back down on her bed as Mac made his way over to sit in her desk chair.

"I'm just so mad at your friend Joe Stillman I could scream!" she began with obvious anger coloring her words.

"I just know that he's going to get Louie in trouble again and I can't stand it! How could he do that?"

Jenny could see Mac's brow furrow and a confused

look appear on his face. "Joe? How is Joe going to get Louie in trouble? This doesn't make any sense at all."

With her signature rush of words, Jenny recited her earlier conversation with Louie, about how excited he was to learn how to work Joe's new metal detector, and how she was sure they would be going back to Choctaw Creek to look for the lost gold. She had just begun her tirade when Mac leaned forward in the chair and began shaking his head side to side.

"No, no, you've got it all wrong, Jen. This isn't even Joe's first metal detector and I really don't think he has any intention of going to the creek. At least he's never mentioned it to me, which I'm sure he would have by now. Joe's hobby is treasure hunting. As far as I know, he hasn't found anything that would really qualify as treasure, but he really likes to look for stuff with his metal detector. He's shown me all kinds of things he's found around here like old horseshoes, rusty harness buckles, and even a few old coins. It's his hobby, Jen, that's all, and I guess he wants to share it with Louie."

Mac stood up, straightened her desk chair, and began to walk to the door. As he passed his twin sister, who hadn't moved from her seat on the bed, he reached out and affectionately thumped her on the arm.

"I'm sure they're not going to the creek to look for gold, Jen, but if it will make you feel any better I'll ask Joe about it tomorrow at football practice, okay?"

Jenny nodded silently as she watched her brother step out of her room.

While Mac's words were somewhat reassuring, Jenny was still unsure about Joe's intentions with his new metal detector. As a result, her concern for Louie's safety caused her to sleep fitfully.

It was still too early for the sun to peek through Jenny's east window when the alarm on her cell phone sounded promptly at 6:02 a.m. Although she was still half asleep Jenny managed to make her way into the bathroom for a quick shower. She was nearly dressed when she heard her mother's voice calling from the foot of the stairs.

"Mac, Jenny, you guys had better hurry and get down here if you want to eat breakfast," Meghan Joulian called from the foot of the stairs. "It's almost 6:30 and you have to be at school in a little over an hour."

Almost before she could finish talking, the twins raced down the stairs and rushed into the kitchen. Mac grabbed two pieces of buttered toast and a large glass of orange juice practically inhaling both before picking up his backpack and darting out the door.

"See you tonight, Mom," the tall blonde teenager shouted as he bolted out the door. "I've really got to hurry or I'm going to be late!"

Trailing behind Mac, Jenny made her way to the counter and picked up a plate near the stove. She scooped a large spoonful of scrambled eggs onto it, picked up a piece of toast, and sat down at her regular place at the table.

"Why is Mac in such a hurry?" Meghan asked as she handed Jenny a glass of orange juice before sliding into her chair at the table.

"All I know," Jenny said between bites, "is that the football team is having some kind of a quick meeting before class. I guess he'll tell us about it later."

Breakfast over, Jenny waved goodbye to her mother and walked outside into the bright Oklahoma sun. A feeling of happiness had replaced the gloom of the night before and she found herself smiling as she tossed her bright yellow backpack into the backseat of her white Ford Focus.

Louie was sitting on the porch steps watching as she pulled into the circle drive in front of his house. Before her car had rolled to a stop, he stood up, and reached for his well-worn camouflage-colored backpack. After pitching it into the backseat of the car, he climbed into the passenger seat and slammed the door.

"Please don't slam the door," Jenny scolded. "You know I hate that. If you keep doing that, it's going to make the door rattle."

"Oh, yeah, sorry about that. I forgot. I guess I just can't wait to get to school today."

Before she put the car in gear, she turned to glance at her cousin. The sunlight was bouncing off the young Argentine-American's shiny auburn hair and he was grinning broadly. Suddenly her cheerful mood vanished.

"Why are you in such a rush to get to school?" she asked, already knowing the answer.

"Because I'll probably get to talk to Joe again. I think he wants to get together this weekend, but I'll find out."

"This is about that metal detector, isn't it?"

"Yeah! I can't wait to see what that thing will do. I think it's really powerful."

"Louie," Jenny said turning to him as she stopped the car at a red light, "I want you to promise me that you and Joe will not go to the creek and look for that gold under any circumstances. Will you give me your word that you won't go down there?"

The young man looked surprised and hesitated before responding.

"I mean it, Louie. I don't care how big and tough Joe is, we nearly lost you down there a few weeks ago. I don't want to go through that again. Will you promise me that you won't go down there? Will you?"

The light turned green before Louie responded, which aggravated Jenny even further.

"Well?" she asked. "Are you going to promise or not?"

Knowing it was hopeless to argue with his best friend, he mumbled, "Yeah, I promise."

"Okay, then I want to hear you say it. Say, 'I won't go to the creek with Joe.' Go on, say it." Jenny's tone left no room for argument.

"Okay, okay. I promise. I promise that I won't go to the creek with Joe to look for the lost gold. Are you happy now?" he asked with a touch of sarcasm in his voice.

Sixteen-year-old Jenny was obviously not happy. She wasn't happy about the metal detector and she wasn't happy with Joe, which upset her even more. Without a word, she pulled into the school parking lot and parked the car. The two teens retrieved their backpacks and walked toward the front door of Choctaw High School in stony silence.

Louie was already waiting at the car five minutes after the final bell had rung, nervously tracing the yellow parking stripe with his right foot. The thought of another confrontation with Jenny over the lost gold at Choctaw creek was so upsetting that if he could have found another ride home, he would have certainly taken it. He looked up just in time to see Jenny striding rapidly toward the car her backpack slung over her left shoulder. And she was smiling. Suddenly he stopped tracing and straightened up to greet her.

"So how was your day?" she asked cheerfully as she opened the rear car door and laid her backpack on the seat. "Mine was awesome!"

Obviously relieved to discover the unpleasantness of the morning ride was gone, Louie dropped his backpack in the back and climbed into the passenger seat.

"Oh, it was okay I guess. Nothing special."

"Did you get a chance to talk to Joe?" Jenny asked.

At the mention of the older boy's name, Louie slumped in his seat and turned to look out the side window.

"No, I didn't see him today. I don't know where he was," Louie said clearly disappointed.

"Oh ....." she started to say something else about Joe but decided against it. "I guess you heard it's supposed to rain this weekend."

"Really?"

Suddenly Louie's demeanor noticeably brightened. "No, I didn't know that. Maybe that's why I didn't see him. I don't think using a metal detector in the rain would work very well, do you?"

"Probably not." Jenny did her best to hide the smile that was threatening to give away her delight that any possibility of searching for gold at the creek this weekend was no longer a possibility. If Louie picked up on his cousin's attitude, there was no indication.

"You know what?" her young passenger asked. "I really don't care. Joe hasn't said anything about going to Choctaw Creek, so I have no idea where he is planning to search. But I can tell you one thing; I don't want to go back down there for a very long time – if ever."

Jenny had just turned into the circle drive in front of

Louie's brightly colored two-story house and was slowing to a stop when her best friend made another announcement.

"Actually, there's something else that I want to explore that's a lot more interesting than that stupid old creek."

Before Jenny could respond, Louie was out of the car, backpack in hand sprinting toward the house. Just as he reached the front door, he turned toward the car.

"See you tomorrow!" he called before he disappeared into the house.

CHAPTER TWO

Jenny was so surprised by Louie's last remark that it took a moment for her to refocus enough to drive home.

'What was he talking about?' she asked herself. 'What could be more interesting than that "stupid old creek" as he put it?' The short drive to the Joulian home was over before she could come up with an answer.

Back in her room, Jenny changed into her favorite pair of faded blue jeans and the red shirt she was wearing the day her seven-year-old cousin, Emma fell down the bank at Choctaw Creek cutting herself on the sharp rocks. Although her shirt had been washed several times, a few of the blood stains were still faintly visible. Fighting the impulse to call Louie, Jenny decided to go downstairs instead and help her mother fix dinner.

Meghan was making homemade chicken salad sandwiches when Jenny entered the kitchen.

"I'm afraid it's just going to be us tonight," she informed her daughter. "Mac called a few minutes ago and said that he wouldn't be home in time for dinner and your father is still at the vet clinic. I think there was some kind of an emergency this afternoon."

"I'm not surprised," Jenny said as she helped herself to one of the sandwiches. "They don't know what they're missing. These sandwiches are great, Mom!"

"Thank you!" her mom replied taking a theatrical bow before she took her place at the table. "That recipe has been handed down from my great-grandmother and I don't think there's any way to improve it."

Jenny was nearly finished with her sandwich when her mother stopped eating and stared at her attractive blonde daughter.

"Isn't that the shirt you were wearing when Emma fell down the bank and got hurt?" she asked. "I'm surprised you still want to wear it."

Jenny laughed. "Why? Just because that little imp bled all over it? I'm glad she's okay, but I'm sure she's probably still mad at me for not letting her borrow that old skull I found at Choctaw Creek for Show-and-Tell at school. I know she's only seven, but that child is impossible."

Before the conversation could continue, Jenny's cell phone rang. Again, she let the phone ring a few times to enjoy her new ringtone. The caller ID showed that it was Louie.

"It's Louie, Mom. I really need to take this," Jenny said as she stood up and pushed her chair back under the table. "I'll see you in a little while, okay?"

Leaving her mother sitting alone at the kitchen table, Jenny accepted the call as she dashed up the stairs and disappeared into her room.

"I'm so glad you called!" she said breathlessly into the phone as she kicked off her athletic shoes and collapsed onto her full-sized bed.

"Couldn't stand it, could you?" Louie teased. "I'm surprised that you haven't called me. You should have seen your face when I told you that I had something more interesting to explore than that old creek. Admit it, you were shocked, weren't you?"

Jenny's enthusiasm instantly turned to irritation which was clearly noticeable in her tone.

"Shocked? I don't think so. Actually, I was annoyed that you'd make a statement like that and then run off with no explanation."

"Oh, come on, Jen. I just wanted to get your attention, that's all. Wait till you hear what I'm planning to explore," the teenager said excitedly. "Are you ready? Wait for it ..."

"I'm not waiting for anything, Louie!" she said emphatically. "Either tell me now or I'm going to hang up. I'm tired and I don't feel like playing stupid games."

Louie's voice was suddenly serious. "Okay, okay, Jen, no games. "Here's what I'm going to do. I want to go back and really explore that old shack where I was imprisoned when I was kidnapped by that crook Danny Collie and his friend Bud. There's some neat stuff in there, Jen. I just know there is, but there wasn't any light, so I couldn't really see anything. If it doesn't rain very much this weekend, I'd really like for you to go with me if you're free Sunday afternoon."

During the conversation, Jenny had propped herself up on her overstuffed pillows and was trying to get comfortable. Her cheery yellow-flowered comforter which matched the wall paint never failed to raise her spirits, but not this time. The seriousness of Louie's proposal canceled any delight she normally would have taken in her room.

"No, you can't Louie; you just can't go back there. You almost died in that old shack. Everyone, including Mr. George, told you not to go back there, remember?"

At the mention of Mr. George, the boy paused. Watson George, Louie's math teacher and Boy Scout leader, had saved his life by rescuing him from the old shack a few weeks ago. He had also warned the young Boy Scout about how dangerous the old building was and told him not to ever go back there.

"Yeah, I know," Louie said halfheartedly shaking off the warning. "But that was before anyone knew about that old shack except Mr. George. Now everyone knows where it is, so there's no way I could be lost in it again. That would be the first place they would look."

For what seemed like an eternity, neither teen spoke. Finally, Louie broke the silence.

"Well, I'm going back there probably Sunday afternoon if it doesn't rain too much. Are you going with me or do I have to go by myself?"

Jenny sighed audibly as she pushed one of the pillows out of the way and sat up on the edge of her bed.

"Please don't go back there, Louie," she pleaded. "I have a horrible feeling something terrible will happen again. I can't imagine anything in that run down old wreck of a shack being worth risking your life for." She paused for a moment before continuing. "Didn't Mr. George make you promise that you wouldn't go back there when you were in the hospital?"

"I have no idea – maybe," the boy laughed. "Maybe not. Remember that big guy beat me so badly that I was out of it for days. I can't remember what I promised anyone, but it doesn't matter. I'm going back either with or without you."

Even though she didn't respond immediately, he knew she was still there listening and probably trying to make up her mind.

Finally, she said, "It's only Tuesday. I'd like to think about it for a few days. I guess you know that going back there makes me very nervous."

"Sorry about that, but I've got to see what's inside that shack. You can't even imagine what it was like to spend an entire night in total darkness not knowing what was in there with me. There could have been a wild animal, a rabid skunk, snakes, or anything in there. I was soaking wet, cold, and in pain from the beating that guy gave me.

"When Mr. George opened the door the next day, it let in just enough light that I could see that there was a lot of stuff packed in there. I just want to see what's in there, that's all. We wouldn't have to stay very long."

Jenny switched the phone to her other hand and said, "It's getting late, Louie. I promise I'll think about it. Okay? I'll see you in the morning." She ended the call before he could respond.

For the next three days, the weather in central Oklahoma couldn't have been better. As it often does in mid-to-late October, the sun shone brightly, highlighting the clear blue sky with not a storm cloud in sight.

Louie had been determined not to say anything about the shack until Jenny mentioned it. But now it was Friday afternoon and the subject had not come up. As the two walked to Jenny's car in the parking lot, the boy decided to hint at the Sunday visit to the shack.

"I saw online this morning that the rain is going to miss us," he began trying his best to be as casual as possible. "It's supposed to be a really nice day on Sunday too, hardly any wind, and about 65 degrees."

Jenny knew exactly where he was going with his weather report, but decided not to comment. Ducking her head so that he couldn't see the smile that was beginning to spread across her face, she opened the back door of her car and carefully set her bright yellow backpack on the seat. Louie literally threw his camouflage-colored backpack into the back and climbed into the passenger seat. Jenny had driven out of the school parking lot and had just turned onto the highway to head home before the boy spoke again.

"Well, I still have my job babysitting Emma tomorrow," he offered. "I was afraid they would fire me after Emma fell down the creek bank and got hurt, but they didn't."

Jenny looked straight ahead at the road. She knew if she were to look at Louie, she wouldn't be able to hide her amusement at his attempts to get her to mention the shack.

"That's great, Louie!" she enthused. "I'm sure Uncle Martin and Aunt Nala have every confidence in you, especially after you were able to use your first aid skills to help stop her bleeding."

"I didn't do all that much," he said quietly looking out the side window. "I wish I had a different job, but they pay me pretty well and I don't have to do all that much. The only thing is, it takes up almost half of my weekend. By the time they get home from work, Saturday is pretty well shot."

Jenny turned into the circle drive in front of the Morales home and stopped the car beside the sidewalk. Before her young passenger opened the door, he turned to his cousin and best friend.

"Since I'm going to be tied up tomorrow," he said with a determined look on his face, "I might as well find out now. What did you decide about going to the shack with me Sunday afternoon?" he asked pointedly. "I'd like to go about 2:00 o'clock and maybe stay for an hour or so – not all that long. So will you go with me or not?"

Still gripping the steering wheel, Jenny turned her head to gaze at the grim-faced boy beside her.

"You know how I feel about that, Louie," she said sternly.

She could see that her response was immediately disappointing to him. His shoulders slumped and he stared at his hands clasped tensely in his lap.

"I think it's dangerous to go back there, and I really think it's a mistake, but there's no way that I'll let you go to that horrible old shack by yourself. So, yes, against my better judgment, I will go with you Sunday afternoon."

Surprised and relieved at her decision to go, Louie suddenly sat up ramrod straight and grinned.

"Thanks, Jenny!" he all but yelled. "I'm so glad that you decided to go with me. It wouldn't be any fun at all without you!"

He bolted out of the car and slammed the door, forgetting Jenny's instructions to close the door gently. Then he retrieved his backpack and proceeded to slam the rear car door as well.

As Louie began to dash toward the front door, Jenny rolled the window down and shouted after him.

"If you keep slamming my car doors, you're going to have to walk to the shack!" she warned.

The young Boy Scout was too excited to pay any attention to Jenny's threat.

"Sorry, see you Sunday!" he called over his shoulder before vanishing into his parents' house.

Jenny had just returned home from soccer practice late Saturday afternoon when her cell phone rang. She was sure it would be Louie before confirming it on the caller ID.

"Hey, Jen," he began the moment she answered. "I've been thinking about what we should take to the shack tomorrow. Have you given that any thought? We probably need to round stuff up tonight to be ready for tomorrow afternoon. What do you think?"

She hadn't given any thought to their trip to the old shack at all, so his questions caught her completely unprepared. Before responding, she walked to her desk chair and sat down.

"Stuff? What kind of stuff are you talking about? Why do we need to take anything? I thought we were just going to look around."

"Oh, no," her cousin protested. "We are, but we always have to take stuff. I'm taking a heavy-duty flashlight, my first aid kit, bug spray, plastic garbage bags, a rope, and of course, my phone. Do you think we should take any tools or maybe a shovel?"

"Tools? A shovel?" Jenny exclaimed. "Seriously? You said that we're just going to look around, so why do we need tools and a shovel?"

"You just don't know when you might need something," he tried to explain. "I always try to be prepared like they teach us in Scouts. Don't you have some kind of a tool kit in the trunk of your car?"

Jenny thought for a minute.

"I think so, but it's not much of one. I haven't checked lately, but the last time I saw it I think there were a couple of screwdrivers, a pair of pliers, and a little adjustable wrench. That's about it."

"Excellent! Then all I'll need to bring is a hammer and my camp shovel." The boy was nearly giddy with excitement. "I think we're all set! Can you pick me up at 2:00 o'clock?"

The sixteen-year-old athlete's reaction to Louie's plans was just the opposite.

"Yeah, sure," she said glumly. "I'll be there."

For a moment after the call ended, Jenny didn't move from her desk chair.

"I can't believe this!" she said shaking her head. "What am I getting myself into?"

Sunday morning dawned clear and bright just like Louie's online weather forecast had predicted. Even though it was nearly Halloween, the temperature was unusually warm for mid-October in Oklahoma.

At 8:30 a.m., Jenny sleepily crawled out of bed and slid her feet into her fuzzy leopard-print house slippers which perfectly matched her pajamas. Before she could go downstairs for breakfast, a strong feeling of dread washed over her. It was so intense that she decided to sit down on the edge of her bed for a minute to try to figure out what was happening to her.

Five minutes later, still sitting on her bed, the only impression that she had been able to come up with seemed to center around the old shack that she and Louie were going to explore later in the afternoon.

'That's crazy,' she chided herself. 'Why would that old shack make me feel like this? I know that Louie could have very easily died in it a few weeks ago, but he didn't. It's nothing. It's just an old wreck of an abandoned shack that nobody has lived in for 50 years. So what's the deal? Why do I feel like this?'

Nothing made any sense. Finally, she decided that she might feel better if she went downstairs to join her parents for breakfast.

Sunlight was streaming through the east windows of the big country kitchen when Jenny entered the kitchen. Her parents, Carson and Meghan Joulian, had finished breakfast and were still talking and drinking coffee at the table.

"Well, look who's here!" her mother teased. "There's some breakfast casserole left in the oven if you're hungry."

Jenny nodded and helped herself to a large serving of the egg and sausage dish before picking up a glass of orange juice and taking her place at the table.

"So what are you and Mac up to today?" her father asked. "I presume he's sleeping in since he hasn't been down here yet. You look a little tired yourself."

Between bites, Jenny acknowledged that she was a little tired. Quickly she realized that she didn't dare mention that she was planning to go to the shack with Louie.

"I have no idea what Mac is planning to do today," she said. "He's probably going to the gym or he might hang out with some of his friends. I really don't know. What are you guys going to do?"

"I've got to go back to the clinic for a little while this afternoon and your mom is going with me," Carson said.

"Yesterday morning a man brought in a yellow Labrador retriever that had been hit by a truck. One of the dog's hind legs was broken in two places and he also had some internal injuries. He was in a lot of pain when his owner brought him in, but I think we got him stabilized enough to pull through. One of the vet techs has been sitting with him, but I want to make sure everything is okay."

An animal lover from an early age, Jenny was always concerned about her father's patients, especially when it was a life and death situation.

"Oh, that poor dog!" she said sadly. "I hope he makes it. It's just so sad that he has to go through this, but at least I know he's in good hands."

"What are you planning to do today, Jenny?" her mother asked.

"Oh, not too much," Jenny said carefully making sure that she was looking down at her plate when she answered. "I've got some reading to do after breakfast and then I promised Louie that I would help him with a project later this afternoon. That's about it."

"Well, have fun," her mother said cheerfully as she stood up from the table to collect the breakfast dishes. "I guess we'll see you later then."

The teen nodded before she drank the last of her orange juice. 'She wouldn't be this happy if she knew that Louie and I were going back to that old shack,' she thought to herself with a twinge of guilt.

Jenny had just returned to her room after breakfast when her cell phone rang. Kicking off her slippers, she climbed back onto the bed before answering.

"Hey, Jen," the excited male voice on the other end of

the line began, "things have changed a little, so I can actually go a little earlier than 2:00 o'clock if you can. I've got everything we need, so I can go anytime that works for you. I just can't wait to see what's really inside that old shack!"

Jenny audibly sighed as the feeling of dread she felt earlier washed over her.

"I'll have to let you know. My parents are going to the vet clinic this afternoon to see how a dog is doing. It got hit by a truck yesterday and it's in pretty bad shape. I probably should wait until they leave."

"Okay, whatever. Just let me know," Louie said. Then after a short pause, "You really don't want to go, do you?"

"No, I don't want to go. The whole thing is just creepy, but I'm going with you anyway."

Before either of them could say anything else, she heard her mother's voice from halfway up the stairs."

"We're off to the clinic, Jen," she called. "See you later."

"They're leaving!" Jenny exclaimed more to herself than to Louie, who was still listening on the phone. "It's not even 10:00 o'clock yet and they're leaving. Oh, no! I hope that doesn't mean the dog is about to die."

"Jenny?" he said after a few seconds of silence. "Can we go now?"

"Yeah, I guess so," she finally mumbled into the phone. "I need to change clothes first. I can probably be there in about 20 minutes."

It only took a few minutes for the tall blonde teenager to find her favorite pair of faded blue jeans and a well-worn blue sweatshirt. Deciding not to wear her good athletic shoes, she dug out an old white pair from the back of her closet. One last sigh and she was ready to go.

Her twin brother, Mac was waiting when she opened her door. He had obviously just gotten out of bed as his golden blonde hair was mussed; he was barefoot and wearing green-and-tan flannel pajama bottoms and a white tee shirt.

"What's going on?" he asked, sleep still coloring his voice. "Where are you going?"

"Louie and I are going to the old shack."

"The old shack?" Mac simply repeated, clearly confused. "Are you talking about that old shack where Mr. George found Louie a few weeks ago? That old shack?" Suddenly Mac was wide awake.

"Yeah, that old shack. It was dark when he was imprisoned there and he just wants a chance to see what's really inside it."

"Awesome! Can I go with you? I want to see inside the old shack, too! I don't think Louie would care if I came with you."

"Don't you have football practice or something?" Jenny asked with a touch of sarcasm in her voice.

"No, not today. I can be ready in two minutes, okay?"

Not waiting for her response, he turned and rushed back into his room.

"I'll be waiting in my car," she called after him, "so you'd better hurry if you want to go with us."

His twin was just ready to start her car when Mac raced up and breathlessly climbed into the passenger seat clutching a protein bar.

"I can't believe that you and Louie are really going back to the old shack!" her twin panted as he fastened his seatbelt. "Didn't his Scout leader, Mr. George tell Louie not to go back there because it was so dangerous?" he asked between bites of his breakfast bar.

"Yeah, but he wants to go anyway. And you know Louie, if he makes up his mind to do something, he'll do it – regardless. I really don't want to go, but I don't want him to go back there by himself, either."

"No," Mac agreed, "he definitely shouldn't go back there by himself."

Louie was standing on the bottom porch step with his bulging camouflage-colored backpack propped up against his leg when Jenny's car pulled up. When he saw that Mac was sitting in the passenger seat, the boy opened the rear door behind Jenny and got in.

"When Jenny told me that you two were going back to the old shack, I wanted to see it too, especially after everything you went through when you were trapped in it," Mac said to his cousin. "I hope you don't mind that I'm going with you and Jenny."

"No problem," the younger boy replied.

The white car turned out of the driveway and drove toward the highway.

"What's the best way to get there, Louie? Should we go back to the pasture and walk through the woods like you did?" Jenny asked.

"No, I think we can get closer than that. Believe it or not, I actually found it on Google Earth last night. If you will go to the bridge over Choctaw Creek and head west for about two miles, we'll be very close. I couldn't tell for sure, but it almost looks like there might be remnants of an old road, too. We'll just have to see when we get there. If not, we can always park and walk."

In a few minutes, Mac spotted the bridge.

"There's the bridge straight ahead!" the blonde football player exclaimed. "Slow down, Jen. You need to turn left at the next intersection. Then we'll have to look for something that resembles an old road or a long driveway."

"Which side of the road is it on?" Jenny asked.

"The old road, if there is one, will be on the left," Louie explained. "It will probably be very overgrown, so we're really going to have to look carefully."

As she neared the two-mile point, Jenny slowed the car to nearly a stop.

"Do you see anything that looks like a road?"

"Not yet," the boys said in near-perfect unison.

"Go on a little further. Maybe we can see it then," Louie suggested.

They had still not seen anything even resembling a path at the three-mile point.

"We've gone too far," Louie said. "Turn around at the next intersection and we'll look for it from this direction."

As they headed back toward the bridge, Mac suddenly shouted.

"Stop, Jen! Look over there! I think I see something that might have been a path or something! Can you see it, Louie? The weeds are a foot high, but I think there's something right over there," the excited teen said pointing to an overgrown field.

"Let's get out and walk," Louie suggested to Mac. Maybe we can see it better on foot."

The two boys climbed out of the car and walked toward the area Mac had indicated.

"You're right, Mac!" Louie exclaimed a few yards into the field. "I see what you're talking about. It's not a road at all; it's only two tires tracks. I don't know how far this goes, but this has got to be it."

Mac walked over to where Louie was standing and looked down at the tracks.

"You're right! This is definitely a path of some kind. Let's try to follow it and see if it leads to the shack. Maybe we can knock down some of these weeds as we walk so that Jen can see to drive if this really goes to the shack. You walk in the left path and I'll take the right one," Mac suggested.

It took the boys almost ten minutes to force their way through the weeds and briars before they stumbled upon what was evidently an old homestead. All that remained was part of a concrete slab and some of the concrete footing that could have been for a house.

As they turned to head back to the car, Louie caught a glimpse of the shack which was nearly obscured by the stand of pine trees surrounding it.

"There it is!" he shouted excitedly pointing to something a few yards away from the concrete remains nearly hidden in the brush and undergrowth. "There's the shack! That's it right over there!"

"Let's go back to the car and see if Jen can drive up here," Mac said breaking into a run back down the path.

When the car came into sight, they could see Jenny standing outside the driver's door staring into the distance.

"We found it! Louie found the shack!" Mac told Jenny while trying to catch his breath.

Louie was trying to determine if her car could safely cross the rough terrain to the shack. Discovering that there wasn't a fence or a deep ditch blocking the way, he decided it was possible for the car to drive down the old path.

"Can you see those tracks?" he asked Jenny pointing to the nearly hidden path. "We tried to knock down some of the weeds, but you'll have to really watch to see them. It doesn't look like anyone has driven over them for a long time. They're not very deep, so your car should be able to make it if you take it slow."

Jenny wasn't sure it was a good idea to drive her car through the sea of weeds, but the boys convinced her that if she would drive slowly and stay on the tracks, the car would make it just fine.

Back in the car, the boys could barely contain their excitement; Jenny could barely contain her fear and misgivings. Inching their way down the ancient path, the trio could hear the weeds scraping against the underside of the car. The roughness of the ride only added to Jenny's gloom. At last, she stopped the car in front of the old concrete slab.

"The shack's over there!" Louie shouted as he bolted out of the car, pointed toward the trees and excitedly took off to force his way through the tangled underbrush.

"What's wrong, Jen?" Mac asked noticing her solemn demeanor as they got out of the car. "Are you worried about your car?"

"No, I'm not worried about my car, Mac; I'm sure the car's fine. I can't explain it, but as soon as we stopped, I just got this weird feeling. Maybe it will go away when we get to the shack."

Her twin walked a few steps in front of her to help her push hrough the fallen branches and brambles instead of running after his cousin, which was his first inclination. Suddenly he stopped at turned around.

"Are you sure you're okay, Jen? he asked. "We really

don't have to go any farther if you don't feel like it."

Jenny shook her head.

"No, it's alright. I really want to see what's inside that old shack, too. It's just that I can't help feeling that there's something terribly, terribly wrong here and it's got to do with that horrible old shack."

CHAPTER THREE

By the time Mac and Jenny had worked their way through the dense foliage to reach the old shack, Louie had already circled it and was standing by the front door.

"So this is the old shack," Jenny said as she approached the old structure, her words halfway between a question and a statement of disbelief. "What a wreck! Look at that! I can't believe it is still standing! Amazing!"

Ignoring her comments, Louie motioned for Mac to join him at the door.

"This is really bizarre. The whole place is about to fall down and someone put a brace like this on the door!" the young Scout remarked as he ran his hand over the heavy 4" x 4" brace.

"Maybe someone put this heavy beam across the door because there's not a door knob or anything to hold it shut," he suggested as he examined the brace.

As the two boys continued to study the brace, Jenny decided to take pictures with her cell phone camera. It occurred to her that it might be important to document everything about the old shack and its surroundings. Forcing her way through the trees and undergrowth, she took pictures of the badly deteriorating and weather-beaten wooden siding of the old shack from as many angles as possible. Hoping to get a little better shot of the roof, she climbed onto the trunk of a large tree that had fallen over a few feet back from the structure.

Satisfied that the dozens of photos she had taken were sufficient, Jenny made her way to the door to join Mac and Louie who were struggling with the heavy wooden brace.

"There you are!" Mac exclaimed as she walked over to them. "Let me have the keys to your car, Jen. This thing is nailed to the door with bridge spikes or something. We think we can pry the brace off if we use the tire iron in your trunk. Somebody doesn't want anyone to go inside the shack, that's for sure!"

The girl retrieved the keys from her jeans pocket and handed them to her twin.

"There's not much we can do until he gets back with the tire iron," Louie told her. "This is the only door into the shack and as you can see, it's not going to open without some work. There are two windows, one on each side, but they're boarded up and probably have been for years, so we can't get in that way."

Jenny walked up to the door, put both hands on the brace, and tried to move it.

"It looks like this thing ought to just slide up out of the two iron brackets on each side of the door, but I can see why it won't with those huge nails someone has driven into it."

She turned away from the door, walked to the edge of the shack, and looked back at her cousin.

"I'm really surprised. I was expecting the shack to be much larger than it is. How big do you think it is, Louie?"

"I don't know, Jen, but since we have to wait for Mac to get back with the tire iron, I'll try to step it off. It won't be 100% accurate, but it will be pretty close."

He walked to the edge of the shack and turned back walking heel to toe to the other edge, counting each step out loud for Jenny to hear.

"The front of the building is about 16' wide," he said before turning to step off the side of the shack. "The side is going to be much harder to step off since the brush is so heavy, but I'll give it a try."

Jenny watched as he forced his way through the thick underbrush to the end of the shack. She couldn't hear his count for all the noise the snapping of the bushes made.

"That was hard to step off," the young Scout admitted when he returned to the door. "I would say this shack is about 20' by 30', or roughly the size of a double-car garage."

"Do you think someone actually lived here?" she asked trying to imagine how much room there would be in a double-car garage. "Or do you think whoever owns it, just used it to store stuff?"

"I don't know," Louie said furrowing his brow. "It would be pretty primitive if someone had actually lived here. There are about 600 square feet of empty space with four walls, two windows, a door, and a dirt floor. My best guess is that they either used it for storage or maybe used it as a bunk house for a hired hand. Then again 70 or 80 years ago, this might have looked totally different than it does now."

Before they could continue their speculations, Mac emerged from the underbrush tire iron in hand.

"This ought to do the trick," he announced stepping up to the front door. He shoved the pointed end of the tool between the brace and the door and pulled. The door groaned, but the brace did not budge.

"Let's try putting the tire iron closer to the nails," Louie suggested. "Maybe we can work them loose."

"Good idea," Mac said, moving the iron toward the end of the brace. Once again, he pulled on the tire iron. This time there was a tiny bit of movement. Encouraged, he pulled again as hard as he could. The huge nails holding the brace slowly began to loosen.

"Want to give it a try?" he asked handing the tire iron to Louie. "Maybe I got it started for you."

A year younger than his cousin Mac and physically smaller, Louie made up for his lack of brute strength with his quick mind. Using the iron tool as a lever, he moved it to a slightly different spot on the brace and gave it a quick pull. This time the nails visibly moved. Over the next few minutes, the boys took turns loosening the spikes with the tire iron. Finally, the nails had moved enough for them pry the brace off the door.

Jenny had perched on the fallen tree trunk she had used earlier to watch the boys work on the brace. When it finally came off, she clapped and cheered.

"Way to go, guys!" she shouted.

"Wait a minute," Louie cautioned. "I need your car keys, Jen. I want to get my backpack out of the car before we open the door. It's going to be very dark, and there's no telling what we're going to find inside; there could be anything. Just don't go in until I get back, okay?" he said as he turned toward the clearing where the car was parked.

In what seemed like seconds, Louie returned with his backpack. Propping it up against the side of the shack, he extracted his powerful military-style flashlight and opened the door.

The interior was pitch black with only a speck of light peeking through a few of the broken shingles.

"See how dark it is in there?" Louie asked activating his flashlight. "That's how dark it was the entire night I was trapped in here. It wasn't very pleasant, I can assure you."

The three teens paused at the door before entering the inky blackness. The boys were obviously excited at the prospect of adventure while the feeling of dread Jenny had experienced earlier resurfaced.

Louie aimed the beam of his powerful flashlight into the shack. The intense light bounced off the walls and the many items scattered about creating eerie shadows.

"Sorry I don't have another one of these," Louie apologized, holding up his flashlight.

"Not a problem," Mac said activating the flashlight on his cell phone. "Jen has one of these too, so we're good."

For a few moments, no one spoke as they tried to make sense of the cluttered interior. Each pointed a light in a different direction.

"There's a huge stack of old newspapers and magazines against that wall," Louie said running his light over the stash. "I don't think I would have made it that night without the newspapers. I used some of them as a towel to dry off; I sat on some of them and covered up with some of them to try to keep warm. I was really happy when I found them. I couldn't see any dates on the newspapers, but I know they must be very old since many of them were too fragile to use."

"There's a broken chair and some random pieces of furniture over there," the Boy Scout said, flashing his light against the opposite wall. "I used that chair right there to dry my clothes on after Danny Collie threw me in the creek. I have no idea what's in the back of the shack because I only had a few matches for light and I didn't want to waste them."

The interior of the old shack was so full of discarded items that it was impossible not to step on some of them. After a brief survey, the teens concluded that the majority of items consisted of cast-off furniture and a variety of clothing and personal items.

"It smells terrible in here!" Jenny exclaimed clearing her throat. "I can't decide if I smell **MOLD** and mildew or if something died in here."

"I'll bet there's a body hidden in here somewhere," Mac teased. "Keep looking, Jen. Maybe you'll get lucky and find it."

"I don't know about a body," she responded, "But I was lucky enough to find this. Here catch!" she said before sending a small leather bag flying in his direction.

"Stop it you two!" Louie warned. "We don't have a lot of time. Let's see what else is in here."

Mac headed for a back corner, while Jenny explored the furniture and other items stacked against the wall.

"I found a desk!" Louie exclaimed as he rummaged through the items stored in the center of the shack. "I wonder if there is anything left in the drawers."

Excited by the possibility of the find, he carefully

opened each drawer. The shallow middle drawer contained a couple of crudely sharpened lead pencils, a broken fountain pen, and a dried up bottle of ink. The small side drawers were either empty or contained a few scraps of discarded yellowed paper. When he pulled open the large bottom drawer something clanged. Shining his light into the depths of the drawer, he saw what appeared to be a large rusty coffee can. Most of the red and yellow paint had rusted away including the brand name of the product. Instead of a modern plastic lid, the antique coffee can had a metal lid.

Louie laid his flashlight down on the desk to examine the old can. It took several attempts to open it, but he finally succeeded. Inside he found a roll of papers wrapped inside a newspaper. Being careful not to tear the old documents, he gently spread them out on the desk for a better look. Suddenly he realized that he was staring at some very old papers that appeared to be important.

"Mac, Jen! Come here quick!"

"What is it, Louie?" Jenny asked before she dissolved into a fit of coughing. "I can't breathe in here!"

Mac was right behind Louie and simply turned to see what had prompted his shout.

"You guys will never believe what I just found in this old desk! I found the deed to the ranch!"

Louie's light was bright enough for the teenagers crowded around the desk to make out the large word "DEED" at the top of one of the pages.

"Do you think it's real?" Jenny asked between coughing spells.

"Looks real to me," Mac said. "I think you'd better roll those papers up and put them back in the can before they get torn, Louie. Somebody might really need these."

"I'm definitely going to take this coffee can with us," Louie said. "It would be a mistake to leave it here. Why don't we take one more look around and get out of here."

Mac turned back to the corner he was exploring while Jenny worked her way to the opposite corner. A loud crash followed by a shout and a groan broke the silence.

"What was that?" Jenny called. "Are you okay?"

"Yeah, I'm fine. I just tried to move this huge piece of furniture and it fell over," Mac replied. "I don't think anything broke, but I don't think I can move it back either."

"Guys, come look at this!" Jenny called. "I think someone must be living here. There was a table pushed out from the wall and when I looked behind it, this is what I found," she said motioning to a pile of fast food and candy wrappers. "I think it's a female, too, because there's a hot pink sweatshirt with a red heart embroidered on the front of it and what looks like a pair of ladies' jeans with rhinestones on the back pockets draped over that chair."

Louie suddenly dropped to one knee and directed his flashlight beam to a large cardboard box that was sitting next to the chair.

"Look at this! It's full of drugs, syringes, and who knows what else. There is some pretty heavy stuff in here," he said tensely, holding up a prescription bottle.

Louie dropped the prescription bottle back into the box and stood up.

"I don't want to meet whoever owns this," he said. "People get killed over stuff like this every day! We've got to get out of here! Now!"

"We've got to get out of here – right now!" Louie repeated stepping away from the box of drugs and shining his powerful flashlight toward the door. "Whoever owns this stuff could be back at any second and we don't want to be here when that happens! Let's go!"

The intense darkness inside the shack combined with the eerie shadows created by the flashlights was scary; finding the illegal drugs was terrifying.

As Louie retrieved the rusty coffee can and turned toward the door, Mac reached out and grabbed his arm.

"We can't leave yet," he protested. "I dropped my phone when I accidentally knocked over that huge piece of furniture. It's too heavy for me to move by myself and my phone is under it. If you can help me shove it to the side just a little, I think I can get it."

Jenny had started to pick her way through the discarded items and was nearly to the door when a strange noise shattered the silence. Seeing daylight through the partially open door, she scrambled to the opening, bolted outside and hid behind a nearby pine tree to wait for the boys.

The sound seemed to come from the boarded up window close to where the boys were standing. Louie motioned for Mac to follow him. They had just reached the door when they heard another sound like a heavy window opening. Once outside, Louie quietly closed the door and grabbed his backpack while Mac silently replaced the heavy brace. Then the three frightened teens crashed their way through the underbrush to the clearing where the car was parked, jumped inside and locked the doors.

Jenny was trembling so badly that she could barely start the car and then gave it so much gas that she nearly flooded the engine.

"It's okay, Jen, just relax," Mac said trying to sound brave. "We're safe now. Just take it slow. Follow those tracks. We don't want to get stuck out here."

Once back on the highway, Jenny caught a quick glance of Louie in the rear view mirror. His shiny auburn hair was glistening in the afternoon sun, but his face was ghostly white as he sat in the back seat bear-hugging his backpack.

"Are you okay?" she asked him, turning her head slightly toward him.

"Yeah, I'm fine," the boy answered although his voice sounded a little shaky and a bit higher than normal.

Mac leaned back in the passenger seat, pressed his head against the headrest, and took a few deep breaths to calm his jittery nerves before he spoke.

"I can't believe that we made it out of there without whoever owns all those drugs seeing us! That was too close! We were really lucky!" he exclaimed.

For a few moments no one spoke until Mac suddenly broke the silence.

"Oh, no!" he moaned. "My phone! My phone is under that piece of furniture I knocked over at the back of the shack. How am I going to get it? If they find my phone, I'm a dead man! They will be able to find me and probably do me in because I know too much! I've got to get my phone back! How am I going to that?"

For a few minutes, none of the teens spoke. Suddenly Jenny had an idea.

"I know what we can do until we can figure out how to get your phone, Mac," she said excitedly. "It's simple. All you have to do is to call the phone company and tell them that your phone is temporarily lost and ask them to turn it off. That way it won't ring until you call them back. What do you think about that idea?"

"That's exactly what you should do, Mac," Louie agreed. "Here's my phone. Give them a call. Now no one will know it's there but us."

The anxious teen was visibly relieved as he reached for Louie's phone and made the call.

"There are just so many questions about all this," Louie finally offered after Mac had finished his call. "I think we need to sit down and try to sort it all out before we go home."

"Yeah!" Mac said enthusiastically. "Let's go to Burgers 'n More. I need a burger. The little protein bar I had a while ago is long gone. I'm starving."

"Sounds good to me," Jenny said as she turned onto the highway leading into town. "It's after 2:00 o'clock. Actually, I could use something to eat, too."

The questions started as soon as the three teens had picked up their food and drinks and were settled around a table at the back of the restaurant.

"I want to know who nailed the door shut with those giant spikes," Mac said between bites of his cheeseburger. "Was it nailed shut when you were kidnapped by Danny Collie and his friend, Bud when you discovered them searching for the lost gold at Choctaw Creek a few weeks ago?"

"No, it wasn't nailed shut and there wasn't a heavy brace, either," Louie said as he took a long drink of soda. "Bud just opened the door, they threw me inside, secured the door again and left. So no, there's no way it could have been nailed shut. It just opened too easily."

"Know who I think nailed it shut?" Jenny asked. "I think it was your Boy Scout Leader, Mr. George. Think about it, Louie. He gave you a lecture about not going back to the shack, so he probably did it to keep you out. The two crooks are in jail, so they couldn't have done it. So who else would know about that old shack? No one; that's why it has to be Mr. George."

Louie squirted ketchup onto a French fry and popped it into his mouth before he spoke.

"I don't know, Jen. I guess it could have been Mr. George, but I just don't think so. He gave me the impression that he really didn't want to go back to that old shack either."

"Well, I think we know one thing for sure," Mac declared as he wadded his French fry sack and put it into the empty cardboard box that had contained his cheeseburger. "I'm sure it wasn't the druggies. Why would they nail the door shut and then have to climb in the window every time they came back?"

Louie frowned as he looked across the table at Mac. "I think it might have been the druggies, Mac," Louie said. "That brace would certainly keep most people out. I actually saw that boarded up window twice when I walked around the shack and there was no indication that it wasn't permanently boarded up.

Jenny abruptly stood up and pushed her tray to the edge of the table.

"I'm going to the ladies' room," she announced. "I'll be right back."

While she was gone, the boys continued to discuss the brace securing the door. In a few minutes, she was back at their table. As she approached her seat, she carefully slipped a small square of folded paper into Louie's hand. As soon as she caught his eye, she put her finger to her lips indicating not to say anything.

He unfolded the paper on his lap and read: "The two guys at the table behind you are listening intently to everything we're saying. I think we need to be very careful." His eyes widened and he nodded.

Suddenly Jenny stood up again and picked up her tray with her soda cup.

"Hey, I've got a great idea. It's so nice out, let's refill our drinks, and go across the street to the park for a little sun. What do you think?"

"Great idea, Jen! Let's do it," Louie said as he picked up his tray and followed her to the trash bins.

It was obvious to Mac that something was happening, but he hadn't a clue as to what. Not wanting to be left behind, he picked up his tray and followed Louie.

Once outside and resettled at a picnic table in the park, Louie handed Mac the note that Jenny had given him. His eyes also widened as he read the words she had written.

"What do you think that was all about?" he asked, handing the note back to Jenny.

"I don't know, but those guys seemed to be too interested in everything we said. For all I know, they could be part of the drug dealers working out of the old shack. We just need to be very careful, that's all."

The incident at Burgers 'n More had been so unsettling for all three teens that for a few minutes no one spoke. Instead, they looked around to see if anyone else was watching them. The small park, nestled in a grove of shady trees, was empty. The picnic table Jenny had selected was set apart from the others, so there was no chance of being overheard. Finally, everyone was convinced that they were alone.

Mac was first to break the silence. After taking a long, loud slurp of his large soda, he looked at Jenny and Louie who were seated across the table and asked, "So how am I going to get my phone back? Got any ideas?"

"I'm afraid you can't get it back, Mac, at least anytime soon," Jenny said. "It's way too dangerous to go back there. I think you should just give up and get a new one."

Her idea didn't go over well with her twin.

"I don't want a new one. I want that one. I can't afford another one! It's got too many pictures and too much information on it to start over. I'm going to figure out some way to get back in there and move that furniture. Will you go back with me, Louie?"

Mac didn't respond, but rather took the lid off his soda cup and poured a couple of ice cubes into his mouth. Then he replaced the lid and waited for the ice to melt.

"I don't know, Mac. I think it might be too dangerous. Jen might be right; maybe you should just forget it and get a new phone."

"No, I'm not getting a new phone! Can we at least talk about it and maybe come up with some kind of a plan? Remember it was your idea to go to the shack in the first place."

"Sure we can talk about it."

Jenny rolled her eyes and shot Louie a 'Please don't encourage him' look, but it was too late. She knew all too well that Louie was not one to walk away from challenges no matter how daunting they might seem.

"Okay," he began, "here's what we know. There's a box with drugs in there. A female is living or at least camping in the old shack. We don't know if she's 15 or 50. We don't know if she is a drug dealer or maybe just a drug user, so we don't know how dangerous she might be. We also don't know how often she goes to the shack and how long she stays there. And we don't know if she has friends that go there with her – maybe even those guys at the restaurant."

Mac was clearly encouraged. "Yeah, you're right! I just thought of something else. I think there must be another way to get to the shack. No one has driven over the path we took for years. So that means she's not using the door, especially since it was nailed shut!"

"I know of at least one other way to the shack," Louie said. "That girl would have had to park in your grandparents' pasture and walk through the trees like Bud and Danny Collie did when they kidnapped me. I don't think she did that because if there was a strange car in the pasture your grandparents would call the cops.

"There's an idea, guys," Jenny said with a touch of sarcasm. "Why don't we just call the cops and let them get your phone, Mac."

"No!" both boys protested in unison.

"We can't do that, Jen," Louie explained. "We don't want anyone to know that we went into the shack. First of all, they might get us for trespassing, or even worse, they might think the drugs were ours and that we were part of the drug deal."

Jenny was obviously concerned at the direction the plans were going.

"I'll get on Google Earth when I get home to see if I can find another route," Louie offered. "As soon as I do that, Mac, maybe we could try scoping out any other paths to see if we can find out how that girl is getting to the old shack. We should be able to tell by looking for broken branches, or trampled vegetation, and stuff like that."

They were obviously determined to make a workable plan and Jenny was horrified.

"You can't be serious!" she objected. "What if you run into her?"

"Doesn't matter," Louie said. "We don't know what she looks like and she has no idea who we are. Anyway, it's public property."

"No, it's not!" Jenny protested. "The land around that old shack belongs to somebody. You should know that; you've got the deed in that old coffee can. You'll be arrested for trespassing!"

Ignoring her, Louie continued, "As soon as we can find her path, then we can try hiding close to it and watch for her coming and going. Once we know that, it will be safe to enter the shack and retrieve your phone."

"That ought to work!" Mac exclaimed. "When can we start? We know that she went to the cabin about 1:30 this afternoon and she's probably still there."

"Right. It's going to be tricky since we don't get out of school until late afternoon, but I guess we could try to go tomorrow if you want to."

Mac's face reflected his disappointment.

"I probably can't go anytime after school for a while," he confessed. "Football practice."

"Guess what, Louie!" Jenny said suddenly sounding unusually excited. "I don't have football practice tomorrow. I'll go with you and we can go as soon as school is out. If anyone catches us out there in the bushes, they'll probably think we're on a date or something. I think we can pull this off. Bring your map tomorrow. Let's do it!"

CHAPTER FOUR

"No!" Mac nearly yelled as he slid off of the picnic bench and stood up. "There's no way I'm going to let you go back to that old shack, Jen. This is incredibly dangerous! Anyway, you're not strong enough to help Louie move the furniture to get my phone. No, you're not going! That's it!"

He crumpled his large soft drink cup and threw it in the direction of the trash container. It hit the rim and bounced off."

"You missed," Jenny said calmly as she, too slid off the bench and walked over to retrieve the cup and toss it into the container. "Nobody said anything about going into the shack, Mac," she said as she walked back to the table. "Louie and I are just going to do a little spying to see if we can find out when she comes and goes or if anyone else goes with her that's all. Then maybe if we can figure out when she won't be there, you and Louie can go in and get your phone. It's not going to be all that dangerous for me."

"I still don't like it," Mac mumbled as the trio walked back across the street to retrieve Jenny's car.

No one talked about the shack on the way home. Instead, Louie asked Mac if he had talked to Joe Stillman about what he was planning to do with his new metal detector.

"No, not yet, but I may see him at the gym later this afternoon. If I get a chance, I'll ask him about it, okay?"

The tall blonde boy was so irritated that both Jenny and Louie decided that any further conversation would be a waste of time, so the three rode to Louie's home in silence.

As soon as the twins returned home, Mac got out of the passenger seat without a word and walked to his blue Malibu, which was parked under a tree.

"Are you going to the gym?" Jenny called after him.

Without turning around he answered, "Yeah."

It was after 3:00 o'clock when Jenny returned to her room. Her parents were apparently still at her father's veterinary clinic where they had gone earlier that morning to check on the injured dog. Jenny thought about calling her mother to see how things were going, but decided to call Louie instead.

The Boy Scout answered on the first ring.

"Hey," Jenny began as she stretched out on her queen-size bed being careful to keep her shoes off the new plush comforter. "I guess you could tell that Mac's very unhappy with me."

"Yeah, that was pretty obvious," Louie agreed. "I guess he's mad because he can't go with us tomorrow or is he mad because he lost his phone?"

Jenny untied her neon pink and lime green athletic

shoes and slipped them off before answering.

"I'm not sure he's really mad, Louie," she said curling up in the middle of her bed. "I think it's a combination of things. He's disappointed that he can't go with us tomorrow, he hates it that he lost his phone and won't be able to get it back for a while, and he's worried that we might get into trouble or hurt. It just seems like he's mad."

"Whatever," he said clearly unimpressed with her analysis. "If he's so disappointed about not going with us tomorrow, why doesn't he just skip football practice and come with us? I'll bet they have enough players to get along without him."

"Didn't he tell you?" Jenny asked obviously shocked at his suggestion. "He's the starting quarterback this year! He can't just randomly skip practice."

"No way!" the boy exclaimed. "He didn't tell me that he was the quarterback."

"Have you ever been to a game?" Jenny asked rolling her eyes.

"No, I really haven't. You know I don't like sports very much, but since he's the quarterback maybe I'll try to make a game or two this year."

"Yeah, I think you should do that."

Before the conversation could continue, Jenny heard the back door slam and her mother's cheerful voice announcing that they were home.

"Guess I'd better go," she said. "I just heard my folks come in. I want to hear how the dog is doing, so I'll see you tomorrow, okay?"

Jenny bounded off her bed and hurried down the stairs to greet her parents.

"How's the dog?" she asked as her dad was hanging up his jacket.

"He's still heavily sedated, but his vitals seem to be improving. It's going to take a long time for his bones to heal, but he's a young dog, so that gives him a much better chance," the vet explained.

"What kind of a dog did you say he was?"

"He's a Labrador retriever. Even as hurt as he was, I could tell that the dog had a wonderful temperament when the man brought him in. The poor pup kept trying to wag his tail. It really breaks your heart to see a dog hurt like this."

"Listen, Jenny," her mother interrupted, "we're going to get cleaned up, and then we're going to pick up Juan and Katie. We're going to that new Argentinian restaurant in the City. Juan's parents are from Argentina, you know."

"Yeah, I know. Is Louie going with you?" the girl asked.

"No, he's not going with us I'm afraid you kids are going to be on your own for dinner. Maybe you can order a pizza or something."

"Does Aunt Katie like Argentinian food?"

"If I were guessing, I'd have to say yes. My sister seems to like everything. I've never had that kind of food before, so I hope I like it."

"Sounds interesting," Jenny managed to say before a severe coughing spell erupted.

"Are you alright, Jenny?" her mother asked, concern coloring her voice.

'Yeah. Just allergies," she said as soon as she recovered. "I'm fine."

Back in her room, Jenny decided to review the pictures she had taken of the old shack earlier that afternoon. 'I can't believe I actually took 61 pictures! Wow, some of these are really cool, too! I'll bet Allison would like to paint some of these. She's really into old buildings and trees and stuff. I need to go through these again and pick out a dozen or so that she might like and send them to her.'

Allison Canary had been one of Jenny's best friends since the second grade. Even though as they grew older and many of their interests had changed, they still remained friends. Allison was a talented artist and played clarinet in the school band. Jenny, on the other hand, was a superb athlete and the captain of the girls' soccer team.

As Jenny continued to scroll through her cell phone pictures, she suddenly felt sick. Then she had violent coughing spell that left her whole body aching.

'I think I'll do this tomorrow,' she said to herself. 'I feel horrible.'

She plugged her phone into the charger by her desk, and flopped down on her bed. The large red digital numbers on her nightstand clock told her that it was 5:21 p.m. 'Maybe I'll feel better when Mac gets home and we can order a pizza or something,' she thought to herself before she fell into a deep sleep.

Shortly before 10:00 p.m. Meghan and Carson came through the back door laughing and talking about the wonderful food and entertainment at the new Argentinian restaurant. Since it was a school night, they were pleased to see Mac's blue Chevy Malibu and Jenny's white Ford Focus parked near the house, a comforting sign that both kids were safe and at home.

"Mac, Jenny, we're home!" Meghan called from the living room. "Did you two get something to eat?"

The tall football player came out of his room and walked to the top of the stairs.

"I don't know where Jenny is, Mom," he said. "Joe and I stopped for a burger before I came home about 7:30 and her car was here, but her light was off. I knocked on her door, but she didn't answer, so I don't know where she is."

Meghan set her purse down on the end table by the sofa and took off her sweater.

"She didn't text you or leave a note or anything?" the concerned mother asked her son as she started up the stairs. "It's not like her to be out late without telling anyone. Do you think she could be asleep?"

"Jen doesn't normally go to sleep at 7:30, so when she didn't answer, I just figured she must be out with Louie or one of her friends."

Meghan walked up to Jenny's door with Mac close behind her.

"Jenny?" she called as she turned the doorknob and slowly opened the door. "Jenny? Are you asleep?"

In the dim light, they could see Jenny still wearing her faded jeans and yellow sweatshirt sprawled in the center of the bed apparently passed out.

"Jenny!" Megan said rushing to her daughter's side. "What's wrong? Are you sick?"

As Mac stood frozen in the doorway, Meghan began to gently shake the girl's shoulder while calling her name.

Finally, the girl groaned and tried to roll over.

"Turn the light on, Mac," Meghan instructed. "Something is wrong with Jenny. I think she must be ill."

Her worried mother reached over and put her hand on the girl's forehead. It took only an instant for her to realize that her daughter had a very high fever.

"She's burning up, Mac! We need to get her fever down as quickly as possible. Go downstairs and get a glass of cool water and bring it back up here."

Meghan stood up and quickly walked toward the door. In a matter of minutes, she returned with a digital thermometer, a bottle of acetaminophen and a cold wet washcloth at the same time Mac reappeared with the glass of water, which he set on the nightstand.

"Roll over, Jenny," she said. "I need to take your temperature. Just hold still."

A minute later, her mother looked at the thermometer, shook her head, and frowned.

"103 degrees," she said grimly. "I'm going to put this wet washcloth on your forehead and face for a few minutes Jenny, to cool you off a bit."

Mac had never seen his twin sister this sick and unresponsive before and he was extremely worried. Not knowing what else to do, he walked over to the edge of the bed and put his hand lightly on her arm.

"Is she going to be all right?" he asked nervously as the color drained from his face.

A quick glance at her usually strong athletic son told her that he was also on the verge of tears.

"I'm sure she's going to be just fine, Mac," she said walking over to him and slipping her arm around his broad shoulders. "I'm going to give her a couple of these tablets and a glass of water for now. I'll watch her tonight and if she's not better in the morning, I'll take her to the doctor."

Curious about what his family had been doing upstairs, Carson immediately quizzed his wife as soon as she returned to the living room.

"Do we need to call Martin?" he asked referencing his older brother. "Maybe he could prescribe something for her over the phone?"

"No, Carson, let's not bother him right now. He's an emergency room physician and he might even be on duty tonight. Anyway, I think she might have the flu. I'll check her again before I go to bed and again first thing in the morning."

"Well, if you think she has the flu, sleep is the best thing for her," the tall veterinarian said.

At 6:15 the next morning, Meghan quietly climbed the wooden stairs to her ailing daughter's room. Not bothering to knock, she silently opened the door and discovered that her teenage daughter was still fast asleep. She noticed that the girl had barely moved from the night before.

"Jen," she called softly. "Are you awake? Jen?"

There was no answer or movement, so Meghan moved to the side of the bed, sat down, and leaned over to feel her daughter's forehead.

Finally, after what seemed an eternity, the girl moaned and literally croaked the word "Mom" through very dry lips.

"Well, good morning, Sunshine," her mother said trying to sound more cheerful than she felt. "How are you feeling today?"

The girl managed to whisper the word "terrible" before dissolving into another fit of coughing and sneezing.

"You're still running a temperature, Honey? Do you think you might have the flu?"

After another long moan, the teen rolled over, curled up into a ball, and pulled the lemon-yellow covers up under her chin.

"I don't know. I just hurt everywhere and I am very tired. I just need to sleep."

Her mother stood up and gave her daughter a light pat on her shoulder.

"Do you want to go to the doctor?"

"No. I just want to sleep."

"You probably need that more than anything right now. Mac is going to pick up Louie on his way to school today, so don't worry about that, okay. I'm not going to work today, so if you need anything I'll be here."

An hour later, Mac paused at Jenny's door for a moment and knocked softly before dashing downstairs on his way to school. He wanted to let her know that he was thinking about her if she was awake. There was no answer.

Louie was sitting on the porch steps next to his backpack when Mac entered the circle drive and stopped a few feet from where his cousin sat.

Expecting to see Jenny's white car, he was surprised to see Mac's blue Chevy instead.

"Where's Jenny?" the boy asked as he tossed his backpack into the car.

"Jen is sick today," Mac replied. "I don't know what's wrong with her. She coughs and wheezes a lot and she seems to have trouble breathing. Mom thinks that she might have the flu. Anyway, she also said that Jen was extremely tired and that she hurts all over so she's home in bed. I just hope it's not contagious, that's all."

Louie didn't say anything for several minutes and seemed to be lost in thought as he stared out the side window. Finally, he turned to look at Mac, who had just pulled into a parking space in the school parking lot.

"I don't think she has the flu, Mac," Louie said seriously. "Remember when we were inside the shack and she kept saying she couldn't breathe? Many things in there could have made her sick. For one thing, there was so much **MOLD** in there that I couldn't breathe very well either. I think she could be allergic to it. The roof's been leaking for years, so the place is just one giant mold pit. Didn't you smell it?" the Boy Scout asked.

"Yeah, I guess. It didn't smell very good in there, but I didn't know it was mold," Mac admitted as he turned off the ignition

"I'm worried about her, Mac," Louie said grimly. "She could have had a bad reaction if she's allergic to mold or something even worse than that."

"Worse than that?" Mac repeated. "Like what?"

"That old shack must be home to thousands of mice and probably rats, too judging from the rodent droppings that were everywhere. She might have been exposed to **HANTAVIRUS**."

What?" Mac asked obviously concerned

"Hantavirus. It affects the lungs. She seems to have all the other symptoms, too."

Louie could see the worry deeply etched on his cousin's face.

"Could she die?" he asked softly.

"Well," Louie said trying to appear optimistic, "people can die from it, but we probably caught it in time. I'm sure she will be fine."

CHAPTER FIVE

At 11:37 a.m. Meghan Joulian's cell phone rang.

"Mom!" a hysterical Mac nearly yelled into the phone. "Is Jenny dying? Is she going to live?"

His questions caught his mother totally off guard.

"Mac? What are you talking about? Where are you?"

"I'm at school. Is Jenny going to die?"

Meghan couldn't resist smiling at her son's unfounded concern as she walked back to the kitchen table and sat down at her regular place.

"It's okay, Mac," she said as reassuringly as possible. "Jenny is going to be just fine. In fact, she's sitting at the table with me right now drinking a cup of hot tea. She had a very bad allergic reaction and she also has some kind of a virus that made her very sick, but she's doing much better now."

"So she's really going to be okay? I mean really?" the boy asked with a twinge of doubt coloring his words.

"Yes, she's really going to be just fine. I took her to the doctor early this morning and he gave her a shot and another prescription for the antihistamine capsules that she took before. She's not dying, Mac, she's going to be just fine."

"Was she allergic to mold?" Mac asked.

"**MOLD**? Why do you think she was allergic to mold?"

"I don't know," Mac mumbled. "I probably heard somebody say mold could be very bad for people if they were allergic to it, that's all."

Meghan took a long sip of hot tea from her favorite navy blue mug which was decorated with a brightly colored veterinary pharmaceutical company logo before continuing the conversation.

"I'm sure it wasn't mold," his mother said. "She was definitely allergic to something, but it was the virus that made her sick. Anyway, I don't know where she would find very much mold around here, so I seriously doubt that mold had anything to do with it."

"Yeah, well, good, I'm glad she's okay," Mac stammered. "I've got to go. Bye."

As soon as the call ended, Mac handed the cell phone back to his friend, Joe Stillman and headed for his next class very much relieved.

"You probably guessed that was Mac," Meghan said as she set her phone down on the kitchen table. "He was afraid you were dying from a mold allergy. I don't know where he gets all these crazy ideas."

At the mention of the word "mold," Jenny nearly choked on her last sip of tea because she knew exactly where she had encountered mold – the old shack.

When the final school bell rang at 2:45 p.m. Mac

grabbed his backpack and hurried to his locker hoping to intercept Louie on the way to the front door.

"Louie," he shouted catching up to his cousin midway down the hall. "Let's get out of here. I've got something to tell you."

Once both boys were in the car, instead of starting the engine Mac turned to Louie.

"I talked to Mom at noon today," he said. "Jenny was very sick because she has a virus and she was also allergic to something. I think it might be the **HANTAVIRUS** and the **MOLD**, just like you said. But the good news is she's going to be okay."

"Awesome!" his cousin replied.

"I want to go back to the old shack right now and see if we can get my cell phone. We should have plenty of time before we're supposed to be home."

"Now?" The younger boy was clearly shocked at the suggestion. "Don't you have football practice?"

"Yeah, I was supposed to go to football practice, but I asked Coach if I could be excused today because my sister is very sick and I needed to go home, so it's okay."

Louie was uncomfortable about going back to the old shack so soon since someone was evidently living there.

"Jen and I were going to watch the shack for a few days first before you and I went in, remember?"

"I know, but I changed my mind. I don't want her anywhere near that old shack now. It's just too dangerous for her for so many reasons."

Mac started his car and headed toward the highway and the shack.

"So how are we going to do this?" the Boy Scout wanted to know. "Are you planning to park where we did before at that old homestead and walk in?"

Mac didn't answer immediately, but instead kept his eyes on the road while Louie watched the sparsely populated countryside fly by. It was several minutes before the tall athlete said anything.

"I thought about this all afternoon, Louie," he said. "It's too hard to get in and out of that old homestead if we have to make a quick getaway. I'm positive that whoever is camping in that old shack is coming in from the opposite direction. I think we should drive around by the bridge which is almost directly opposite of the shack and see if we see any cars parked in the area, what do you think?"

"Sounds good."

The two-lane concrete bridge over Choctaw Creek was less than a mile and a half from the old shack, which was totally hidden from the road by the dense woods. After driving up and down the road, they didn't see any suspicious cars, nor any place to leave the car.

"I don't see anywhere to park here, do you?" Louie asked obviously frustrated.

"No, I don't," Mac said. "What if I parked the car in my grandparents' pasture like we did when we were helping Jen with her project? Do you think you could find that old shack in the woods again?"

"I know I can find it! If you park there, we won't have to worry about hiding the car and the shack is not that far away either." Louie exclaimed. "Let's do it!"

On the way to the pasture, the boys tried to work out a plan to retrieve Mac's phone without getting caught.

"I think the first thing we need to do," Louie offered,

"is to see if there is anyone in the shack."

"Yeah, right. That ought to be easy," Mac scoffed.

"No, I'm serious. There are shingles missing all over the roof, especially over the corner where we saw all those drugs. If I could see the stars through it the night that I was a prisoner there, I think we could see if there is any light coming from inside."

"What? Seriously?"

"Yeah, it'll be easy. I'll show you when we get there."

As soon as Mac parked the car, the two boys sprinted to the edge of the densely wooded area. Louie took the lead as they pushed their way through the trees and underbrush. It took nearly 25 minutes before they found the old shack.

"There it is!" Louie whispered as he turned around to Mac and pointed to the clearing. "Whoever is staying here is getting in through the boarded up window on the other side of the shack. Let's work our way over there, but stay in the trees in case there's anyone outside."

"Then what?" Mac asked. "If there's not, are we just going to hide there for a while or what?"

"If we don't see anyone, I'm going to get on the roof and work my way over to the missing shingles to see if I can see anyone," the younger boy said as he began to push forward again.

Mac caught up and grabbed the back of Louie's blue jacket to stop him.

"No way!" he protested. "How are you going to get up there and what if whoever is living in there hears you? Then what?"

Louie turned to his cousin and matter-of-factly stated, "There's a tree on the other side of the shack with a very low branch. I noticed it when I walked around the shack yesterday. It's so close to the shack that it will be very easy to climb up enough to get on the roof. Once I'm on the roof, I'm just going to crawl over to look into the holes. I think that would be a lot quieter than walking."

Mac plainly couldn't believe what he was hearing.

"You're crazy!" he hissed. "It's not going to be quiet at all. As rickety as this place is, they could hear anything on the roof whether it's you crawling or anything else. With so many holes up there, I'm afraid you'll fall through. Then you'd really be in trouble!"

Louie ignored the comment and continued to push his way through the trees, brambles, and brush. When he reached what he considered a suitable hiding place with a view of the side of the shack with the boarded up window, he motioned for Mac to stop.

"Doesn't look like anyone's been here since yesterday," the Boy Scout observed. "I don't see any fresh broken weeds or tracks or anything. I'm going to give it five minutes and then if I don't see anyone, I'm going to the roof."

"Look at all these **BERRIES**!" Mac exclaimed looking around his hiding place. "I'm starving. Do you think it's safe to eat some of these?"

Louie looked around and plucked a handful of wild berries.

"The dark ones are safe enough, but whatever you do, don't eat any white berries. Those could kill you."

When five minutes went by without seeing anyone, Louie indicated that he was going to the other side of the shack and motioned for Mac to stay where he was.

As Louie made his way to the other side of the old

shack, Mac stepped back a few paces into the woods and hid behind a large pine tree. From his position, he was certain that he was out of sight should anyone walk up to the shack or climb out through the boarded up window. His hiding place also gave him a fairly unrestricted view of the old shack's roof. Until something happened or Louie returned, all he could do was wait.

Climbing to the top of the roof wasn't quite as easy as Louie had anticipated. The tree bark was extremely rough which hurt his hands, and the branches were a little higher than he remembered. However with his pride on the line, someway he managed to make it to the edge of the roof.

As soon as he was eye-level with the roof, it was obvious that Mac was right. There was no way that he could safely crawl on it. Many of the old weather-beaten wooden shingles were damaged, broken or entirely missing. He was about to give up when he noticed a hole about half the size of his fist in the wooden siding. It was nearly hidden by the tree branch he was using as a ladder. Instead of climbing onto the roof, he bent down and looked into the hole.

After several minutes of peering through the damaged siding, Louie could see no visible light inside the shack. Convinced that no one was inside, he crawled back to the tree trunk and clawed his way back down to the ground. He was tempted to shout his findings to Mac, but decided against making any unnecessary noise and instead walked quickly back to the edge of the woods where Mac was waiting.

"Did you get on the roof?" Mac eagerly asked as soon as he caught sight of Louie approaching his hiding spot. "Did you see anybody in there?"

"No, you were right about the roof, but I found a big

hole in the siding instead. I couldn't see any light at all in there, so I'm pretty sure no one is there right now."

"Can we go in and get my phone?"

Louie paused for a moment looking intently around the old shack and then at Mac.

"I don't see anyone coming, so if we're going to go in there, let's get in and out as quickly as possible."

The boys silently made their way to the front of the shack and Mac lifted the heavy wooden brace out of the iron brackets. This time there were no large spikes securing the brace to the shack. Dropping it to the ground, Mac carefully opened the door revealing the inky blackness within.

Louie turned on his cell phone flashlight and cautiously ran the beam of light around the interior to confirm that there was no one in the building. Deciding that it was safe to proceed, he stepped inside the doorway.

"My phone fell under that huge piece of furniture in the back of the shack," Mac said quietly trying to tell Louie where to direct the beam of his flashlight. "Can you see it?"

"Is that it over there?" Louie asked pointing his light at a large object at the back of the shack.

"Yeah, that's it. When I accidently bumped into it in the dark, I dropped my phone, and it fell underneath it."

The two boys picked their way through the maze of discarded objects to reach the items stored in the back corner. Louie had to climb over a couple of overturned chairs to reach the back of the fallen piece to see if the phone was visible. While Mac waited, the Boy Scout shone his light around and under it from the back. Finally, he spotted the cell phone lying face down in a small gap between the top of the massive piece of furniture and a small object it was resting against.

"I see your phone, Mac and it looks okay," he announced. "It's about two feet from the top of this thing and toward the center. What is this thing anyway?"

"No idea, but it's really heavy I can tell you that. I couldn't move it by myself."

Louie put both hands on the side of the object and tried to shove it. The massive wooden piece didn't budge.

"There's no way we can lift it. Let's try to push it over enough to get your phone out," he suggested.

"I don't know," Mac said nervously. "I just don't want it to fall on my phone and smash it."

As Louie continued to analyze the angle of the piece in relation to Mac's phone, his cousin climbed over the same two chairs to reach the side.

"If we push it over on its side, it should miss your phone. What do you think?"

"It's going to be close, but don't see any other way," Mac agreed stepping to the front of the piece of furniture.

Louie set his cell phone on the floor a few feet away with its flashlight pointed toward the gap and walked back toward it.

The two boys put their hands on the side of the massive object and planted their feet ready to give it a shove.

"Ready?" Louie asked. "Okay, on the count of three, push it as hard as you can. One, two, three, go!"

The massive wooden piece groaned but barely moved.

"Again," he instructed. "One, two, three, go!"

This time the huge piece of furniture slowly began to slide off the small object at a different angle than Louie anticipated with Mac's cell phone directly in its path. In a desperate attempt to save his phone, Mac reached out and grabbed the top of the piece to redirect its fall. Louie heard a ripping of old wood the instant before he heard his companion scream and the antique piece crash to the hard dirt floor.

"What happened, Mac?" he asked as he leaned down to retrieve the cell phone which had miraculously escaped being crushed by the old piece of furniture. "Are you okay?"

"No, I'm not; I'm really hurt! When that thing started to fall, I grabbed it to keep it from falling on my phone. Part of the top tore off and a piece of it is stuck in my hand. It threw me off balance and I fell and hit my head on something. Can you pull this out?" the tall athlete asked holding out his injured hand. It really hurts!"

Louie stepped back, picked up his cell phone, and pointed its flashlight at Mac's right hand. A large splinter of wood nearly four inches long and over a half-inch wide had broken off and was now deeply impaled in Mac's right hand. The boy's face was ashen and blood was beginning to drip from the wound. He was tightly holding his right wrist with his left hand and looking as though he could pass out at any moment.

"Please, Louie, can't you pull this out?" he begged again gritting his teeth.

Louie shook his head. "No, I can't. If I tried to pull it out, your hand might really bleed and I could cause some serious damage. Come on, Mac, I've got your phone in my pocket. Let's get you to a doctor. Just hang on, okay? Can you hold your hand up? That should slow the bleeding. Can you do that?" The injured boy nodded weakly.

Louie put his arm around Mac's waist to help him navigate over and through the cast-off debris while holding his cell phone flashlight in his other hand to light their way. As they neared the center of the shack, Mac stumbled over a pile of trash and nearly fell again. As his arms flew out to regain his balance, he hit Louie's cell phone and sent it tumbling to the floor. The beam of light was now aimed at the corner where the three cousins had found the stash of drugs the day before. As he bent down to pick up his cell phone, Louie saw something in the dim light that caught his attention. Looking closely, he could see what looked like a body stretched out on the floor only a few feet away.

Terrified, he grabbed Mac's arm and roughly dragged him the last few feet to the door and out of the old shack.

"We've got to get out of here now!" he whispered. "We're not alone!"

As soon as the two boys were out of the shack, Louie could tell that Mac was on the verge of passing out from the pain in his hand. He could barely stand, his face was ghostly white, and his eyes appeared to be rolling back into his head.

"Mac, we've got to get away from here!" the Boy Scout said tensely. "You've got to hang in there. Can you walk?"

Without a word, the normally energetic football player took two steps before his knees buckled nearly sending him to the ground. Louie, who was still standing next to him, was able to catch him before he collapsed and guided him to the fallen tree trunk that Jenny had used to take pictures.

"Sit down, Mac," Louie instructed helping the larger boy to take a seat on the tree trunk. "Lean over as far as you can and try to put your head between your knees. That will keep you from passing out. I'll be right back."

Louie hurried back to the door of the shack which was still standing open. He took a quick glance inside to make sure that there were still no lights and no one was moving.

Then he quietly closed the door and turned around to pick up the brace.

The heavy piece of timber was almost more than the slightly built fifteen-year-old could handle, but some way he managed to lift it up enough to slide it into the brackets. Then confident that the door was secure, he turned and sprinted back to where his injured cousin was sitting. As soon as he saw Louie approaching, he sat up, lowered his hand, and reached out to him.

"Please, please," he begged holding out his injured hand. "Can't you pull this out? It's killing me. I can't even feel my fingers."

CHAPTER SIX

"No, Mac, I can't pull it out. I might really damage your hand if I pulled it out and I would have no way to stop the bleeding. Listen, we've got to get away from here. I'm sure I saw a body on the floor in there. Someone is either passed out or dead. Come on; let me help you stand up."

With Louie's help, the injured teen managed to stumble to his feet. It was painfully obvious to the Boy Scout that the chances of his cousin making it to the car before he passed out were almost zero. Since Mac was much too heavy for Louie to carry, the best he could do was to wrap an arm around his waist and try to hold him up as they staggered through the dense foliage. The pair had gone less than 50 feet when Mac's legs gave away causing both boys to fall to the pine needle-covered ground.

"Sorry," the tall athlete mumbled. "I can't go any farther. I just can't I've got to sit down somewhere."

Louie got to his feet, brushed the pine needles off his hands and jeans, and looked down at Mac lying on the ground. His hand, still impaled with the sharp fragment of wood was beginning to swell and discolor. Blood which had been slowly dripping from the wound now covered his right hand and arm, and was drying on his shirt and jeans.

"Mac, you've got to try. We've got to get out of here and get you to a doctor. I wish I could carry you, but I can't. I'll try to hold you up, but you just have to try to walk. Nobody would ever find us out here."

"I can't do it, Louie, I can't walk any further. Listen, my car keys are in my right jacket pocket. Take my car and go get help. I feel like I'm going to pass out, but I'll be okay until you get back. Just go," Mac said weakly.

"No, I won't leave you here. Anyway, I can't drive your car. I don't have a license and I've never driven a stick shift, so no, that won't work. We're going to have to think of something else."

"Then call my mom," he said softly. "She stayed home from work today to be with Jenny. Maybe she and Jen could come get us."

"Good idea!"

Louie pulled his cell phone from his jacket pocket and hurriedly punched in the Joulian's home number. The phone rang more than a dozen times with no answer.

"No one answered, Mac. Does she have a cell phone? Do you know the number?"

"Yes she has one, but I don't know the number. It's in my phone contacts."

Louie retrieved Mac's phone from his back pocket and quickly found Meghan's cell number. This call went unanswered as well.

"She didn't answer her cell phone either," he said as he slipped Mac's phone back into his pocket.

"I'm going to try Jen," Louie offered. "I've never known her to be without her phone, so I'm sure she will answer."

Again, the call went unanswered.

"I can't believe it!" Louie exclaimed. "She always, always answers her phone!"

Mac didn't respond. He was lying on his back on the bed of needles with his eyes closed. His hand, which was continuing to swell, was lying palm up by his side.

"Mac! Are you still with me?" Louie asked as he walked over, knelt by the boy's side, and gently shook his left shoulder. "Don't go to sleep. You've got to stay awake. Neither your mom nor Jen answered any of my calls. What should I do now?"

The panic in the young Scout's voice was hard to miss.

Mac's only response was a low moan.

"I'm going to call my dad's office," Louie finally said as he stood up. "He's a hand surgeon, so he'll know what to do. I don't know if he's there, but I'll try."

The boy accessed the speed dial on his phone and called his father's office. The receptionist answered the call on the second ring.

"This is Luis Morales," he told her. "May I speak to Dr. Morales, please? He's my father. It's very important."

"I'm sorry," the woman replied. "He's at the hospital right now. Would you like for me to text and ask him to call you as soon as possible?"

"Yes, yes, please, text him now and tell him it's an emergency! Thank you."

Louie ended the call and slowly slipped his cell phone back into jacket pocket before turning his attention back to his injured companion. The boy lying on the ground seemed to be slipping in and out of consciousness. The color was gone from his face, his breathing appeared to be shallow, and his hand was continuing to swell.

"My dad's not going to call anytime soon, Mac," Louie said sadly with a mixture of disappointment and sheer panic in his voice. "He never does if he's at the hospital. That means he's probably in surgery or something. What are we going to do? We've got to get you out of here."

This time there was no response. Mac was still lying face up on the bed of pine needles unmoving and with his eyes closed.

"Mac!" Louie said loudly as he squatted down beside his cousin and gently shook his shoulder. "You've got to wake up. Come on, Mac! Wake up!" There was no response.

Louie stood up and retrieved his phone activating it to see the time. 4:18 p.m. He sighed and returned the phone to his jacket pocket.

"It's almost 4:20. No one is home. No one is returning my calls and I've got to get him out of here. What am I going to do? Please hang on, Mac," he begged. "You've got to hang in there. You just have to."

The boy walked a few steps back through the brush in the direction of the shack to see if anyone had followed them. Seeing no one, he turned back toward Mac.

"Okay, Louie, just stop it! You've got to think," he said out loud to himself. "Get a grip. Quit reacting and think. What would an Eagle Scout do? What would Mr. George do?"

"Mr. George! Yes!" he nearly yelled. "Mr. George! Of

course! I need to call Mr. George. Why didn't I think of that! He will come. I just know he will! He will know exactly what to do to help Mac!" he continued out loud.

Watson George, Louie's math teacher, and Boy Scout leader was still seated at his desk at Choctaw High School grading test papers when his cell phone rang. A quick glance at the phone's screen identified the caller before he accepted the call.

"Well, hello Louie," the former soldier said with a hint of surprise in his voice. "What's going on?"

"Oh, Mr. George, you've got to help us!" Louie began in a voice at least an octave higher than usual and about twice the speed. "Mac is hurt. He's got a huge splinter stuck in his hand, and I think he's unconscious. I can't carry him and he needs help. I'm afraid he's going to die if we don't get him to a doctor. Will you come help us? Please," the boy pleaded.

"Of course I'll come and help you, Louie. Just slow down. Where are you?"

"We're in the woods not too far from Choctaw Creek. We're almost to that old shack where you rescued me a few weeks ago. Mac's got a huge splinter in his hand and he's too weak to walk so we had to stop. Oh please hurry!"

"Okay, Louie, I know exactly where you are. I'm on the way. Try to stay calm and keep Mac warm. I'll get there as quickly as I can."

As soon as the call ended, Louie rushed back to Mac's side and sat down beside him.

"It's going to be okay, Mac!" Louie excitedly told the semi-conscious boy. "I called Mr. George and he's on his way to get us and take you to a doctor. Just relax, okay. I'm going to sit here with you until Mr. George gets here. You just rest."

Although it seemed to take forever, it was less than 30 minutes before Louie heard someone pushing through the underbrush toward them. He jumped to his feet and walked quietly toward the sound of twigs snapping and underbrush moving. Though he was confident that it was his mentor coming to rescue them, he didn't want to take any chances in the event it was someone else. It wasn't until the boy spotted a familiar figure approaching that he knew it was his teacher.

"Mr. George?" Louie called out hesitantly turning back toward the spot where Mac was lying. "Over here."

As soon as the powerfully built man reached the injured teen, he dropped to one knee and gently shook the boy's shoulder.

"It's Watson George, Mac. Can you hear me? We're going to take you to the Emergency Room to get that splinter out of your hand. You're going to be okay."

No response.

He then gently picked up Mac's injured hand, took a quick look, and softly whistled.

"Louie," he said looking up at the boy standing beside him, "you were absolutely right not to attempt to remove that splinter. It is in so deep and the wood is so disintegrated that it would break apart and cause even more damage if you tried to pull it out. I'm glad you were smart enough not to try to remove it yourself."

As the muscular former soldier stood up, he noticed the horrified look on his young student's face and put a hand on the boy's shoulder to reassure him.

"It's going to be okay. I know that it looks very serious right now, but I'm sure the medics can fix it. An Eagle Scout couldn't have done any more than you did. Now, take off your jacket and let's secure Mac's arms across his chest with it to prevent any further injury to that hand."

As soon as he was confident that Mac was ready to travel, Watson George bent down and slid his powerful arms under the unconscious boy and lifted him up.

"Lead the way, Louie. My truck is parked next to Mac's car in the pasture."

Fighting their way through the brush and brambles, they were nearly to the truck when Mac's phone rang. It rang a half dozen times before Louie was able to retrieve it from his back jeans pocket and answer it.

"Hello?"

"Louie?" the female voice on the other end of the call asked. "Where's Mac? Why are you answering his phone? I need to talk to him for a minute. He was so worried about me that he called mom at noon to see how I was. I think he thought I was dying, can you believe that? I just want to tell him that I'm okay and there's no need to worry about me. Is he there?"

"Jen? Listen, I can't hear you very well. I need to call you back in a few minutes."

"What? How come? What's going on?"

The call ended abruptly. before any of her questions were answered.

Mac began to regain consciousness as they approached Watson George's pickup parked in the pasture near Choctaw Creek. Noticeably confused as to what was happening to him, he began to writhe and moan in pain.

"Be still, Mac, it's Mr. George," he said. "I've got you. Louie and I are taking you to the Emergency Room to get that splinter out of your hand. I know it hurts, but you've got to be still. We'll get there as fast as we can."

The injured boy apparently understood as he stopped moving and relaxed in the man's arms.

"The keys to the truck are in my left jacket pocket," the Scout leader told Louie. "Get them out and unlock the doors. I'll put Mac in the back seat. I want you to ride back there, too, and hang on to him until we get to the Emergency Room. Can you do that?"

As soon as the boys were safely settled in the back seat of Watson George's crew-cab pickup and headed to the hospital, the Boy Scout leader spoke.

"I'd like to know what happened to Mac, Louie, but I think you'd better call Jennifer first and tell her and her parents that we're going to the hospital."

"Oh, yeah," the rattled teen said digging his cell phone out of his pocket. "I need to call her. She'll be mad if I don't. I almost forgot."

Jennifer Joulian answered on the first ring.

"Louie! What is going on? Where is Mac?"

"Mac got hurt, Jen, Mr. George is taking us to the Emergency Room in his truck."

"Got hurt?" Jenny probed. "What happened? Is he going to be okay?"

"He has a huge splinter stuck in his hand and the pain was so bad that he passed out. I tried to call you and your mom to come and get us, but neither of you answered, so I called Mr. George."

"Sorry, we were at the doctor. I'll tell mom and we'll meet you there," Jenny said grimly. "Then you can tell me what happened." She ended the call without another word.

After riding in silence for a few miles, Watson George

looked up to see Louie in his rear view mirror.

"You know, Louie, I'd really like to know how Mac got such a large splinter in his hand out in the middle of those woods. Will you tell me what happened?"

For a few seconds Louie said nothing. He squirmed in his seat, and then he nervously blurted out, "I am so sorry, Mr. George. This is all my fault. I am so sorry."

"Oh really? Why is this your fault, Louie?"

"Mr. George, you told all of us not to ever go to that old shack because it was dangerous, but we did anyway. It's my fault because I wanted to see what was inside it and I talked Mac and Jen into going with me yesterday afternoon. We were checking out all the trash and stuff that's in there when we heard a noise and it scared us. We were hurrying to get out of there when Mac dropped his phone. It fell under a huge piece of furniture and he couldn't get it.

"He really needed to get his phone back, so he asked me to go to the shack with him after school today to help him get it. We were trying to move a huge piece of furniture to get his phone when it started to fall. Mac reached out and grabbed the top of it to keep it from smashing his phone and a huge splinter broke off and stabbed into his hand and then he fell and hit his head. I am sorry, Mr. George. I feel terrible that I disobeyed you. It's my fault that I talked the others into going as well. I am so sorry about everything," the boy said with genuine regret.

"I see," the former soldier said without a trace of emotion in his voice.

Another quick glance in the rear view mirror confirmed to Watson George that the teenage boy in the backseat was visibly upset and probably on the verge of tears.

For nearly five minutes, no one spoke. Finally, Louie broke the silence.

"Please don't be mad at me, Mr. George. I'm sorry and I'll never do it again, I promise."

"I'm not mad at you, Louie. I'm sad that Mac's hand was so badly injured, but I'm not mad at you or anyone else."

"You're not mad at me?" Louie was clearly relieved.

"No, I'm not mad at you. Actually, I'm not even very surprised because I knew you wanted to see what was in there from the day I rescued you. I'm a little disappointed because I was trying to keep you and your cousins from getting into trouble. Do you know why I told you not to go back to that old shack?"

"You said it was dangerous."

"That's right. I'm not sure anyone ever really lived in that old shack, but I am sure that no one has used it much if at all for at least fifty years. **DUST-BORNE DISEASES** could easily cause breathing problems and many other health issues. There's no telling how many varmints are living in there, either. I'm sure there are plenty of rodents, **SPIDERS**, and probably snakes, not to mention **TICKS** in all those weeds. With as many holes as there are in the roof and the siding, anything could have gotten in there. And, as you discovered, besides being bitten or stung by something there are also many other ways to get hurt."

"Yeah, I know," Louie mumbled.

"You probably didn't think about this, either, Louie, but you guys were trespassing. That old shack is on private property. I don't know who owns it, but obviously, somebody does. You could have been arrested and charged with a misdemeanor. Did you realize that? I'd hate to have to bail you out of jail!"

Before the boy could respond, his cell phone rang.

"It's my dad," he said as he accepted the call. "Hello?"

Watson George could only hear Louie's side of the conversation, but it was obvious that Dr. Morales was returning the teenager's earlier call.

"Yes, I did ..... About 4:30 ...... I called because Mac's hand got hurt this afternoon and I wanted to see if you could pick us up and take us to the Emergency Room .... Yes, it's bad ..... That's what I thought ..... The receptionist said you were at the hospital, but she would text you .... That's okay. ..... Mr. George, my math teacher is taking us right now ..... Oh, that's great! .... I'll see you there."

Louie was so exuberant over his father meeting them at the Emergency Room that he totally forgot his remorse and the previous conversation with Mr. George.

"My dad is going to meet us at the Emergency Room as soon as he's through at the hospital," he said. "He's a hand surgeon, so he knows everything about hand injuries. He'll be able to fix Mac's hand for sure!"

Suddenly the injured boy began moaning loudly. As soon as his eyes focused and he saw who was sitting next to him, he again pleaded for the Boy Scout to remove the splinter that was sticking out of his hand.

"Mac! You're awake!" Louie exclaimed. "We're going to the Emergency Room and they will get that piece of wood out of your hand. Just hang in there for a few more minutes, okay? We're almost there."

Within minutes, Watson George turned into the Emergency entrance and stopped close to the automatic doors. Not waiting for medical assistance, he got out of the driver's seat, opened the back door, picked up Mac in his powerful arms, and rushed inside. Approaching the desk, he pushed past two people waiting to check in and requested immediate help for Mac. A nurse standing behind the clerk recognized the seriousness of the situation and immediately ushered him into the treatment area.

"You stay here," he told Louie as he turned to follow the nurse through the double doors. "You'll need to be here when his family gets here. I'll let you know as soon as I know what they're going to do." In an instant, he and Mac disappeared behind the double doors.

Louie was much too agitated to sit down in the waiting area, so he walked outside and paced up and down the sidewalk trying to catch sight of either Jenny and her mother or his father. He had just turned back toward the entrance when he saw his mentor walk through the automatic doors.

"Mr. George!" he exclaimed, surprised to see the man so soon. "Are they through with Mac already? Is he ready to go home?"

"Not yet. They are still working on him. Let's go back into the waiting room. I'm sure his parents and Jennifer will have many questions when they get here. I'll stay with you until they come, but I need to move my truck first."

The math teacher had barely finished speaking and had just fished his keys out of his jacket pocket when they caught sight of Jenny and her mother rushing toward them from the parking lot.

"Louie!" the girl called to him. "What's going on? How is Mac?"

Both women were nearly breathless when they reached the two waiting on the sidewalk.

"Mrs. Joulian," Watson George said addressing Mac's mother, "your son is in the Emergency Room. He has a large splinter stuck in his hand and part of it needs to be surgically removed, but they can't do it without parental consent since he's a minor. You need to talk to the lady at the check-in desk. She has all the information."

The others noticed the color drain from Meghan's face as she turned without a word toward the automatic glass doors and disappeared.

"Thank you very much for helping Mac," Jenny said. "We really appreciate everything you've done for him."

"You're welcome," the math teacher said with a smile. "I'm just glad Louie thought to call me. I'm glad I could help."

In less than a minute, Mr. George was gone.

"Come on, let's go," Meghan said rushing the two teens into the Emergency Room. "I need to sign papers for Mac's treatment. You two can wait for me inside. Your dad will be here in a few minutes, Jen. When he gets here Louie, I want to hear what happened to Mac."

"Of course, Aunt Meghan?" Louie said. "While you sign the papers, I'll go to the restroom."

"I need something to drink. Do you want anything, Mom?" Jenny asked

The concerned parent shook her head as she turned toward the check-in desk.

The two best friends didn't say a word as they walked toward the restrooms and vending machines. As soon as they were out of earshot, Jenny motioned for Louie to join her in a small alcove near the soft drink machine.

"What really happened to Mac?" the tall blonde teenager quietly asked suspecting there was a lot to the story that he didn't want to tell. "How did he get hurt?"

Even though there was no one in the vending area, Louie looked around from side to side to make sure no one was listening.

CHAPTER SEVEN

"Mac asked me to go back to the old shack with him after school today to help him get his phone," Louie began as if telling a great secret.

"What?" Jenny said obviously shocked. "I thought you and I were going to watch it first to see if we saw anybody before you went in."

"Yeah we were, but Mac needed his phone and you were sick."

"That was stupid, Louie! How did you know that whoever owns all those drugs wasn't in there? You could have been killed!" Jenny was livid at the revelation.

"It's okay, Jen. We were trying to move that huge piece of furniture to get his phone, but it started to slide. He was trying to keep it from falling and smashing his phone, so he grabbed the top of it and it splintered and went into his hand. He was in so much pain that he passed out."

Jenny was horrified.

"Does Mr. George know that you and Mac were at the old shack?"

"Well, yeah."

"Did you tell him about the drugs?"

"No, I didn't say anything about that."

"Good! I don't think we should tell anyone about that. It's bad enough that we went back to the old shack without mentioning the drugs."

"What am I going to tell your mom about what happened to Mac?" Louie asked nervously.

"You're going to have to tell her everything except about finding the drugs."

Louie groaned. "We are so busted!"

"Yeah, seriously."

Jenny stepped out of the alcove and over to the soft drink machine. She put in some change and selected a bottle of water while Louie turned toward the restroom door.

"Hey," she said to him as he walked past her, "what are you going to do about that girl and all those drugs?"

Jenny returned to the waiting room just as Louie's father, Dr. Juan Morales walked through the automatic glass doors. He immediately walked over to the corner where his sister-in-law, Meghan Joulian was sitting, nervously twisting her purse handles.

"Meghan, I got here as quickly as I could," he told the woman sitting in the gray padded chair. "I got a call from Louie telling me something about Mac's hand getting hurt. He didn't give me any details, but I gathered it was serious since his teacher took them to the Emergency Room. What's going on? Do you know what happened?"

It was easy to see the anxiety written on the Argentinian surgeon's face as he pulled another gray padded chair around to face his sister-in-law.

"Thank you for coming, Juan," Mac's mother said as she greeted him. "I really appreciate it. I don't know very much about what happened, either. Mr. George was getting ready to leave when Jenny and I got here. All he told us was that Mac had some kind of an accident that resulted in a large wooden splinter that's stuck in his hand. It must be serious because his hand is going to require surgery. I just signed the consent forms."

The surgeon nodded to Jenny as she took a seat next to her mother and glanced around the waiting area.

"Where is Louie? I thought he was here."

"Oh, he is. He just went to the restroom," Jenny said. "He should be right back."

"I called Carson, too," Meghan said. "He was just finishing up at the clinic, so he should be here any minute."

Jenny was the first to see Louie as he turned the corner from the vending machines and walked slowly toward the group waiting in the corner. She could see that his face was much paler than usual and an obvious look of dread seemed to distort his features.

"Hi, Dad," he said trying to sound normal as he sat down in a chair beside Jenny.

"What happened, Louie?" Dr. Morales began turning to face his son. "How did Mac get hurt? What happened?"

His father's "doctor voice" as he described it to his friends never failed to fluster the boy, causing him to speak faster than normal and jumble his thoughts.

"Well," Louie said clearing his throat before launching

into his explanation. "Mac dropped his cell phone and he really needs his phone because all of his pictures and contacts are on it and he can't call anybody without his phone, but he dropped it and it went behind this big old wooden thing. And we couldn't even see it for a while and then when we did see it, his phone was so far under that thing that we couldn't even get it unless we moved it. And it was so heavy that it took both of us to move it and when we finally got it to move, it started to fall over like we didn't want it to and Mac was afraid that it was going to smash his phone, so he grabbed it and tried to move it in another direction and this giant splinter tore off and went into his hand. And it was so painful that I think he actually passed out for a little while. I hope that his hand is going to be okay because it really looked terrible when Mr. George brought us here in his pickup truck."

Dr. Morales simply stared at his teenage son for a few seconds after he finished his rambling explanation. Then he exhaled loudly, took off his glasses, and ran his right hand over his face. He had just put his glasses back on and was preparing to stand when Mac's father entered the waiting room and walked toward them.

A quick look at the grim faces of his family members told him that whatever had taken place was serious.

"What happened?" the veterinarian asked of no one in particular.

"Louie just told us that apparently the boys were fooling around and Mac dropped his phone. It fell under something and when they tried to move it to get the phone, it started to fall so Mac grabbed it and a splinter tore off and punctured his hand. Louie couldn't get in touch with anyone, so he called his math teacher, Mr. George who drove them here in his truck. At this point, that's all I know," Juan said as he got to his feet.

"Where is Mac now?" Carson asked.

"It sounds as though he may be in surgery. I'm going to see what I can find out. I'll be back as soon as I know something."

As Dr. Morales walked toward the check-in desk, Carson walked over and sat down next to his wife and put his arm around her shoulders.

"He's going to be okay, Honey. He's a tough kid. At least it was his hand and not his head, right?"

Meghan tried to smile, but her heart obviously wasn't in it. Instead, she reached over and softly patted her husband's knee.

"Now aren't you glad that my sister Katie married a hand surgeon?" she asked.

Jenny was in shock that Louie had managed to give a fairly accurate though abbreviated version of the accident events without mentioning the old shack even once. She took a long sip from her bottle of water and turned her head to take a quick peek at her best friend. The color had not returned to his face and he was sitting with his head bowed and his hands clasped between his knees. Suddenly she felt the need to encourage him.

"Mac's going to be just fine, Louie. Stuff like this happens all the time. It's just a good thing you were with him, that's all. Who knows? You might have even saved his life."

The boy just shrugged his shoulders and leaned further back in his chair."

"Was it a large splinter that broke off into his hand?" Jenny's dad asked.

"Yeah, it was," Louie said flatly. "I didn't measure it or anything, but I'd guess it was about 4 inches long and maybe a half-inch wide at the end where it went in. It was huge and it had to be really sharp to go in as deeply as it did. It almost went through his entire hand."

Jenny heard her mother gasp at Louie's graphic description, so she reached over and patted her hand.

"It didn't bleed very much, though," he said becoming more animated with each sentence. "Mac kept begging me to pull it out, but I knew better than to do that."

"That was very wise on your part, Louie. Pulling out a jagged splinter could have torn nerves, blood vessels, muscles, anything," Carson said.

"I know. That was the hard part because I knew he was in a lot of pain and he just kept begging me to do it."

Suddenly the double doors leading to the emergency treatment area opened and Dr. Morales walked back into the waiting room to the corner where the family was seated.

"I talked to the ER doctor that saw Mac when he first came in. He said that the splinter was large and disintegrated and that it penetrated so deeply that it nearly went completely through his hand. He removed most of it, but the wood was so old and decayed that it kept breaking and splintering into tiny shards when he tried to remove it. He said that there was no way that he was going to continue since it was such a major injury, so they called a hand specialist. Mac's in surgery now."

No one with the possible exception of Louie was expecting a diagnosis that severe.

Carson asked what everyone else was wondering.

"Did the doctor tell you how long he was expected to

be in surgery?"

"From the description of his injury, it's going to be awhile. I'm sure it's going to be at least a couple of hours before they take him up to a room, maybe longer. Since infection is a possibility, he'll have to stay tonight and possibly several days."

"Did the ER doctor say who is doing the surgery?"

"Yes, he did, and I was really glad to hear that it is Dr. C. B. Ashe. I've known Charlie Ashe for a long time. He's an excellent surgeon, so I can tell you for sure that the man knows what he's doing."

"That's wonderful news," Meghan said as she squeezed her husband's hand.

"How long do you think it will take for his hand to heal, Juan? I don't know if you know this or not, but Mac is the starting quarterback on the football team this year, so he really needs that hand," Mac's father said.

Juan shook his head. "No, I didn't know that. Good for him! I'm sorry to admit that we're not much of a sports family," he said before continuing. "Back to your question Carson, I really don't know. I haven't seen the injury or even any x-rays. My best guess is that if the splinter went in as deep as they said it could have damaged nerves and maybe even an artery. If that happened, he might not be able to feel his fingers and I'm sure that would affect his throwing ability. The splinter, either going or coming out, could also damage or tear muscles and tendons. All I can tell you at this point is that we will have to wait and see. I know that's not very comforting right now. I'm sure Dr. Ashe will give you all of the details as soon as the surgery is over."

Carson pushed his chair back, stood up and stepped

closer to his brother-in-law.

"Thank you, Juan. It means a lot for you to help us through this."

"Of course, I'll be happy to do anything I can to help," he said. "Also, I called Katie and told her what happened. Louie and I are going to go home now, so why don't you give me a call as soon you talk with Dr. Ashe."

The two men shook hands and Juan and Louie headed to their car while Carson went back to his seat next to Meghan to wait for the doctor.

Juan had pointed out the surgery waiting room to them before he and Louie went home, so the three went in there to wait.

"They always keep these rooms so cold," Meghan complained. "I hope that Dr. Ashe comes soon or I just might freeze to death."

Her husband laughed and offered her his jacket before choosing a large green chair near the corner to wait.

"At least these chairs are more comfortable than the ones in the emergency waiting room," he said.

"Considering that people might have to sit in here for hours, they'd better be more comfortable," she remarked.

Jenny watched her parents settle in for what could be a long wait.

"Mom's right," she said as she moved toward the door. "It's freezing in here! I'm going to walk around for a little bit, but I'll check back in a few minutes to see if the doctor has been in yet, okay?"

Neither parent commented as they silently watched their sixteen-year-old daughter slip out of the waiting room. Jenny had no intention of walking very far, only as far as the chairs in the corner of the Emergency Room away from anyone that might overhear her conversation. As soon as she sat down, she reached for her phone to call Louie.

"Can you talk?" she asked as soon as he answered.

"Sure. Did the doctor come in yet?" he asked.

"No, it might be a while before he finishes with Mac," she said. "I haven't had a chance to talk to you since all this started and I've been worrying all day about the drugs we found Sunday at the old shack. What are we going to do? Should we say something to the police or something?"

The boy on the other end of the line was quiet for so long Jenny thought the call had been dropped.

"The drugs are the least of our problems right now, Jen," he said grimly when he finally spoke. "When I was trying to help Mac out of the shack, it was so dark that I was using the flashlight app on my cell phone. When he stumbled, he knocked it out of my hand. When I picked it up, the light was pointing toward the corner where we found the drugs. Jen, there was a body back there lying on the floor. I don't know if that person was dead or just passed out."

"What?" Jenny was clearly horrified. "A body? Was it a girl? Could you tell?"

"No, and I didn't want to stick around to find out," Louie said. "I just wanted to get out of there as fast as we could before something else happened."

"Did Mac see it?"

"No. He was all but unconscious and in terrible pain. I had to just drag him out."

"What are we going to do? Are you going to report it to someone?"

"I really don't know what to do."

"Maybe you should tell Mr. George."

Louie paused for a moment before answering.

"I just don't know what to do," he repeated. What if that person was alive when we left and then he or she died. Do you think I could be arrested for not getting that person some help?"

Jenny tried to think of something encouraging to say to her best frind, but the possibility of a dead body in the old shack was just too frightening. This time the girl could't think of anything to say.

"I'm really afraid Jen. I know that I should have gone back to check on that person, but I didn't. All I could think about was getting help for Mac. I just hope he'll be okay and that everything went well with the surgery."

"I'm sure it did, Louie," Jenny said. "Especially since your dad has so much confidence in the surgeon."

"Yeah, I'm sure it did, too, but I'm really worried about him, Jen," the boy on the other end of the phone said. "Remember what my dad said about possible nerve damage? When we were out in the woods just before he passed out, Mac was begging me to remove the splinter. The last thing he said to me was, "I can't feel my fingers."

CHAPTER EIGHT

Jenny was visibly shaken about the thought of someone dying in the old shack. She ended the call and slowly walked back to the waiting room to join her parents. Her mother was the first to notice her daughter's troubled demeanor and paler than usual color as she sank into a chair near her dad.

"You're really worried about your brother, aren't you?" she asked.

"Yes, I really am. Louie's description of Mac's injury just makes me hurt all over. I guess the doctor hasn't been in to talk to you yet."

"Not yet, but it's been over an hour, so I would imagine it won't be much longer."

Carson stood up and began to pace back and forth in front of his family. Suddenly he stopped in front of Jenny.

"It just occurred to me," he said to her. "If Mr. George

took Mac and Louie to the hospital, where is Mac's car? Did they leave it somewhere?"

The puzzled look on his daughter's face told him that she didn't know.

"Call Louie and find out," he told her. "We need to pick it up. Mac must have the keys in his pocket."

Jenny picked up her phone and stepped out of the room to call her cousin.

"Mac's car is in the pasture where he parked when we were working on my school project," Jenny told her dad.

"That's odd," he said. "Why would he leave it there?"

"I guess you'll have to ask them," she said trying to avoid mentioning the old shack. "I wasn't with them."

For the next 45 minutes, no one spoke. Jenny surfed Facebook, her father alternated between sitting and pacing while her mother leafed through some of the magazines piled on the small table next to her chair.

Even though they were nervously waiting for the doctor to walk through the door to report on Mac's surgery, it was still a bit of a surprise when a tall slender man in blue scrubs entered the room.

"Mr. Joulian?" he asked looking around at the men in the room.

"I'm Carson Joulian," the worried father said getting to his feet. "This is my wife, Meghan and my daughter, Jenny."

"I'm Dr. Ashe," the man said as he walked over to the corner where Mac's family was waiting. He greeted the women and shook hands with Carson.

"First of all, your son did just fine. He has a very serious **PENETRATING INJURY** to his right hand. I understand that you didn't see it, but a very large splinter of old dirty wood broke off of something and pierced his hand going almost completely through it. He is very lucky. There are two arteries that cross in the center of the palm," he said holding up his hand and illustrating the position of the arteries with his fingertip.

"When the jagged splinter entered his hand, it only nicked one artery but didn't sever it, which is good. As the tip of the splinter entered his hand, it also violently pushed muscles and tendons into the nerves that control his fingers. Fortunately, only the one artery was damaged and nothing inside his hand was severed. However, that's not to say this wasn't a serious injury. The inside of his hand sustained major trauma and is badly bruised. No bones were broken, but some of the muscles and tendons had to be repositioned and there was some tissue damage."

For a moment, Jenny seriously thought that her mother was going to faint as she listened to the doctor's recital of Mac's injuries. The normal color had drained from her face and she was gripping the arms of her chair so hard that her knuckles were also white.

"A big concern is contamination," the doctor continued in a calm voice. "The splinter was very dirty and could have easily been contaminated with something that could cause a major infection such as tetanus or even gas gangrene. We irrigated the wound as best we could, but we will have to do it at least once more as soon as the swelling begins to subside to make sure all of the dirt and foreign material has been washed away."

"Do you think he will get the feeling back in his fingers?" Jenny interrupted as she stood to face the surgeon. "He's the quarterback this year, so he really needs his hand."

Carson frowned and gave his daughter such a stern disapproving look that the worried teen simply sat down in her chair and looked anxiously at the doctor not daring to ask anything else.

"I don't know," Dr. Ashe answered noting her concern. "That's a good question. Since nothing was severed, I think there's a good chance that when the swelling goes down and his hand heals, he will get all or at least some of the feeling back in his fingers."

"Dr. Ashe, can you tell us how long he will be in the hospital and maybe some idea as to how long it will take for his hand to heal?" Carson asked.

"No, I really can't. His hand injury is so severe that until we're sure there is no contamination remaining in the wound and that no infection has developed, we can't even stitch the wound together. The only thing we can do is lightly cover it with a bandage to keep it clean. How long he stays in the hospital will depend on what happens in the next day or two. He will need physical therapy after his hand has healed.

"We're also concerned that he might have suffered a mild **CONCUSSION** when he fell and hit his head when the splinter injury occurred."

"Oh!" Meghan exclaimed. "A concussion?"

"I have no way of knowing how he was injured, but it appears that he either fell or something fell on him as there is a knot on the side of his head the size of a goose egg."

"That would explain why Louie said that he was nearly unconscious when Mr. George brought him here," Jenny said softly to herself.

"Do you have any other questions?" Dr. Ashe asked as he looked at the stunned faces of Mac's family. "If not, they have moved your son upstairs to room 446. He's heavily sedated right now, but you're welcome to go up to his room if you would like."

"I have a question, Dr. Ashe," the worried mother asked as the surgeon prepared to leave the room. "Is it alright if I spend the night with my son in his room?"

"That's entirely up to you; I don't have a problem with it. Just be aware that he will not be awake for several hours."

The instant Dr. Ashe was out of the room, Jenny sprang to her feet.

"Come on," she insisted. "Let's go see Mac."

As the trio exited the elevator on the 4th floor and walked toward Mac's room, they passed room 427.

"There's Louie's old room," Jenny said pointing to an open door on her left. "It's hard to believe that we were all up here just a few weeks ago to see Louie after that awful Danny Collie beat him so badly. Now we're here in the same hospital and even on the same floor to see Mac. This is just insane!"

The door to room 446 was closed. Meghan knocked softly before pushing the door open. The interior of the room was dimly lit, but bright enough for them to see Mac in the bed tucked under the covers fast asleep. A closer look revealed that his right hand was wrapped in bandages and propped on a pillow. Several tubes were attached to his left hand which led to machines and a bag of fluids.

Meghan immediately walked to his bedside and began stroking his hair while Jenny lightly touched his shoulder and whispered his name. Carson stoically stood at the foot of the bed and gazed down at his unconscious son.

"Are you really going to spend the night here?" Jenny

whispered to her mother, who silently nodded. "Can I stay, with him, too?"

"No, you can't," her mother whispered back. "You've got school tomorrow. Carson, there's no point in you and Jenny staying any longer. Mac is not in any danger and he won't be awake for hours so you might as well go home."

Carson nodded then walked over to the closet and opened the door to see if Mac's clothes were inside. His shirt, jacket, and jeans were all neatly hanging inside the closet. A quick search in the pocket of Mac's jacket produced the keys to his car.

"Meghan," Carson said to his wife as he joined the women at Mac's bedside, "do you need to go home before you stay for the night?"

"No, I'll be fine. I'll go home in the morning," she said without taking her eyes off her only son.

"Then Jenny and I are going to leave. I want to stop by the pasture on the way home and pick up Mac's car. I found his keys so Jenny can drive it home."

He put his arm around his wife's waist for a quick hug and softly kissed her cheek. Jenny gave her twin brother's arm a gentle squeeze and whispered "I love you" to her sleeping twin.

As soon as they were seated in Carson's SUV and back on the highway headed toward Choctaw Creek, the veterinarian turned to his daughter.

"I can't understand why Mac's car is in the pasture," Carson mused. "That absolutely makes no sense to me at all unless he and Louie went back down there to look for the lost gold again. I also can't understand how he could get that splinter in his hand if they were exploring the creek. Did

Louie say that's what they were doing?"

Suddenly it was crystal clear to Jenny that there was no way the boys were going to be able to keep their visit to the old shack a secret.

"No, they weren't exploring the creek or looking for the gold. Louie told me that he had asked Mac to go with him to explore that old shack. He just wanted to look around since it was too dark to see anything when he was locked in there. Mac parked his car in the pasture because it's not very far from the old shack."

For a long moment, her dad did not comment on her explanation but instead drove with his eyes intently focused on the highway.

"Well, I knew it had to be something like that after listening to Louie's explanation," he finally said. "I don't think Mac could have gotten a large splinter through his hand exploring the creek. Also, I distinctly remember Mr. George talking about that old shack when Louie was in the hospital and how dangerous it was to go back there. Didn't he make you kids promise not to go back to the old shack?"

Jenny sighed deeply.

"Yes, he did," she admitted.

"Besides getting hurt, do you realize that Mac and Louie were trespassing which is against the law? I'd hate to have to bail them out of jail. Just remember that even though no one has lived there for a long time, it's against the law to break into someone else's property no matter how old it is."

"Yeah, I know."

"Jen, Mr. George wasn't kidding when he told you kids not to go back to the shack. There are just so many ways to get hurt in there. You could be bitten by a varmint or pick up germs that could also make you sick. It's just too dangerous."

'You just have no idea,' she thought to herself as she nodded agreement.

Mac's car was parked in the pasture a few yards from Choctaw Creek just like Louie told her. Carson handed his daughter the car keys as he slowed his SUV to a stop close to his son's older blue Malibu.

"I'm going to follow you home in case you have any trouble," he told her. "I don't anticipate anything, but you never know. This pasture is very rough, so take it slow."

It had been a while since Jenny had driven her brother's car and even though she was almost as tall as her twin, she still had to move the seat forward and adjust the mirrors. Finally ready to go, she started to call Louie to talk on the way home, but decided it wasn't a very good idea and put her phone back in her purse.

The little blue digital lights on Mac's dashboard clock had just changed to 8:47 when Jenny stopped the car in the front drive, turned off the engine, and got out of the car. Her dad was already out of his SUV and halfway to the back door.

"It's going to be strange without Mom and Mac here tonight," Jenny said as they entered the kitchen.

"Sure is," her dad agreed. "I don't know about you, but I'm worn out. I'm going to take a hot shower and turn in. I'll see you in the morning."

"Okay, sounds good," the teenager said as she started toward the stairs. "I have a headache and I'm very tired, too."

Once inside her bedroom, Jenny closed the door and flopped down on her bed. Retrieving her cell phone from her purse, she called Louie.

Even though he answered on the second ring, it

seemed to her that it took forever.

"I wanted to call you earlier, but I just didn't have a chance," she began as the words rushed out of her mouth.

"The surgeon came in and told us that Mac's hand is probably going to be okay, but he's not sure. He said that there was some damage, but nothing was broken or cut up too badly although the nerves between his 3rd and 4th fingers are badly bruised. That's the good news. The bad news is that I'm afraid you're in serious trouble."

Jenny repositioned herself on her bed propping herself up on the oversized pillows before resuming the conversation. "I'm really sorry," Jenny said apologetically, "but there wasn't anything else I could do. I had to tell him."

"What are you talking about? Louie asked genuinely puzzled. "Why am I in trouble?"

"Actually, I don't know that you're in trouble, but you just might be."

For a long moment, the boy on the other end of the line didn't respond. Jenny knew instantly that she had irritated her cousin with her mysterious remarks because he had complained about it before.

"What I mean is," she said rushing to explain, "I had to tell my dad that you and Mac were at the old shack when he got hurt. And I'm sure he will tell your dad, so it might get you in trouble. Anyway, I'm really sorry because I didn't want to say anything, but he asked where Mac got hurt and I had to tell him. I hope I didn't get you in trouble."

She could hear him exhale loudly before he spoke.

"I'm sure that they would have found out soon anyway," Louie said. "I'll probably get a stern lecture, but I don't think I will be grounded or anything."

"That's good! Listen, I know it's still fairly early, but I'm exhausted and I don't feel very well. I'm going to bed. I'll pick you up in the morning as usual, okay?"

"Sure. I'm glad you're well enough to go back to school. I'll see you tomorrow."

Jenny awoke nearly an hour before her alarm sounded. Hurriedly slipping her feet into her comfy slippers, she rushed downstairs expecting to see her father sitting at the table sipping coffee. Instead she found a note telling her that he had gone to the hospital to see Mac before he went to the veterinary clinic.

Disappointed because there was no one at home and that she didn't have time to go to the hospital before school, she grabbed a banana and a glass of milk and headed back upstairs to get ready for school.

Jenny arrived at Louie's house a few minutes early and had just leaned back in her seat to wait for him to come out when her cell phone rang. She knew immediately from the special ringtone that it was her mother calling.

"Hey Mom, how is Mac?" she asked excitedly with her signature rush of words. "Is he awake yet? Is he doing any better this morning?"

"Good morning, Jenny. Yes, Mac's awake, but he's still groggy. The doctor hasn't been in yet, so I don't know anything else to tell you. I know you're on your way to school, but I thought you might like to know that he is awake. I'll call you over your lunch hour and let you know what the doctor says. I don't want you to worry about him; he's going to be just fine, okay?"

Jenny had just finished the call when she saw Louie bounding down the steps to her car. He flung his backpack in the back seat and climbed into the front seat, carefully closing both doors without slamming them.

"I can't believe it!" Jenny exclaimed. "You didn't slam my doors."

"Yeah, well I sure felt like it," he grumbled. "At least you warned me. Your dad called my dad last night and told him all about what happened at the shack. I knew I was in for it when he called me into his study about 10:00 o'clock last night. He wasn't mean or anything, but I sure got a lecture and a half. But, good news! I'm not in trouble or grounded or anything. He just told me not to ever go back there again and why. Same old stuff we've heard before."

"That's about the same thing I got from my dad and he doesn't even know that I was there. Have you given any more thought to what we should do about the drugs and that body you think you saw? What should we do?"

"I don't know."

The instant the final bell rang, both kids hurried to Jenny's white Ford Focus parked near the front of the school parking lot.

"Do you want to go to the hospital with me to see Mac for a minute before I take you home?" she asked as soon as they were ready to go.

"Yes, I would," he said. "I've been worried about him all day."

On their way to room 446, the two best friends again talked about what to do about the drugs and the body at the old shack.

"The only thing that I've been able to come up with is to tell Mr. George," Louie confessed. "He certainly knows that we were at the old shack, so that's not an issue. I just can't decide. Have you come up with anything?"

"No, not one single thing. I don't know if your idea is a very good one or not, but at least you have one; I don't have any ideas at all."

"There is one thing that makes me feel a little better," Louie continued. "Don't you think if someone had actually died in the shack we would have heard about it?"

"Well, no," Jenny said surprised at his comment. "You were only there yesterday. To tell you the truth, I'm really concerned that someone might be in serious trouble because nobody but the three of us knows about what you saw. I think you should tell Mr. Geroge."

The door to room 446 was partly open when the two arrived. Jenny didn't bother to knock, but simply pushed the door open quietly and stepped inside with Louie close behind. Mac was sitting up in bed with his right hand propped up on a large pillow. His mother was sitting in the recliner in the corner opposite the bed. Even though it was only late afternoon, both looked extremely tired.

"Mom?" Jenny asked quietly. "May we come in?"

Mac spotted the two visitors first.

"Jenny! Louie! Get in here you guys." Mac could barely contain his enthusiasm.

Neither waited for a second invitation, but rather rushed to his bedside. Jenny reached over the rail to give her brother a heartfelt hug while Louie settled for lightly touching his arm.

"How are you feeling?" Jenny asked. "Are you in lots of pain?"

Mac shook his head and tried to smile.

"To be honest, I can't really feel much of anything

right now. See all those tubes? There's so much pain medicine and stuff going into me that I can't feel my hand at all." Jenny glanced at the bags of fluid hanging from the metal stand and frowned.

"Do you know when you can go home and get off all this stuff?" she asked.

"Not for sure. I guess it all depends on what happens with my hand," he said.

Meghan stood up and walked over to Jenny and Louie.

"The doctor was in this morning and said that because the injury to Mac's hand was so severe he wanted to keep an eye on it to make sure no infection set in. They can't even close the wound until they are sure it's healing properly. I know he is staying here tonight, but I don't know after that. I'm sure we'll find out tomorrow.

"I don't know what they gave him, but it really knocked him out. He's only been awake for a couple of hours."

"Oh, no!" Mac suddenly groaned. "I didn't show up for football practice today. Coach is going to be so mad at me. He doesn't know that I'm in the hospital, so will you call him tomorrow and tell him for me, Mom? Tell him that I don't know when I can come back, okay?"

"I am so sorry, Mac. I should have called today, but with everything going on, it didn't even occur to me. I'll call him tomorrow and also the principal's office to let them know why you're not at school."

Visibly relieved, the boy smiled and mouthed the words "Thank you" to his mother.

"Hey, I brought your phone with me," Louie said with a touch of pride in his voice. "The battery may be run down, but at least it's here and it's not hurt or anything," he said as he handed the phone to his cousin.

"Jenny," Meghan said as she turned toward the door, "since you and Louie are here, if you'll excuse me, I'm going to step down the hall for a minute. I'll be right back."

The instant his mother was out of the room and the door closed, Mac suddenly became animated.

"Louie, I've got to ask you something. Yesterday was pretty much a blur after I fell and my hand got hurt, but something has really been bothering me since I woke up. Did I hear you say that we had to get out of the shack in a hurry because you saw a body or did I just make that up?"

"No, you didn't make it up, Mac. When I was trying to help you walk, you stumbled and knocked my phone out of my hand. When I bent over to pick it up, the flashlight was pointing to the corner where Jenny found the drugs. I couldn't see it very well, but I'm certain there was a body stretched out on the floor. I don't know if it was a man or the girl that Jenny thinks might be camping there. And I have no way of knowing if that person was dead or alive. So, no, unfortunately, you didn't make it up."

CHAPTER NINE

Mac sank back on his pillows and groaned.

"That's what I was afraid you were going to say. Have you told anyone about it, like your dad or Mr. George or anybody?" he asked.

"No, we haven't told anyone," Jenny said jumping into the conversation. "Actually we don't know what to do."

"Jenny and I have talked about it a lot since yesterday, but we really don't know what to do. We even talked about calling the police," Louie offered.

His cousin's remark prompted Mac to frown and shake his head.

"I don't think you should call the police," he said. "What do you think, Jenny?

"We talked about it, but we weren't sure that would be a good idea either," she said.

"With all those drugs in the shack and maybe even a

dead body, I'm afraid it might get us all in trouble especially since we really weren't supposed to be in that old shack in the first place," Mac continued.

"Yeah, that's right, but there's the other thing," Louie said in a very serious tone. "What if we don't say anything and they find out that we knew about the drugs? What if someone was **ABUSING DRUGS** and overdosed or even died, could we be guilty of a crime and maybe go to prison?"

Mac and Jenny stared at each other clearly concerned about Louie's question.

"Well, we obviously knew about the drugs, there's no question about that. We all saw them," Jenny said. "I even took pictures of them and I think I have one picture of you, Louie, holding a syringe or something. You and I didn't see the body, Mac but we both knew about it because he told us, so I think we're probably guilty, too."

Louie was horrified. "You have a picture of me holding a syringe or something? Please delete that photo right now, Jen! If anyone sees a picture of me holding any of that stuff, they will naturally assume it's mine. We're in enough trouble as it is."

Jenny reached into her purse to retrieve her phone, but couldn't find it.

"I can't believe it!" she said. "I left my phone on the charger in my bedroom. I never do that. I'll delete the photo as soon as I get home, I promise."

"If you don't" Louie warned, "I could be in serious trouble. That picture could send me to prison for life."

By the time Meghan returned to the room, the three cousins were so worried about the possibility of getting into trouble for drug offenses and failure to report a dead body or someone passed our from a drug overdose that they had run out of things to say to each other. Jenny and Louie were still standing next to Mac's bed holding on to the rail in the exact same location as when she left the room.

"Did you three have a good visit," she said cheerily as she made her way back to the rust-colored recliner in the corner of the room.

"Yes, we did, Aunt Meghan," Louie said trying to match her mood, "except Jenny needs to take me home now. I'd like to get there before my parents get home."

"I understand, Louie. Thank you for being here. I know Mac was happy to see you."

Jenny gave her brother another bear hug and turned to speak her mother.

"Is Dad coming up after work, too?" she asked. "If he is, maybe I should just take Louie home and then come back so we could eat together."

"Yes, that would be nice. Your dad is planning to be here about 6:30 unless things didn't go well at the clinic. You know that poor dog that got hit by a truck Saturday? He had to have another surgical procedure this afternoon, so I'm sure your dad will be tired. By the way, if you could stop by the house on the way back and pick up my maroon sweater I would really appreciate it."

On the way home, neither Jenny nor Louie felt like talking after the emotional conversation that had just taken place with Mac. She was nearly ready to turn into the circle drive in front of Louie's house when he began to speak.

"I almost forgot something really important!" he said enthusiastically. "I saw Joe Stillman in the cafeteria at lunch today. And guess what? He's invited me to go with him on

Saturday afternoon to show me how his new metal detector works. Isn't that awesome! I can't wait!"

Jenny was visibly interested at the mention of her heartthrob's name.

"Where are you going? Did he say? Remember you promised me that you wouldn't go back to Choctaw Creek to look for gold with that thing. Remember?"

"Yeah, I remember," he said as he climbed out of the passenger seat. "If it will make you feel any better, we're definitely not going to the old shack either."

The girl was so distracted by the mention of Joe's name that she nearly forgot to stop by the house to get her mother's sweater before going back to the hospital.

Mac was sitting up eating his dinner when she returned to the room. The first thing that she noticed was that it appeared to be a struggle since he had to eat with his left hand. Meghan had already cut his food into bite size pieces, so all he had to do was to scoop them up with a spoon.

"That's really doing it the hard way," his twin sister teased him as she walked over to give him a hug. "It smells really good and I'm starving, so you'd better not stop."

"You shouldn't be hungry for very long," their mother said from her seat on the recliner. "Your dad called a few minutes ago and he's stopping by Burgers 'n More to pick up our dinner if you can wait that long."

Mac groaned as he tried to eat another spoonful of mashed potatoes.

"Why didn't you tell me? I would have much rather had a burger than this stuff."

"Just hush and finish your dinner," his mom told him. "I'm not sure you're ready for a burger yet."

As soon as Carson arrived and distributed the hamburgers, the conversation immediately turned to Mac and Louie's ill-fated trip to the old shack. As the discussion progressed, it soon became clear to Jenny that neither of her parents had any idea that she had also paid a visit to the old shack the day before. With his dinner over, Mac was getting sleepy.

"I don't think there's any reason for you to spend the night up here tonight," Carson said to his wife. "Mac needs to sleep. You might as well go home and get some rest, too. You can come back first thing in the morning and see him when he's awake."

His family barely had time to wish Mac a good night before he drifted off to sleep.

Jenny arrived home before her parents and immediately rushed to her room to call Louie and tell him her secret.

"Guess what?" she said as soon as he answered the phone. "Mom and Dad have no idea that I was with you guys Sunday afternoon. They spent the whole time we were having burgers in Mac's room tonight talking about you and Mac, so they don't know that I was at the shack, too. I think that's a good thing, don't you?"

"Yeah, I guess."

Ignoring his lack of enthusiasm, she continued with the reason for her call.

"I forgot to tell you when I took you home this afternoon that I need to stay after school tomorrow for 15 or 20 minutes. The soccer team is having a short end-of-season meeting and since I was the team captain this year, I've really got to be there."

"No problem."

"I just wanted you to know where I was so that you wouldn't be waiting at the car."

"Okay, thanks."

Jenny could tell from the lack of his usual enthusiasm that something was amiss.

"What's wrong, Louie? Are you okay?"

"Yeah, I'm okay."

"No, you're not. What's wrong?"

"I'm just a little bummed over everything that happened to Mac not to mention the drugs and maybe even a dead body lying there in that old shack."

"Mac is going to be fine and as for the drugs and maybe the body, we'll figure all that out later. It's going to be okay. For now, just get some sleep and I'll see you tomorrow."

The next morning when Jenny stopped at the Morales' home to pick up Louie for school, he came down the front steps carrying his backpack and another plastic bag containing the old coffee can which he carefully set in the backseat.

As soon as school was out, Jenny headed for the gym to meet her soccer teammates while Louie went to his locker to retrieve the plastic bag before paying Mr. George a visit.

The former soldier was helping one of his math students with a problem when Louie walked into his classroom. Without stopping his explanation, he motioned for Louie to take a seat in the front row.

As soon as he finished with the other student, Mr. George closed his classroom door and walked over to where Louie was sitting.

He pulled out the student desk next to Louie and turned it to face the boy before sitting down.

"What can I do for you, Louie? Did you need help with

the graphs we were doing in class this morning?"

"No, Mr. George, I think I understand them. I came by because I wanted to show you this," he said handing the plastic bag to his teacher.

"What is it?" Watson George asked as he opened the plastic bag and peered inside. "It looks like an old rusty coffee can."

"Yes, that's what it is," Louie said. "But look inside. It's what's inside that I wanted you to see."

The teacher carefully removed the can from the bag and examined it. The original paint and lettering had worn off the can years before leaving only a few patches of red and blue paint on the rusty tin can and there was no lid. Inside the can were several sheets of paper that had been rolled up and stored inside for safe keeping. Noting the delicate nature of the ancient paper, he gently removed the papers from the can and unrolled them on the top of his desk. Louie saw his body stiffen as he read the words on the documents.

"Do you know what this is, Louie?" the man asked.

"Well, not for sure," he said clearly uncomfortable with his teacher's reaction to the papers. "I've never seen anything like this before, but it looks like it might be the deed to the ranch since it has the word deed at the top of the page. It's hard to read, but it looks like the names written on it are Caleb and Matilda Schnickel or something and it's dated 1910. Can you believe that? It's over 100 years old!"

"Where did you get this, Louie?"

The tone of his teacher's voice and his reaction to the documents frightened the boy. Suddenly he desperately wished that he hadn't brought the coffee can to Mr. George. He realized that his only option was to confess that he found it at the old shack. For a minute the boy simply stared at the coffee can sitting on Mr. George's desk but didn't respond.

"Where did you get this, Louie?" Watson George repeated sensing the boy's discomfort. "It's okay. Just tell me where you found it."

"I found it in the old shack," Louie admitted clearly uncomfortable. "It was in an old desk that was shoved up against some other furniture. There were a lot of interesting things in there, but we didn't have much time to explore anything else before Mac got hurt."

"Like what?" his teacher persisted. "What else did you find in there?"

Scrambling to come up with other items he saw that didn't involve the drug cache, he hesitated for a moment and then continued.

"It was very dark in there and the only light I had was from my flashlight, so I couldn't really see very much. I found stuff in the desk that I had never seen before. There was a bottle of what looked like dried up ink or something and some old pens that might have used the ink if that's what it was. What I saw looked like junk."

Mr. George returned his attention to the old papers and the coffee can sitting on his desk before he spoke.

"These papers are very interesting, Louie," he said holding the papers up to the light. "You don't see antiques like this very often. Would you mind if I borrowed them for a little while? I promise that I'll take good care of them and I'll get them back to you in a couple of days, okay?"

The teacher's genuine interest in the old papers was so disarming that Louie immediately nodded his consent before continuing.

"Those papers are really valuable, aren't they? That would explain the heavy brace on the door. I'll bet somebody put it on there to keep people from getting in and finding other valuable antiques."

"There was a brace on the door?" Watson George asked obviously puzzled. "What kind of brace, Louie?"

Encouraged by his mentor's curiosity, the boy excitedly launched into a detailed description of the brace.

"I've never seen anything like it, Mr. George. It was huge! This heavy piece of wood fit into iron brackets on each side of the door. I couldn't believe how heavy the brace was and that it was actually nailed onto the door with gigantic nails, too.

"Mac and I couldn't get it open with our bare hands. We finally got the tire iron out of the trunk and pried it off. That would keep anyone out for sure!"

For a long moment, the Boy Scout leader seemed lost in thought.

"Why do you think the door was braced like that, Louie? When I found you locked in that old shack a few weeks ago, the door was secured, but there wasn't anything like that holding the door shut. What would make someone go to all the trouble of putting up a brace like that? I can promise you that there are no valuable antiques in that old shack."

Suddenly Louie realized that he had said too much.

"I don't know, Mr. George. Maybe whoever owns the shack might have found out about me being locked in there and wanted to make sure it didn't happen again."

"No, Louie, I can assure you there's more to it than that," the tall teacher said looking intently at his student. "Somebody is protecting something or they would not have braced the door like that. What did you and Mac find in there, Louie? I have a pretty good idea, but I want to hear it from you. What did you and Mac find in there?" he repeated. "Whatever you tell me will just be between us, okay? I won't tell anyone else."

The color had drained from the boy's face and he was staring at the floor as he listened to his leader's comments. The fear and panic on Louie's face were easy for Watson George to see as the boy sat motionless. The teacher walked back to the front row and looked down at his student.

"I'm guessing that you and Mac found some illegal drugs in there and now you don't know what to do. You don't know whether to call the police or just forget it. Am I right?"

Louie lifted his head and nodded mutely.

"It's okay, Louie. I was pretty sure after hearing your description of the brace on the door that someone must be using the old shack it to sell drugs. I don't know what you found in there, but it doesn't matter. You and Mac aren't in any kind of trouble. Would it make you feel better if I took care of this for you?"

Obviously relieved, the boy slid out of the student desk and picked up his backpack.

"Oh, thank you, Mr. George! We didn't know what to do and we were afraid we might get into trouble after seeing that box of drugs. We were glad that we didn't run into whoever they belonged to, which could have been dangerous."

"Dangerous? It could have been deadly. You were very lucky. You and Mac won't need to worry about this anymore; I'll take care of it. Besides the drugs, Louie, is there anything else you want to tell me?"

CHAPTER TEN

As soon as Jenny's soccer team meeting was over, she went to find Louie for the ride home. She knew he would probably be waiting in Mr. George's room.

"I thought I might find you in here," she said as she opened the door to the math classroom and stepped inside.

Her cousin was still seated in the student desk on the front row. Mr. George was seated at another desk turned to face him and the two were engaged in an animated conversation including mysterious hand gestures.

"I hate to break up the meeting, but I've got to go home," she told them. "I'm anxious to see if Mac got to go home today."

"Louie told me that Mac had surgery on his hand, but they expect it to be back to normal soon. Let me know how he's getting along, will you?" the teacher asked Jenny.

"Absolutely! That was so kind of you to rescue him and take him to the emergency room. I know he appreciates it, too."

"I was glad to do it."

"See you tomorrow, Mr. George," Louie said as the two kids hurried out the door.

Louie was in such high spirits that he was almost jogging before they had even reached the front door of the school.

"What's with you?" Jenny said trying to keep up with him. "Slow down, will you?"

"Can't or I might explode! Race you to the car!"

"Okay, what's this all about?" Jenny asked as soon as the two best friends were seated in the car. "You and Mr. George were having quite the conversation. What was that all about?"

"I told him that Joe Stillman invited me to go with him Saturday afternoon to search for stuff with his metal detector. I just can't wait! Mr. George told me that his cousin had one when they were kids and they found all kinds of neat stuff. They even found some really old coins. Isn't that awesome? When you came in he was giving me some ideas about how to use it and what to look for."

At the mention of Joe Stillman, Jenny's attention immediately centered on the ruggedly handsome football player. While she heard Louie's words, she didn't grasp any of the content past his name.

"Joe Stillman?" she asked. "Did you talk to Joe Stillman today?"

"Yeah! I couldn't believe it!" the boy said excitedly. "He actually came over to my table in the cafeteria and asked me if I was still planning to go with him to try out his new metal detector Saturday. I told him that I was looking forward to it and he even offered to pick me up as soon as I finished taking care of Emma."

"Did he say where you guys were going?"

"Not for sure, but it sounded like he wants to start at that old metal bridge outside of town, the one that they're going to tear down. Can't wait! This is going to be awesome!"

Jenny had noticed that Louie was not carrying the plastic bag with the old rusty coffee can.

"Hey, what happened to the coffee can with the papers in it that you brought to school today? Did you leave it in your locker?"

"No, Mr. George has it."

"What? You gave the can with the deed to the ranch to Mr. George?" Jenny exclaimed. "Why?"

For a minute, the boy frowned, tugged at his seatbelt and looked out the side window. Then he looked at Jenny.

"I didn't actually give it to him. He asked to borrow it for a day or two and I said it would be okay."

The boy interrupted his explanation when he caught sight of his friend grimacing.

"I really didn't want to let him have it, but it was so weird when he took the papers out and looked at them. He asked me where I got them and I had to tell him that I found the coffee can in the old shack."

Jenny couldn't stop herself from reacting to Louie's comment and groaned.

"I had to tell him, Jen. Anyway, he already knew that we had been inside the shack since that's where Mac got hurt. It was so strange, almost like he'd seen a ghost or something. I don't know if he knew who Caleb and Matilda Schnickel were or what, but he became very serious and that's when he asked to borrow it. There's no way that I could say no, especially when he promised to take care of it. I mean, after all, he is my Boy Scout leader."

It was immediately obvious to Jenny that he must have said something else about the old shack because the boy was no longer sitting still in the passenger seat. Knowing what high regard Louie had for Mr. George, he might have even told him about the drugs, or that someone was camping there and maybe even about the body.

"Louie, what else did you tell Mr. George?" Jenny asked sternly. "Did you tell him about the drugs?"

"I didn't actually tell him; he guessed it. I wish now that I hadn't told him about the huge brace on the door. He told me that no one would put up a brace like that unless somebody was protecting something and he guessed it was drugs. He asked me if we had found drugs and I couldn't lie, so I told him we had found some."

Jenny groaned again.

"The good thing is we're not in trouble, and we don't have to worry about it anymore. He said that he would take care of it. I'm really glad, too, because we didn't know what to do."

Jenny had just turned into the circle drive in front of the Morales home and stopped the car. She immediately reached out and grabbed Louie's arm to prevent him from getting out of the car.

"What did he mean when he said that he would take care of it? Is he going to call the police or what?"

"He didn't say, Jen. He just said that he would take care of it. I'm sure he will do whatever is right."

"I'm sorry Louie, but I don't like the sound of that. I'm

sure it will probably be okay, but this makes me very nervous. I just wish I knew what he was planning to do and if we are completely in the clear."

"He doesn't know about you, but I'm sure none of us are in trouble now."

Louie was halfway up the walk to his house when Jenny jumped out of the car and raced after him. He heard her coming and stopped in the center of the sidewalk with his backpack slung over one shoulder.

"Wait a minute, Louie," she panted as she reached his side. "I just had a horrible thought. Maybe the drugs are Mr. George's. Did you think of that? Remember he made such a big deal out of us never going back to the old shack. Remember? He made it sound like it was because we might get hurt, but what if it was because we might find his drugs?"

Before responding, the boy dropped his heavy backpack on the sidewalk and turned to face Jenny.

"No way!" he growled in an emotionally filled voice. "There's just no way that those drugs belong to Mr. George. He's against using any kind of drugs. He even teaches that in the Scouts, so don't go accusing him of being a drug dealer or something. He saved your brother, remember? He just told us not to go there because we might get hurt and he was right! It had nothing to do with drugs!"

It was clear from his words that Jenny had managed to highly offend her best friend.

"I'm sorry, Louie. I don't think Mr. George is a drug dealer, but it just seems to me that something is not right with this picture. I don't know what it is, but I just know something is definitely wrong here."

"Wrong or not, you leave Mr. George out of it!" he

snarled as he grabbed his backpack and sprinted toward the porch steps.

Jenny sighed and returned to her car. The short trip home didn't give her enough time to make sense of this new development. Louie's harsh words made her feel guilty and unhappy all at the same time and she didn't like it at all. She couldn't even think of anything to say to her cousin that might make things better.

The first thing she saw when she arrived home and walked into the kitchen was her twin brother who was sitting with his back to the door.

"Mac!" she nearly yelled with excitement. "You're home! How are you feeling? How's your hand? When did you get home?"

Before he could answer, she hurried to his side and gave him a hug.

"I've been so worried about you," she said. "What did the doctor say about your hand?"

"We're going to have an early dinner, Jen, so go upstairs and wash up. I'm sure Mac will be happy to answer all of your questions when you get back," her mother instructed.

Without a word, the girl turned toward the stairs and disappeared into her room. She was back in the kitchen in record time.

"So how is your hand?" she asked sliding into her chair at the table.

"It's beginning to hurt a little," he said propping his bandaged hand up on the table. "The nurses woke me up early this morning and wheeled me somewhere to wash the inside of my hand out again. You should see it. There's a huge gash right down the center of my palm and you can actually see inside my hand. Weird, huh?"

Jenny winced as she listened to her brother's description of his injury.

"Dr. Ashe, the surgeon who worked on my hand, came in this morning and gave us the details. Mom spent the night with me last night in the recliner, so she was there when he came in. Do you remember what he told us, Mom? I don't think I was awake enough to remember it all."

Meghan quickly dried her hands on the blue-checked towel hanging by the sink and walked over to join the twins at the table.

"You know how Mac got the splinter in his hand, Jen, so I'll just start when he got to the hospital. We found out later that the wood was so old and rotten that it literally exploded into several fragments when it pierced his hand and that presented a problem. The Emergency Room doctor took out the splintered pieces and washed the wound, but it was too deep and fragmented for him to feel confident that all of the debris was cleaned out. He also noticed that one of the arteries had a small cut, at least big enough to require a few stitches. That's why Dr. Ashe was called in.

"When he talked to us this morning, he said that Mac was very lucky. None of the fine bones in his hand were broken and no muscles, nerves, or tendons were severed. He repaired the small cut in the artery, which wasn't a big deal. However, when that large splinter penetrated his hand, it moved things around and severely bruised the nerves, muscles, and tendons, especially those between his third and fourth finger. That's why Mac couldn't feel his fingers when he got to the Emergency Room."

Jenny was visibly distraught as she listened to her

mother detail Mac's injuries. With both of her hands pressed against her mouth and her elbows firmly planted on the table, his sister subconsciously began to lean toward her twin.

"Oh, this is terrible . . . I'm so sorry," Jenny repeated softly under her breath.

"They might not have kept him for two nights, except that Mac had a large bump on his head and was nearly unconscious when Mr. George brought him in. They were afraid that he might have suffered a mild **CONCUSSION**, but thankfully that was not the case. He was also in a lot of pain and they wanted to get him started on some powerful antibiotics to make sure that any germs from the dirty wood in his hand wouldn't start an infection. That's why he was hooked up to all those tubes."

"Is your hand going to be all right?" Jenny asked.

"Yeah, but it's going to take a while," Mac said clearly depressed. "I have to go to Dr. Ashe's office again in the morning to have the gash in my hand washed out. It sounds like I may have to go several times to make sure all the dirt and micro splinters are gone."

"Didn't he stitch the gash together?" she asked.

"No. He wants to keep it open so that any foreign material can work its way out. So basically I have an open wound under this bandage."

Jenny glanced at her mother and rolled her eyes.

"Did he say how long it is going to take for it to heal?"

"Not really. It just depends on how fast my body knits it back together."

Jenny knew the primary question on Mac's mind was whether his hand would be well enough for him to play football before the season ended. She wanted to ask, but decided against it.

"I asked him if I could play football in a few weeks, and all he would say was 'Maybe, we'll have to see.' That doesn't sound very encouraging to me," the tall teen said sadly.

"I'll bet you get to play again," Jenny said trying to encourage him.

Mac shook his head and looked at his bandaged hand.

"I doubt it," he said. "There are only ten games in the season and we've already played eight of them. I'll have to heal really fast if I get to play in any of them."

"Don't worry, Mac. I just have a feeling you'll play again and I'm usually right."

"Jen, would you help me?" Meghan asked as she stood up from the table and walked back to the stove. "Dinner is almost ready."

"Sure," the girl replied taking another long look at her depressed brother.

The table was set and the meal was ready to serve in a very few minutes. A cheery blue and white plate in a country design was set in front of each chair and a steaming bowl of chicken and dumplings, a crisp green salad, and dinner rolls filled the center of the table.

"I hope you can eat this with your left hand," his mother said. "I know that chicken and dumplings are one of your favorites, but I didn't think about your hand."

"Don't worry about it," Mac muttered as he tried to chase a small dumpling around his bowl with his left hand. "I'll get the hang of this pretty soon."

The twins and their mother were still seated at the table talking and finishing dinner when Carson walked in the back door.

"That smells so good!" he exclaimed as he took a seat at the table. "I hope you saved me some."

"How is the dog?" Jenny asked, referring to the Labrador retriever that had been struck by a car late Saturday afternoon. "Is he doing better?"

Her father picked up his napkin and unfolded it over his knee before answering.

CHAPTER ELEVEN

"To answer your question, the dog is actually doing better than I expected. He's a young dog, probably not more than a year old, which is probably why he's doing so well. He's also a very sweet dog. It just breaks your heart to see him try to wag his tail anytime someone talks to him knowing how much pain he's in. I just don't know what to think about his owner."

"Hey, Jen," Mac said, pushing his bowl back from the table, "can I ride to school with you and Louie tomorrow? The doctor said I can't drive for a couple of days because of the pain pills I'm taking."

"Absolutely," his twin said. "But what about football practice? Do you need to stay late or anything?"

Mac grimaced and shrugged his shoulders.

"I don't know. Obviously, I won't be practicing, but Coach might want me to watch the drills or something, I just don't know yet."

Jenny smiled at her brother.

"Not a problem. If you have to stay, maybe I'll take Louie home and then come back or you can call me when you're ready to go. Whatever, we'll make it work."

"Thanks, Jen. I'm really tired. I'm going to turn in. I'll see you in the morning.

"Bright and early the next morning Louie was sitting on the porch with his ever-present backpack waiting for his ride to school. As soon as Jenny's car stopped, he jumped up and hurried to the car, but he didn't notice a passenger in the front seat until he had opened the door.

"Sorry, Louie," Mac said. "I've got your seat."

The boy paused for a moment before he realized who was sitting in his seat. Grinning from ear to ear, he opened the back door, tossed his backpack on the seat, and climbed in beside it.

"Wow, I didn't know that you were going to school with us today, Mac! Awesome!"

As soon as they arrived at school, Mac turned to his sister before opening the door.

"As soon as I know what Coach wants me to do about football practice, I'll text you, Jen. If he wants me to stay and watch the other guys practice, could you pick me up later?"

She nodded as the three made their way to the front door barely in time for the first class. Jenny didn't receive a text from Mac until her lunch period was almost over. She was about to pick up her tray and go to her next class when her cell phone chimed with a text from Mac.

Coach wants me to stay for practice.

I'll text you when it's over.

Louie was waiting for Jenny at the front door after the last bell rang.

"Where's Mac? Is he going to ride home from school with us?" he asked.

"No, he's going to stay for football practice, so I'll have to pick him up later. I'm probably going to have to do this for a few days until he can drive. If you're not in a hurry, I need to put some gas in my car on the way home."

Louie was still talking excitedly about his plans to meet Joe Stillman Saturday afternoon for a metal detecting lesson when Jenny stopped the car in the first lane at the Gas and Grub convenience store.

"I'll buy you something to drink if you'll pump the gas for me," she offered.

"Anything?" he asked laughing at the face she made in response to his question.

Once inside the store, she handed the clerk a $20 bill and asked her to set the gas pump for $10.00 worth of gas. Then the two best friends headed to the cooler to make their drink selections. Jenny chose a bottle of spring water while her cousin found his favorite soft drink.

As soon as the clerk rang up the drinks, Louie grabbed his soda and headed outside to pump the gas. Jenny had just put the change in her purse and had turned to walk outside when another shopper nearly bumped into her.

For a long moment, she simply stood and stared at the young woman, who was making her way to the snack aisle. Jenny could feel her heart go into overdrive as she hurried out of the store.

Louie had just hung up the gas pump hose when Jenny rushed up to him.

"It's her! Get in the car quick," Jenny told him in a loud whisper.

"Who?" he asked obviously puzzled once he was back inside the car.

"It's the girl who is camping at the old shack and she's very much alive!"

"How would you know that?" Louie asked skepticism coloring his words.

Jenny's eyes were wide with excitement as she put the car key into the ignition and started her car.

"Because I knew who it was the instant I saw her clothes. Remember the orange sweatshirt and jeans I saw at the old shack? That's what this girl is wearing."

"There's got to be a million pairs of jeans and sweatshirts that match that description," Louie protested.

"Not a neon orange sweatshirt with a red heart embroidered on the front of it and torn up blue jeans with rhinestones on the back pockets."

Before the two cousins could finish their discussion, the dark-headed young woman walked out of the store carrying a white plastic bag. The two watched as she walked over to an older gray car parked in the front of the store and got in. As she started the car and began to back out of the parking space, Jenny made a snap decision.

"I'm going to follow her," she declared. "If that girl goes to the old shack, we'll know for sure that she's the one who's living there."

"I don't know . . ." Louie began as Jenny's car pulled behind the beat-up older model car. "Don't let her know that we're following her, okay?"

"I won't," Jenny said excitedly. "I've never followed anyone like this before. It's just like in the movies!"

Louie got a good look at the girl's car as she turned out of the convenience store parking lot and onto the street with Jenny close behind.

"I've seen that car before!" Louie suddenly exclaimed. "I've seen it down by the bridge where people leave their pickups to go fishing."

"Are you sure?"

"Positive. One of the back side windows was broken out with plastic taped all over it and the car looked like it had been in a serious hail storm."

"Write down the license number just in case. There is a pad of paper and a pen in the glove compartment."

By the time Louie had written the tag number and the car's description on the pad, they could see the car pull across the highway and park near the bridge.

"I don't want to park down there," Jenny said. "Try to keep an eye on her while I drive up a little further and turn around."

They could see the young woman standing by the side of the highway waiting to cross as the two drove slowly by.

"She's headed to the shack!" Louie all but shouted as he watched her cross the road and disappear into the woods. "Are we going to follow her?"

Jenny turned the car around at the first intersection and started back to the bridge.

"Maybe she won't notice if I park on this side of the bridge," Jenny said as she turned off the highway and parked in the grass.

The two teens bounded out of the car and ran across the highway toward the shack. They made it into the woods and behind a large pine tree just in time to see her pry open the boarded up window and disappear inside.

"Oh, wow!" Louie whispered. "It was her!"

"Told you," Jenny whispered back.

"How old do you think she is? Maybe 17 or 18?"

"That would be my guess, but it's hard to tell. I'm just glad that she's alive. Let's get out of here before she decides to leave again."

As the two cousins quietly slipped out of their hiding place and started toward the highway Jenny suddenly stopped.

"Wait a minute, Louie. A bug or something is crawling on my leg."

Jenny stopped at the edge of the woods and pulled up her left jeans leg. A black bug was clinging to her leg about two inches above her ankle. She instantly knocked it off her leg and shuddered.

"I hate bugs!" she declared. "What was that thing?"

Louie watched it fall onto a dead leaf and immediately picked it up.

"It's a **TICK**, Jen," he said examining it closely. "Did it bite you?"

"No, I don't think so, I just felt it crawling. I think I knocked it off before it had a chance to bite me. Surely I would have felt it if it had bitten me."

"At least it's not an American Dog Tick," he said as he carefully examined the black insect. "There are several kinds of ticks found in Oklahoma, but it's the only one that carries the bacteria that causes Rocky Mountain Spotted fever. Even if it bit you, there's less than a 3% chance that you would become infected. Anyway, this one isn't colorful enough to be an American Dog Tick."

"How to you know stuff like that?" she asked.

"I'm a Scout, Jen, and I want to be an Eagle Scout someday, so I've got to know about all kinds of things."

"Come on, let's get out of here before we get caught," she said as they ran across the highway to where the car was parked. "I need to take you home."

They were talking so excitedly on the way to Louie's house that Jenny missed the text from Mac.

"What are we going to do now that we know about that girl?" Jenny asked.

Louie thought for a minute before answering.

"Maybe I should tell Mr. George," he said. "He already knows about the drugs in the old shack, so maybe he needs to know about this, too."

Jenny didn't answer for several minutes obviously pondering Louie's suggestion.

"That might not be a bad idea," she said slowly. "He probably knows how to trace car tags, so that would be a good place to start."

"Yeah!" the boy said excitedly. "That's awesome! If he traced the tag, he could find out who owns the car. Then we would know who that girl is and why she is camping out at the old shack. I'm going to tell Mr. George tomorrow."

Jenny had just pulled into the circle drive in front of Louie's house and was about to stop when she turned to him.

"Do you want me to stop by his room after school so that we can tell him together?"

"Yeah, I guess, if you want to," he said somewhat less

than enthusiastically.

Louie had just retrieved his backpack and was starting up the sidewalk when Jenny's cell phone chimed with an incoming text.

WHERE ARE YOU??? ARE YOU GOING TO PICK ME UP??? PRACTICE IS OVER!!!!!

Jenny's heart sank as she read Mac's desperate message. She immediately texted back.

ON MY WAY. SORRY I'M LATE! BE THERE SOON.

As she approached the football field, she could see two boys sitting alone in the first row of the bleachers. She identified Mac immediately, but couldn't tell for sure who was sitting with him. As she pulled into the parking lot, the boys started walking toward the car.

"It's about time you got here," Mac complained. "Practice has been over for almost 45 minutes. I would have had to sit out here all by myself if Joe hadn't volunteered to stay with me until you showed up. He offered to take me home, but I told him that you were on your way. I'm sure he was beginning to think I made that up."

Jenny could feel her face turning bright red.

"I am so sorry, Mac," she said. "Time just got away from me."

"You need to apologize to Joe, too," Mac scolded her. "I'm sure he has other things to do besides sitting out here with me."

The girl was almost too embarrassed to sprak.

"Thank you for staying out here with Mac, Joe," she managed to mumble. "I'm sorry I was late. I hope it didn't mess up your plans too much."

'Why did it have to be Joe Stillman?' she thought to herself. 'He probably thinks I'm a complete idiot.'

"No worries, Jen. I understand," the tall good-looking football player said smiling warmly at her. "I'll see you later."

As soon as she had driven out of the parking lot and turned onto the highway Mac began his questions.

"Where were you? What was so important that you couldn't break away and come get me?" he demanded.

"I'm sorry you had to wait so long. I really am, but it was important," Jenny said. "Louie and I discovered the woman that's camping out in the old shack at the Gas and Grub and we followed her back there. It's a long story; I'll tell you when we get home."

After supper, Jenny knocked on Mac's bedroom door.

"If you've got time, I'll tell you everything that happened this afternoon."

An hour and a half later, Jenny was still sitting in Mac's desk chair while he was propped up on his bed listening to her story.

"I didn't know you told Mr. George about the drugs we found," he said. "When did you do that?"

"Louie told him yesterday. Tomorrow we're planning to tell him about the woman we saw at the convenience store. So how did you get along at football practice?"

"All I could do was watch, but Coach said it was important for me to be at practice every day to keep up with the team. So can you pick me up after school for the next several days until I get off these pain pills and the doctor clears me to drive?"

"Sure, and I'll try not to be late next time. If I'm running late I'll text, okay?"

"By the way, Mom is taking me to the doctor at noon tomorrow to get my wound washed out again. There was so much debris and tiny pieces of wood in it that it was hard to get it all cleaned out. I think I have to go in another time or two until they are sure there is no contamination or infection. I still have to keep taking these antibiotics, too. Dr. Ashe wants to keep a close watch on my hand to make sure it's healing properly. I hope it hurries up because I still can't feel my third and fourth fingers."

"I am so sorry about your hand," Jenny said as she stood up and began to walk toward the door. "I want it to heal quickly so that you can play football again. The team really needs you."

Before Mac could respond, Jenny's cell phone rang.

"It's Allison," she said as she opened the door. "I sent her pictures of the old shack that I took last Sunday because she likes to paint old buildings and stuff. I'll see you in the morning."

The next morning when Jenny stopped to pick up Louie, he remembered to open the back door even though he couldn't see Mac in the front seat.

"I'm a little worried about today," he announced as he climbed in and gently closed the car door.

"Oh, yeah? Why is that?" Mac asked.

"Jen and I are planning to stop by Mr. George's room after school today and tell him about the woman we saw at the Gas and Grub who seems to be camping at the old shack. I don't know why, but I'm a little nervous about telling Mr.

George. I guess because he acted very strange when I showed him the coffee can with those old paper deeds in it. I don't know. It's just weird, that's all."

"Why don't you and Jen think about it this afternoon and decide whether you want to tell him when school is out," Mac offered.

"Good idea, Mac! Louie, we can meet by the water fountain on the first floor by my locker and decide if we want to go through with it or not. Okay?" Jenny asked.

Both teens were so anxious about the decision to tell Mr. George about the girl in the shack that neither of them could concentrate in class. At first, Jenny was almost certain that they should tell him everything, but now she wasn't so sure. As soon as the final bell rang, both of them rushed to the water fountain.

"What do you think we should do?" she asked as soon as they had stepped out of the way of the noisy students leaving for the day.

"I don't know," he said in a solemn voice. "I've gone back and forth on it all day. I just don't know. Right now, I don't want to tell him anything. What do you think?"

"I did the very same thing. I don't even have an opinion right now. Why don't you want to tell him about that girl we saw?"

Louie stopped and looked around as if to see if anyone was listening to their conversation before continuing.

"There's something creepy here, Jen. I don't know what it is, but if you could have seen his reaction to that old coffee can with the deed inside it, you'd know what I'm talking about. If it's okay with you, I think we should wait for a while."

"Works for me!" she said enthusiastically. "To tell you the truth, I was really dreading it. Let's get out of here!"

Both teens were nearly giddy on the ride home.

"Guess who found me in the cafeteria today?" Louie asked grinning broadly. "Joe Stillman! He came over and sat down at my table to ask what time I wanted him to pick me up Saturday afternoon to check out his new metal detector. I couldn't believe it!"

"Awesome! Did he give you any details?"

"Yeah, he did. You know that old railroad bridge north of town? He wants to look around in that area since that bridge is so old. He's going to pick me up about 2:00 o'clock when I'm finished babysitting Emma. I just can't wait!"

"Are you talking about that rusty old metal bridge that they keep talking about tearing down?"

"That's the one. Joe told me that he thought it was built during the depression sometime during the 1930s. It might even be older than that. The railroad still runs trains over it, so I guess it must be in pretty good shape even though it looks terrible. I don't know what he thinks he might find out there, but whatever it's going to be fun."

CHAPTER TWELVE

When Jenny stopped for a traffic light, she looked at her friend and laughed.

"Well, I can tell you one thing," she chuckled. "That old bridge is going to be pretty busy Saturday afternoon. Too bad I wasn't invited."

When she saw a puzzled look appear on his face, she continued.

"This is really strange, Louie. You know those pictures I took with my cell phone when we were out at the old shack Sunday? Allison Canary likes to draw and paint old stuff like that, so I sent some of the pictures to her. Here's the weird part. When she called me last night to thank me for sending the pictures, she told me that she was afraid they were going to demolish that old railroad bridge before she could paint it. So she's going out there Saturday afternoon with her boyfriend, Josh, and a couple of other people to take pictures."

"Seriously?"

"Yes, seriously. Does Joe know that?"

"He didn't mention it. I'd be surprised if he knows Allison very well since she's only a sophomore. I don't know her very well either, so this should be interesting."

As soon as Jenny stopped the car in the circle drive at the Morales home, the boy jumped out, grabbed his backpack from the back seat, and sprinted toward the steps. She put the car in gear, turned back toward the highway, and retraced her route to the football field. She knew that it was much too early for football practice to be over, but she also knew that Joe Stillman would be practicing with the team and as far as she was concerned, it would be worth the wait.

Jenny could see the team running plays on the field as soon as she turned into the parking lot. As soon as she parked the car, she grabbed her jacket and headed for the bleachers. It didn't bother her that she was the only spectator, but what did bother her was that she couldn't figure out which player was Joe.

'Where is #59?' she asked herself carefully scanning each player on the field. Mac had told her that Joe was a running back on the offensive team and they were on the field, but there wasn't any #59. Where was Joe? Across the field, she could see her brother dejectedly sitting on the bench watching his teammates practice.

For over an hour, she watched the team run up and down the field. After examining each player's number, she was sure there was no #59 on the field. To make matters even worse, all of the players looked pretty much alike with their pads and helmets. She tried to concentrate on the players catching passes, but she couldn't tell which one was Joe.

She finally gave up and sat back in her seat to wait until the practice was over.

By the time the players left the field, it was beginning to get chilly. Jenny zipped her jacket, turned up the collar, and stuck her hands in her pockets to keep warm. She had nearly decided to give up and wait in the car when she saw two boys walking toward her. The boy with the bandaged hand was obviously Mac; the other was Joe. She could feel her face beginning to flush as the two approached her seat on the first row of the bleachers.

"Look who's here?" Joe laughed pointing at her. "It's your late sister, who's not even late anymore. Hi, Jenny."

Before she could return his greeting, Mac reached over and thumped her arm.

"You look like you're freezing. Have you been out here the whole time?"

She couldn't seem to find words, so she simply nodded her head.

"I think you guys played pretty well today," Mac said to Joe. "Didn't you think Damien played much better today than he did last week?"

"Who is Damien?" Jenny asked when she finally found her voice.

"Damien Venn," Joe told her. "He's our backup quarterback. He's pretty good, but he's not nearly as good as Mac. He's only a sophomore and he doesn't have very much experience. I'll just be glad when Mac can play again."

"Did you practice today, Joe? I didn't see your #59?" Jenny asked.

"Yes, I did, but something happened to my practice jersey a couple of weeks ago, so they gave me another one. I was #27 today."

'No wonder I couldn't find him,' Jenny thought to herself. 'I wish I had known that.'

"Gotta go, guys," Joe said as he turned to leave. "I'll see you tomorrow Mac. Bye Jenny."

"Come on, Jen. Let's get you to the car," Mac said as he put his good hand on his twin's shoulder. "We can't have you turning into an ice cube."

Jenny turned on the heater the moment the car started. At the same time, her brother rolled down his window.

"I hope you're not planning to run that thing full blast all the way home," he complained. "It's already hot in here."

"I'll turn the heater down if you'll roll up the window," she offered.

Jenny was in such a good mood after seeing Joe for a few minutes that she really didn't care if it was hot or cold.

"Hey, Mac," she asked before they reached home. "What do you know about that old railroad bridge that's north of town?"

"That rusty old thing? I thought they were going to tear it down and build a new one. Why do you ask?"

"Because Louie and Joe are going out there with Joe's metal detector Saturday afternoon and Allison Canary and her friends are going out there too, to take pictures."

"Good for them. I'm glad they didn't ask me to go. I don't want any part of that old bridge."

Mac caught a quick glance of his sister, who was clearly confused.

"Jen, that thing's a death trap, it needs to be destroyed. Maybe you should do some research on it before your friends get sucked into its evil spell."

"Evil spell? You mean like something cast by an evil spirit?" Jenny exclaimed as she parked her car in front of the house. "I've never heard of a bridge having an evil spirit. You've got to be kidding."

"Why don't you ask Dad," Mac said as he climbed out of the passenger seat and sprinted toward the house.

Dinner was ready and both parents were preparing to eat when the teens took their places at the table.

"Dad, what can you tell me about that old railroad bridge north of town?" Jenny asked as soon as she sat down. "Mac says it has an evil spirit and it cast an evil spell on it."

Carson finished filling his plate with homemade meat-loaf and mixed vegetables before he answered his daughter. "An evil spirit?" he asked as he picked up his fork. "I don't know anything about an evil spell. Why do you think it has an evil spirit, Mac?"

"Because of all the people that died on it," the teen said confidently.

His mother laughed out loud before she could catch herself.

"Mac if you're trying to scare your sister, I don't think it's going to work. First of all, as far as I know, there are no documented deaths associated with that bridge. I've heard urban legends about hobos back in the 1930s who were trying to read graffiti on the side of the bridge and being run over by trains. I've even heard some wild tales about a few broken-hearted lovers climbing the bridge and taking a swan dive to the rocks below. Sorry to disappoint you, Mac, but I'm positive that there are no evil spells or evil spirits associated with that old bridge."

Jenny made a face at her brother and stuck her tongue

out at him.

"What's with the hobo thing, Mom? Are there still any hobos around?"

Meghan finished her last bite of meat loaf and pushed her plate out of the way.

"Do you know anything about the Great Depression, back in the 1930s, Jen?"

The girl nodded her head.

"Back then no one had very much money and a lot of men were out of work. Sometimes those men would hop into boxcars on passing trains for a free ride to other areas of the country hoping to find a job. They called those men hobos. They even had some kind of a code among themselves. I've read that they would write notes to each other on the insides of bridges and other places with information on where to find a free meal and things like that."

Mac and Carson had also finished eating and were leaning back in their chairs listening.

"You asked me about that bridge, Jen," her father said. "That's a type of truss bridge that was probably made sometime between the late 1800s and the late 1930s. It was mostly made out of iron, which is why it's so rusty. I've never seen a date on it, but it could probably be close to a hundred years old. I don't think they make tall bridges like that anymore."

"Did you and your friends ever try to climb it when you were a kid?" Mac asked.

"I'm sure we might have thought about it, but that thing is probably 20' tall and there are not a lot of things to hold on to. None of my friends were brave enough to try it."

"It just doesn't look like it would be that hard to climb," Mac continued.

"Yes, I know. Especially since the sides are open and braced with about five X beams on each side. But you've got to remember, too that it's another 20 or 30 feet down to the creek. That could do damage if you fell."

Jenny was clearly fascinated with the history of the old railroad bridge.

"No wonder Joe wants to look around it with his metal detector Saturday afternoon," she said. "Louie is going with him, too. What do you think they will find?"

No one answered for a moment. Finally, after he finished a long sip of ice tea, her father responded.

"My guess would be not much," he said. "If he's really lucky, he might find some old bolts or something the builders discarded."

"Maybe one of the hobos threw something out of a boxcar before it went over the bridge," Jenny offered.

"You're dreaming," her brother scoffed. "They were poor, remember?"

"Say, Mac," Carson interrupted, "how is your hand? Is it feeling any better?"

"Yeah, it's getting there. Dr. Ashe said that he will probably take the bandage off next week," the boy said.

"Did he say if you might get to play football before the season is over? I know that there are only a few more games before the big championship game."

Mac frowned and stared at his empty plate.

"He didn't really say if I can play or not, especially since I still have very little feeling in my third and fourth fingers right now," Mac said softly. "Probably not, but he did say as soon as the bandage is removed next week I can do a little PHYSICAL CONDITIONING with the team as long as I don't try to throw the ball or get tackled or anything."

"I know you're disappointed, Mac," his mother said. "I'm just so thankful that your hand is healing so well. You'll have plenty of games to play next year, but I know it's hard right now."

Friday morning dawned crisp and cool, perfect football weather. Louie was standing on the sidewalk when Jenny pulled into the circle drive. He instinctively opened the back door and climbed inside.

Mac turned around in his seat to talk to his cousin. "Dr. Ashe said I might be able to drive next week, so you'll get your seat back."

"Awesome! Do you get to play football again, too?" Louie asked.

"No, not yet."

"Mac, are you staying for football practice after school today?" Jenny asked.

"No, I'm riding home with you and Louie. There's a game tonight, so there's no practice, remember?"

"Okay, sorry. You don't need to bite my head off. I can't keep track of your schedule."

As soon as Jenny had parked her car in the middle of the school parking lot, Mac grabbed his backpack, bolted out of the car and sprinted toward the school leaving Jenny and Louie behind.

As the two best friends walked toward the front door of the school, Jenny and Louie began to talk about Mr. George and the old shack.

"Has Mr. George said anything to you about the deed in the old coffee can or anything?" Jenny asked.

"No, and I didn't want to bring it up. I just think he

will tell me when he's ready."

"Does that means you don't want to tell him about that girl we saw at the Gas and Grub, either?" she asked.

"I'm just not ready to say anything yet, okay?"

"Fine with me," Jenny said. "I'll see you after school."

Mac was impatiently waiting at the car when Jenny and Louie joined him for the ride home.

"Guess what, Jen!" he said excitedly as she struggled to get her car key into the door lock. "Coach wants me to suit up for the game tonight! I can't play, but he wants me to at least sit on the bench and be a part of the team."

"That's awesome!" his sister said enthusiastically. "I'm glad. What time does the game start? Do you need me to take you?"

"The game starts at 7:00 p.m. and no, you don't have to take me. Joe is going to pick me up about 6:00 o'clock, so you're off the hook."

"What position does Joe play? I know he's number #59, but that's about it."

"He's probably our best wide receiver, Jen. He's really good at running the routes, so it makes it a lot easier for the quarterback. I just wish I was playing tonight."

"Joe's going to pick me up, too!" Louie said excitedly interrupting the conversation.

"When? Tonight? Are you going to the game?" Mac asked obviously confused.

"No, not tonight. He's going to pick me up about 2:00 o'clock tomorrow afternoon to go treasure hunting with his new metal detector," Louie said. "I can't wait!"

'I wish Joe was going to pick me up,' Jenny thought.

"Jen told me that her friend Allison Canary is going

out to the old bridge, too. I guess she wants to draw it before they tear it down."

"Yeah, Jen told me. She likes to paint old buildings and stuff like that. I guess I'll see you next week, Mac. I hope our team wins," Louie said as Jenny brought the car to a stop. Pausing for a moment, the twins watched the slightly-built boy wrestle his large backpack to his shoulder and walk slowly toward his house. He turned at the front door and waved goodbye.

The next morning Meghan called softly through her daughter's upstairs bedroom door.

"Are you awake, Jen? I just wanted you to know that your dad and I are leaving for the vet clinic."

"Mom," a sleepy voice replied, "I'm awake. What time is it anyway?"

"It's a little after 8:00 o'clock. Go back to sleep, Jen; it's Saturday. You sound exhausted. We'll see you later this afternoon."

CHAPTER THIRTEEN

Jenny heard both doors of her father's black SUV close and then drive away before she could find the energy to climb out of her bed. She knew that her twin brother would not be awake for at least another hour, so she had the house to herself.

Slipping on her leopard-print house slippers and grabbing her cell phone, the tall blonde teen walked silently past her brother's bedroom door and down the stairs.

The minute she walked through the kitchen door, Jenny could smell freshly baked cinnamon rolls. She immediately spotted the large plate of pastries on the counter covered with a blue gingham napkin and helped herself. After pouring a large glass of milk, she sat down at her place at the table to enjoy a leisurely Saturday morning breakfast. She was thoroughly enjoying every bite of her mother's special recipe when a thought flashed through her mind. Setting down her cinnamon roll and picking up her phone, she pushed the speed dial button to call Louie.

"Hey, tell me something," she began as soon as Louie answered the phone. "How do you search for car tags online? Do I just Google the tag number?"

"Yeah, you can start with Google, but it will probably direct you to some other site. Why? Whose car tag are you trying to find?"

"That girl we saw at the Gas and Grub convenience store. You wrote down her tag number and car description on the pad in my car, but we haven't had time to find out who it belongs to. If I go out to my car in a little while and get it, would you have time to help me if I can't figure it out?"

"Sure. I'm waiting for Aunt Nala to pick me up to babysit Emma this morning, but I can talk anytime between now and about 1:00 o'clock. Just let me know what you find out. Don't forget that Joe is picking me up at 2:00 o'clock to go to the old bridge."

'How could I forget?' Jenny thought as she ended the call. Finishing her breakfast, she walked out to her car and retrieved the pad with the information Louie had copied. Back upstairs, she opened her laptop and began to search. Just like Louie had explained, Google directed her to other sites that identified car tags and their owners. In a matter of seconds, one of the sites delivered a description of the car bearing the tag number Jenny had entered. However, discovering the owner of the car wasn't free. She tried other sites with the same result. Frustrated, she called Louie back.

"What did you find out?" he asked as he answered the call. "Did you find out who owns the car?"

"No, not yet. There are several sites that trace car tags. I found out the license tag belongs to a car matching the description of the one we saw. It's a 1994 gray 4-door Honda Accord. It also gives the VIN number, but to get the owner's name costs money."

"We already knew most of that except for the year the car was made," Louie said. "So how much does it cost to get the owner's name?"

"The cheapest site I found costs $2.95 for a trial subscription, but it takes a credit card to set it up. I don't have one. Do You?" Jenny asked.

"No, I don't have one either. We're going to have to figure this out. Listen, I've got to go. Emma's calling me. We'll talk soon."

Jenny turned back to her laptop and ran site after site with the same results. Finally, accepting defeat, she closed her laptop and flopped down on her bed to think. Question #1: Who among her friends had a credit card? And Question #2: Would that person consent to making an online purchase for her? She closed her eyes and inventoried every one of her friends. As far as she knew, no one had a credit card.

Her mental exercise was interrupted by the slamming of Mac's bedroom door next to her room. 'Mac!' she thought. 'He knows everybody. I'll bet he knows somebody with a credit card!' Springing from her bed, she excitedly dashed downstairs barefooted.

"Mac!" she panted as she burst into the kitchen. "I need to ask you something."

Her twin had just discovered the plate of cinnamon rolls and was trying to pick out the largest one for his breakfast. Her request was ignored.

"Mac!" Jenny said again a little louder this time. "Listen to me! This is very important!"

Still concentrating on the unexpected pleasure of a homemade cinnamon roll, Mac placed his selection on a paper towel and opened the refrigerator to retrieve the carton of milk. Then he set his roll, the milk carton, and a large glass on the table and sat down to enjoy his breakfast.

"Mac!" Jenny repeated loudly for the third time.

"Oh, hi Jen," her brother said finally noticing his sister. "Check out these rolls. Mom must have made them this morning. They are amazing!"

"I know, they're delicious, but I need to ask you something. Do you know anybody that has a credit card?"

"What?" the surprised teen asked between bites. "A credit card? Why do you need a credit card?"

Jenny walked over to the counter, treated herself to another roll, picked up the glass that she had used earlier, and sat down at the table across from her brother.

"Remember the girl that Louie and I followed back to the old shack? He wrote down her car tag and a description of her car. I found websites online that can identify the car and the car's owner, but it takes a credit card to access the information. Do you think any of your friends might have one we could use to access the information?" she asked.

Mac took a long drink of cold milk before answering her question.

"I'm pretty sure none of my friends have a credit card. I think you might have to be 18 to apply for one. Let me think about it and I'll let you know."

"Mac, if that girl is hiding out in that old shack and using drugs, her life could be in danger. She's already passed out or maybe overdosed at least once. We need to find out who she is as soon as possible and get her some help."

"Why don't you and Louie forget about all this spy stuff and just call the cops?"

"Because I think she's too young to die and we want to get her some help, not get her arrested. Are you going to help us or not?"

Mac finished his second cinnamon roll and walked over to put his milk glass in the sink and his paper towel in the trash.

"Do you need a ride to the gym or anything today?" Jenny asked as she followed him to the sink with her glass.

"No. I can't really do very much in the gym until I get this bandage off my hand. There's no football practice today either since we had a game last night," Mac said sounding very dejected.

"So what are you going to do this afternoon?"

"Obviously not very much since I can't drive and my friends are all doing other things. I'll probably just play games on my computer this afternoon."

"I don't have anywhere to go either, so I guess I'll just do some work on my computer, too for a while."

Mac wiped his hands on his green-and-tan flannel pajama pants and walked out of the kitchen toward the stairs. Jenny put the drinking glasses in the dishwasher and cleaned up the kitchen before following her brother upstairs.

Back in her room, Jenny opened her laptop and resumed her search for the mysterious car tag. She searched every site she could find including the State Department of Motor Vehicles website. Every website either led to a dead end or to a promise of the desired information requiring a credit card. Once again she gave up and called Louie.

"Can you talk for a minute?" she asked as soon as he

answered the call.

"Yeah, this is a good time. Emma is watching her favorite TV shows and I'm working math problems for class Monday. What's up?"

"I can't find the owner's name online without a credit card," Jenny admitted. "I asked Mac if he knew anyone that might have one. He's supposed to be thinking about it, but I don't have a lot of hope. Have you come up with anyone?"

"No, but I do have a question. What are we going to do if we find out who owns the car? Are we going to tell Mr. George about the girl in the old shack or what?"

Jenny thought for a minute as she closed her laptop.

"I don't know, Louie, I just don't know. I've been thinking about that, too. Maybe we should make that decision when we find out who owns the car."

"Yeah, you're probably right. Listen, I've got to go. Aunt Nala is ready to take me home. I'll talk to you later."

The call ended sooner than Jenny expected. As she looked around her bedroom with its cheery lemon-yellow painted walls, she realized that she was not interested in continuing to search the web. Instead, she stepped into her closet and grabbed a pair of jeans and a sky-blue sweatshirt with the words "Choctaw Soccer" and a soccer ball imprinted on the front. In a matter of minutes, she was dressed and ready for a new adventure. Picking up her purse and cell phone, she stepped into the hall and stopped in front of Mac's door. The door was open and she could see him seated at his desk playing a video game still barefoot and wearing his flannel pajama pants and a white tee shirt.

"Hey, Mac," she called knocking on the doorjamb. "I just had an idea."

"Oh, yeah? What's that?" he said turning to look at his sister.

"What would you think about going out to the old railroad bridge and watching Joe and Louie look for stuff with Joe's metal detector? Allison is planning to go out there and take pictures, which means your friend, Josh will also be there, too."

"That sure beats sitting around here, let's do it!" he exclaimed. "I'll meet you downstairs in a minute."

Jenny was waiting with car keys in hand when Mac raced down the stairs and to join. Still wearing a white tee shirt, he had pulled on a pair of sweatpants, his athletic shoes, and a jacket.

"Joe and Louie aren't going to get there until after 2:00 o'clock. We've got plenty of time, so we could stop by Chicken Annie's on the way if you'd like. I'll even buy your lunch," she said with a sly grin."

"I'd never turn that down!" he laughed.

After an enjoyable meal, the two climbed back into Jenny's car and headed to the old bridge. As they approached it, they could see Joe and Louie unloading the metal detector, a shovel, a bag, and something that appeared to be hand tools from the back of Joe's car, which was parked on the side of the highway. The boys were walking toward the railroad bridge when Jenny pulled in behind Joe's car and parked. On the other side of the creek, they could see Allison and her friend, Josh, also walking toward the bridge.

"Hey, Joe!" Mac called as he and Jenny approached the two treasure hunters. "Do you mind if we watch for a little while?"

"Not at all," the tall football player called back. "However, if we find anything, you'll have to dig it up for us. Deal?"

"Deal!" Mac replied with a laugh as he and his sister walked through the bar ditch toward the railroad tracks which paralleled the highway.

Allison spotted Jenny as she walked toward the bridge and waved.

"Hey, Jenny," she yelled. "Thanks for sending the pictures of that old shack. They are awesome. I'm already starting to paint one of them."

"That's great," Jenny called back. "Today is perfect for taking pictures of this rusty old bridge. I can't wait to see how they turn out."

Joe was already testing his metal detector and giving Louie instructions on how it worked when Mac and Jenny reached them.

Jenny was obviously unimpressed with the device that Joe was holding.

"Is that it? Is that the metal detector?" she asked pointing at the device which looked to be about three-and-a-half feet long with a small metal box with black plastic knobs and a handle attached to one end and a round ring on the other end.

"Yeah!" Louie confirmed. "That's it. It's not very big, but this one is really powerful! It can find anything metal even if it's buried several feet deep."

"We're going to walk up and down both sides of the track about five or six feet out for a little ways," Joe explained. After we've explored this side, then we'll move to the other side of the tracks."

"Hope you find something," Jenny said clearly uninspired as she watched Joe adjust the volume on the box and begin to sweep the area with the detector.

From time to time there would be a small chirp which would cause both boys to excitedly stop and locate the source of the sound. After twenty minutes of searching, they had managed to locate a variety of beer can tabs, two rusty bolts, and a few small unidentifiable items that might have been part of a harness or a buckle of some kind.

"Let's trade off," Joe said to Louie as he handed over the metal detector. "You search and I'll carry the shovel. Let's cross over the tracks and start back toward the bridge. If we don't find anything over here, we can try looking on the other side of the bridge."

It was obvious that Louie was thrilled to be operating the metal detector. He very slowly and carefully passed the round locator ring over every small bump and indentation in the search area.

Another fifteen minutes of standing ankle deep in weeds watching the boys play with Joe's metal detector and Jenny was ready to do something else. Suddenly the metal detector began to emit a series of high-pitched beeps.

"What did you find? Mac asked eagerly as he moved closer to the spot where Louie was excitedly passing the metal detector's ring over a small patch of bare ground.

Joe quickly began to shovel the spot where the sound was the loudest. A few inches below the surface of the ground, he discovered the rusty remains of what had been a hunting knife.

"Look at this!" he exclaimed excitedly holding up the mud-encrusted and badly deteriorated knife. "I'll bet this thing is 100 year's old!"

"Let me see it!" Louie said reaching for their trophy.

He carefully took the cylindrically-shaped object from his friend and turned it over and over in his hands. Then he gently rubbed off some of the dirt to examine what could be seen of the old knife.

"You'd think that thing was made of pure gold," Jenny muttered under her breath.

"Do you think it's a Bowie knife?" Joe asked trying to get a better look.

"No, it's too small to be a Bowie knife," Louie said. "Unfortunately, it's just an old hunting knife."

"What's a Bowie knife?" Jenny asked. "Are you saying 'Bowie' like Jim Bowie who fought the Mexican army with Davy Crockett at the Alamo?"

"Exactly," her cousin replied. "Jim Bowie was a notorious knife fighter in Louisiana before he went to the Alamo. He hired knife-maker James Black to custom-make his knife in the mid-1800s. The original Bowie knife was pretty large. It was over 9" long, the blade was an inch and a half wide, and it had an "S"-shaped crossbar to protect his hand. Jim Bowie wore it on his belt everywhere he went."

"Then you're right about it being too small to be a Bowie knife," Mac said as he reached for the rusted knife.

"There's even a famous saying about a Bowie knife," Louie said. "It must be long enough to use as a sword, sharp enough to use as a razor, wide enough to use as a paddle, and heavy enough to use as a hatchet."

"You're just incredible!" Jenny said complimenting her best friend. "How do you know so much stuff?"

"Because I'm interested in a lot of things and I read a lot. You might want to give it a try sometime," he teased.

Jenny rolled her eyes, and shook her head.

CHAPTER FOURTEEN

As Joe reached out to retrieve the knife from Mac, he realized that Jenny hadn't had a chance to examine it.

"Would you like to see it, Jen?" he asked holding it out to her. "I'm sorry we've been hogging it."

"No, that's okay, Joe, but thanks. I really don't care anything about knives. You guys can keep it.

Jenny realized that she had no interest in treasure hunting and even less in old knives, so she turned toward the bridge to see what her friend was doing. Allison was standing in the middle of the bridge with her back to Jenny, cell phone camera pointed at the top of the bridge's rusty iron structure. Her friend, Josh was sitting on the grass outside the entrance to the bridge watching her take pictures. Jenny decided to walk over to the bridge to talk to them. As she turned to tell the boys where she was going, a bright light caught her eye. Even though she couldn't hear it, she instantly knew that it was a freight train rounding the curve toward the bridge.

"Train!" she screamed as loudly as she could. "Train! Allison get off the bridge!"

At the same time, Joe also saw the light approaching. He dropped the old knife and took off running full speed through the ankle-deep grass and weeds beside the tracks toward the bridge in a desperate attempt to outrun the train.

Even though she couldn't hear it, Jenny could see the engine approaching rapidly. Frozen with fear that her friends would be hit and killed by the train, which did not appear to be slowing, all she could do was scream.

"NOOOOOOOOOO!"

Her one-word protest rivaled the loudest, guttural primal scream. Then, in a kind of twisted duet, the train's warning horn sounded to blend with her visceral scream. As if in slow-motion, Jenny could see the entire scene unfold from her side of the train tracks. She could see Joe, the tall, handsome football player she adored, racing against time to save a friend who was oblivious to the mortal danger bearing down on her.

Mac and Louie were frozen in fear as they realized what was happening. Then Jenny on one side of the tracks, and the boys on the other side started sprinting after Joe with the train approaching full-speed between them.

'He'll never make it!' The thought struck Jenny with a sickening horror as she watched Joe running toward the bridge. Unable to turn her eyes away from what she knew was about to happen, she steeled herself for the inevitable. Before the cousins could reach the bridge several yards ahead of them, the train flew by them with the deafening sound of metal-against-metal, sparks flying as the train's engineer frantically applied the brakes. Then, as the train reached the trestle, Joe reached Allison.

It all happened so fast. Once it reached the bridge, it took the speeding freight train less than ten seconds to reach the center of the bridge where Allison stood. Jenny was still at least six feet away from the bridge running as fast as she could and yelling at her friend to move when the train roared across the bridge. The last thing she saw before the freighter blocked her view was Allison, who had turned around and was now facing the oncoming locomotive, obviously frozen in fear. Then she heard her friend's heart-rending scream, something that sounded like flesh hitting metal and a loud splash in the creek below.

The freight train pulling dozens of boxcars blocked her view of the far side of the bridge. She could see the spot where Allison had been standing between the cars as they passed, but there was no sign of her or Joe. Until the train stopped, there was no way for her to reach the other side of the tracks. Even though the noise of the train braking was nearly deafening, she could still hear men's voices shouting above the din. The only word that she could clearly distinguish was "911!" With no way to see what had happened and expecting a double fatality, Jenny sank to her knees in the grass and sobbed uncontrollably.

It took nearly 1800' feet beyond the bridge for the train to come to a complete standstill. As soon as it finally stopped moving, Jenny ran toward the train and climbed over the couplings that joined the boxcars. She could hear sirens in the distance and men shouting as she dashed over the tracks to the edge of the creek bank.

A few feet below, she could see Allison floating face up in the middle of the creek. Joe was swimming at her side trying to hold her head up and to guide her body to the water's edge where Mac and Louie were waiting.

Jenny was so overcome with emotion at seeing Joe alive and Allison possibly not that she didn't hear the train crew race past her and slide down the bank. The commotion below suddenly brought her back to reality.

"Help me get her out of the water," she heard one of the train's crewmen shout.

From her position above the creek, she could see the two men gently lift her friend out of the water and lay her down on the small strip of dry land where the water had receded. Joe climbed out of the water and was bent over gasping for breath.

"Are you hurt, son?" she heard one of the men ask, but she couldn't hear Joe's answer.

Then she heard the other man exclaim, "Good for you! You might just be saving her life!"

Jenny didn't have to look to know that Louie was administering first aid to Allison. A few seconds later, the firefighters rushed past her. Three of them, bags of equipment in hand, hurried to the edge of the bank and made their way down to water's edge. A fourth responder was struggling to get across the couplings with a large flat board. Two paramedics from the ambulance crew were also climbing across the couplings to make their way to the creek bank.

From her vantage point on the bank, Jenny couldn't tell what the emergency responders were doing to Allison or if she was even alive. Mac, Louie, and the train crew were huddled around the men watching. Joe, who was now wrapped in a blanket and shivering, was standing behind the men. Unable to see or hear what was happening below, Jenny was seriously considering sliding down the bank herself when a cheer erupted from the men below.

"What's going on?" she shouted. "Is Allison okay? Is Joe hurt?"

Suddenly Mac and Louie appeared scrambling over the top of the creek bank near where Jenny was standing.

"Allison **NEARLY DROWNED**!" Mac panted. "It's a good thing Louie was with us. He knew to roll her on her side to get the water out of her lungs. He saved her life!"

"No!" Louie protested. "Joe saved her life, not me."

"I couldn't see what happened because the train was in the way," Jenny said. "One instant they were on the tracks and then they were gone. Did the train hit them?"

"No!" both boys said loudly in unison.

"We saw the whole thing," Louie said. "They would have never survived if that freight train had struck them."

"No, they wouldn't have." Mac agreed. "It was just miraculous, Jen! At the very last second, Joe hit Allison with the most amazing flying tackle I've ever seen and they literally flew off the bridge right through the middle of one of those "X" braces. He's a wide receiver; I didn't know he could tackle like that!"

"What about Joe?" Jenny asked seriously. "Was he hurt, too?"

"He said he wasn't," Louie said, "but he was obviously shaken up pretty badly. One of the firefighters wanted him to go to the hospital with Allison, but he refused. He said he was fine and then he just kept saying 'I'm so sorry, I'm so sorry' over and over.

"Finally one of the train crew, I think it was probably the engineer, went over and put his arm around Joe's shoulder, whispered something to him, and asked him what he was so sorry about. He told us before he went back to the train that Joe was upset because Allison was hurt so badly and that he wasn't."

"Yeah, but . . . !" Mac interrupted. "That's just part of it. Joe told me that he was sorry because when he tackled Allison he was off-center, and she hit her arm on the brace so hard that it probably shattered her arm."

"Off-center? That's crazy!" Jenny interjected. "She's very fortunate he had time to save her at all! I actually heard her arm hit the beam, but I thought the train had hit them. Anyway, he should just be thankful they both survived."

"Well, that's not the whole story, Mac," Louie continued. "I think what really, really upset Joe is the fact that when they went off the bridge, he landed right on top of her. It softened his landing, but I think it really hurt her and that is what made him feel guilty."

As the three cousins turned back to the creek to watch, they saw the firefighters secure Allison onto the board and carefully lift her up the bank and across the couplings to where the paramedics were waiting with their stretcher. The EMTs covered the nearly lifeless girl with a warm blanket and hurried toward the waiting ambulance.

As the train crew and Joe followed them up the bank, Jenny had an idea.

"I think Joe needs to go to the Emergency Room, too and at least get checked out, don't you?" she asked.

"Absolutely!" they both agreed.

"Joe," she called as he reached the top of the bank and

walked toward them clutching his blanket. "We all agree that you need to be checked out at the Emergency Room. I'll take you there right now. If you'll give Mac your car keys, he and Louie can retrieve your metal detector and stuff, and meet us there."

"No, don't do that," Joe protested. "I'm okay."

"I just want to be sure that you're okay," Jenny countered, "and besides you're freezing, so come on."

"Hey, Joe, do you still have your gym bag in the trunk of your car?" Mac asked

"Yes. I always keep it in there."

"Come on guys," Jenny interrupted, "hurry up! We've got to get back to the other side of this train before it starts moving again."

As the teens hurried back to the train and climbed across the couplings, Jenny could see the train crew slowly walking back toward the locomotive's engine.

"Jenny, go start your car and get the heater warmed up while we help Joe get into some dry clothes," Mac instructed.

The seriousness of the situation nearly overwhelmed Jenny as she started her car.

'Somebody needs to call Allison's parents!' She reached into her purse and retrieved her phone to call information. She was scribbling their number on a piece of paper when the boys walked up to her car.

Joe was still protesting when Mac opened the passenger door and ordered him into Jenny's car.

"Listen, Joe," Louie began, "we just want to make sure you're okay. It's better to find out if you're injured now when they can do something to help you."

"As soon as this thing moves," Mac said gesturing toward the train, "Louie and I will pick up your metal detector and stuff. I promise not to tear up your fenders on the way to the hospital," Mac joked.

Before Jenny turned her car around to head back toward town, she called Allison's parents. No one answered so she left an urgent message for them to call her.

Then it suddenly occurred to her that Joe needed to call his parents, too, and tell them what was going on.

"Here, Joe," she said handing her phone to him. "Call your parents and tell them we're going to the Emergency Room. They need to meet us there."

The boy hesitated for a moment before taking it.

"It's just me and my dad," he said softly. "My mom left us when I was four or five and I don't even know what happened to her."

Jenny was so stunned by his revelation that for a moment she couldn't think of anything to say.

Finally, she found her voice.

"Then call your dad," she said trying to sound supportive. "I'm sure he will want to meet us at the hospital and know that you're okay."

"There's no point in calling him. I doubt if he could come," the boy said sadly.

"Why not?"

"Because he's been working in Dallas all week and probably won't be home until later tonight."

"I don't care," Jenny said adamantly. "Call him anyway. Just do it, okay?"

Joe slowly began to enter the numbers on Jenny's cell phone. The volume was turned up so high that Jenny could hear a deep male voice answer the call on the third ring.

"Phil Stillman speaking."

"Dad! I almost got hit by a train! I tackled Allison and we went off the bridge and fell into the creek. I know you can't come, so Jenny is taking me to the Emergency Room right now!"

Joe was talking so fast and so loudly that even Jenny had a hard time understanding him even though she was sitting next to him.

"Whoa, slow it down, Joe," the man on the other end of the phone said. "I can't understand what you're talking about. Start over and go slow this time."

Joe repeated his story, but this time ended his message by saying, "I know you can't come, Dad, but that's okay. I'm not hurt or anything."

"Joe, listen to me," his father said. "Calm down. I'll see you in the Emergency Room in a few minutes. Everything is going to be all right. We're going to get through this, okay?"

"I can't believe he's actually going to go to the hospital," the boy said softly. "He's always out of town. He's never been able to make one of my football games, not even one."

Jenny felt like crying as she listened to the pain in Joe's voice and wished that she could give him a hug. She could see that his eyes were beginning to tear up as he laid her phone down on the console.

Since they were still several miles away from the hospital, Jenny decided to try a lighter topic of conversation to pass the time.

"Did Mac tell you that Louie and I saw the girl that's camping at the old shack?" Jenny asked.

"No he didn't, but Louie did. He said that you actually saw her at the Gas and Grub."

"Yes, we did. Not only that, but we actually followed her to the old shack and watched her go in."

Talking about the old shack had taken Joe's thoughts off his father and had visibly brightened his mood.

"Louie said that he even wrote down the description of the car and the tag number. Can't you use that information to find out who owns the car?" Joe asked.

Jenny quickly glanced at her passenger to see if he was showing any signs of trauma before she returned her attention to the road. He appeared to be relaxed and enjoying the conversation.

"Yes and no," Jenny replied. "Yes, the information is available online, and no we can't get it. So we don't know who owns the car. I really think it's important that we find out, too. From what we saw in that old shack, that girl's life could be in danger."

CHAPTER FIFTEEN

"Why can't you get the information? Isn't it a matter of public record?" Joe asked genuinely puzzled.

"Apparently not. I searched all of the public websites I could find for at least two hours and came up with nothing. What I did find were a lot of sites that charge for the information. I even found one site that offered a trial membership with the information for $2.95, but I couldn't use it because it required a credit card and none of us have one," Jenny said frowning, obviously frustrated at the situation. "Can you believe that? Two dollars and ninety-five cents and I couldn't even touch it! I have ten times that much money in my purse, but no credit card!"

Joe found her dilemma and the tone of her rant to be highly amusing and he laughed.

"What? No credit card?" he mocked. "I thought everyone had one of those."

"To apply for a credit card, you have to be at least eighteen years old and have a job. Mac and I are sixteen, Louie is fifteen, and none of us have a real job. So no, we not only don't have a credit card, we can't even get one for two years. Why are you laughing? It's not funny!"

"I'm laughing at you, silly! Steam is almost coming out of your ears over all this. Want to know a secret?" the boy teased.

"Probably not, but what is it?"

"I'm sixteen and I have a credit card! And it's real, too," Joe bragged with a bit of pride coloring his voice.

"No way!"

"Yes, way! Dad got it for me when I turned sixteen so that I would have money to buy gas for my car and other things I might need when he's out of town. So if it's only $2.95 to get the car owner's name, I think I can help you out."

"Oh, wow!" Jenny exclaimed. "That's awesome! Thank you, Joe, thank you, thank you, thank you!"

"Why don't you call me late tomorrow afternoon and we'll see if we can get this puppy to fly."

Jenny paused for a moment trying to process her good fortune. Suddenly she realized there was a problem.

"I don't have your cell number, Joe. Could you add it to my contacts so I'll have it?"

"Sure, not a problem."

He picked up her cell phone from the console and began to enter his cell number when the phone rang.

"Here," he said handing her the phone as soon as he finished entering his number. "Somebody wants you."

"Oh, no!" she groaned as she caught sight of the caller ID on the phone's screen. "It's Allison's parents! What am I going to tell them?"

"Hello?" Jenny said as she took the phone from Joe's hand and put it to her ear.

"This is Cynthia Canary," the woman on the other end of the phone began. "I missed your call earlier. I'm sorry, but I don't recognize this number."

Jenny took a deep breath and tried to concentrate as she merged into heavier traffic.

"Mrs. Canary, this is Jennifer Joulian. I'm one of Allison's friends. I don't know if anyone has notified you or not, but Allison was injured this afternoon. The ambulance took her to the Emergency Room about 30 minutes ago. I'm on my way there now with another friend, Joe Stillman, who saved her life."

Jenny heard the woman gasp when she said the word "injured." For a few seconds, neither woman spoke.

"What happened, Jennifer? Was she in a car wreck?"

"No, she nearly got hit by a train and she fell off that old railroad bridge into the creek when she was taking pictures with her cell phone."

"Oh, no! How badly is my daughter injured?" the distraught mother asked.

"I don't know for sure, Mrs. Canary. Allison nearly **DROWNED** and she might have a broken arm but you'll have to ask the doctors."

"Thank you for calling, Jennifer. I'll leave for the Emergency Room immediately."

Cynthia Canary ended the call before any more words were spoken.

"Well, that was awkward," Jenny commented as she pulled into the hospital parking lot and found a place to park near the door.

"Forget it, Jen. You just delivered some pretty heavy news and she doesn't even know you." Joe said as the two walked toward the door.

"You're right, Joe. This has been a terrible day for all of us, especially for her daughter. I hope I'll be able to identify her when she gets here. Speaking of getting here, how long do you think it will take your dad to get here?"

Joe suddenly stopped walking and turned to her.

"Don't hold your breath, Jen," he said grimly. "I'll believe it when I see him."

Jenny was so shocked at his words that she literally couldn't think of anything to say, so they walked into the waiting room in silence.

There were only three people in the waiting room. Unsure of what to do, the two teens simply stood by the wall at the back of the room and waited. After about ten minutes of standing, Joe began to grow impatient.

"What are we supposed to do?" he asked. "If my dad doesn't show up, do I just check in by myself or what?"

The words had barely left Joe's lips when a tall, dark-haired man wearing a white shirt and a blue striped tie rushed into the waiting room. Jenny saw the man first and immediately knew the man had to be Joe's father.

"Joe!" the man nearly shouted as he spied his son. "What happened? Are you hurt? Have you seen a doctor?"

Jenny watched a kaleidoscope of emotions race over the boy's face before ending in an uncomfortable expression.

"No. We just got here," he said softly. "Jenny brought me. Have you met her?"

The worried father momentarily turned to look at the

girl and immediately held out his right hand.

"I'm Phil Stillman," the man said. "Thank you for looking out for my son."

"You're very welcome, Mr. Stillman. Joe's a very lucky guy," Jenny said as she tried not to stare at the nice-looking man, who was wearing neatly pressed navy blue slacks, a crisp white shirt, and an expensive-looking sports jacket.

"Joe, are you hurt?" he asked again turning back to his son. "If you were almost hit by a train and fell off a bridge into the creek, you need to see a doctor."

"I'm okay," the boy protested. "I don't think I need to see a doctor. It just knocked the wind out of me that's all."

"That doesn't sound very good to me," his father said as he stood up. "I want you to get checked out by a doctor before we go home. Sit down and wait for me while I find out what I have to do to make that happen."

Without a word, Joe walked over to the nearest chair and dejectedly sat down. Jenny could see the boy biting his lower lip as she sat down beside him.

"He never asks me what I want to do. He just barks orders and tells everybody else what to do. I guess that's what he did in the Marine Corps," Joe said sadly.

Jenny could tell that Joe was upset and she desperately wanted to comfort him but was unsure as to how to do it.

"Your dad was a Marine?" Jenny asked quietly.

"Yeah, he told me that he wanted to be a Marine ever since he was a little kid. He went to college, but couldn't get the Marine thing out of his head, so he enlisted as soon as he graduated. He made a career out of it and he's been in wars and everything," the boy said staring at the floor.

"He's not in the Marines now, is he?"

Without lifting his eyes from the floor, the boy continued. "No, he retired from the service when mom left. I don't think he wanted to, but he said he needed to take care of me."

Jenny didn't know what to add to the conversation, so she just sat by her friend's side in silence.

"He was a Lt. Colonel when he retired. It's a whole lot different taking care of a little kid than it is commanding a lot of men."

Suddenly Jenny knew what to say. She leaned over and put her arm around his shoulders and gave him a hug.

"You know what, Joe? No one made your dad retire from the Marines. He did it because he loves you very much and he wanted to spend his life with you. I can tell that he's accustomed to giving orders, but he wants to make sure you're okay. Otherwise, he would have just taken you home. I know that your dad means well and wants the very best for you, but he doesn't know how to show it very well. You're just going to have to give him a little bit of slack."

Before Joe could respond, Mac and Louie burst into the waiting room.

"Joe!" Mac said loud enough for everyone to hear as he hurried toward his teammate. "What did the doctor say? Are you okay?"

"Haven't seen anyone yet," Joe mumbled. "Dad's trying to make that happen."

"You'll be happy to know that your car is safely parked on the third row straight out the front door. No scratches, dents, dings, nothing. We put your metal detector, the shovels, and the stuff you found in the trunk, so it's all good," Mac said as he handed Joe the keys to his car.

"Thanks, Mac, I knew you would take good care of it."

Suddenly Jenny spotted a short, worried-looking woman with short-cropped hair rush into the waiting room and walk straight to the admitting desk. She was certain it had to be Mrs. Canary.

"My daughter Allison Canary was just brought here by ambulance a few minutes ago. I need to see her. Where is she?"

"Let me check," the clerk said as she picked up the telephone and pushed a few buttons. "They're treating her right now, Mrs. Canary. I've let them know that you are here. Please have a seat in the waiting area."

"How badly is she hurt? Can you at least tell me that?" the woman demanded.

"I'm sorry ma'am, but I don't have that information. I'm afraid you will have to wait for the doctor. He will be able to answer all of your questions then."

"Mrs. Canary, I'm Jennifer Joulian," Jenny said as she walked over to the woman. "Would you like to sit with us until the doctor is ready to talk with you? We were all with Allison when she was injured, so we can tell you what happened. The boy in the blue tee shirt is Joe Stillman. He actually saved Allison's life, so I know you will want to talk to him. His dad is also here, but he's stepped away for a moment. He should be right back."

The woman looked dazed and confused but finally agreed to follow Jenny to the back of the room where the boys were waiting.

"I really appreciate you calling me, Jennifer," she said as she sank down into one of the gray chairs.

"Hey, Jen," Mac said as his sister approached the group, "maybe you should call Mom and Dad and tell them-what happened. Louie has already called Uncle Juan and Aunt Katie and told them where we are."

"Good idea," the tall blonde teen said as she stepped away from the group.

By the time she had finished the call and was ready to rejoin the group, Phil Stillman had returned and was ushering his son through the double doors into the treatment area. As Joe turned his head to look at her, she mouthed the words "call me" and held her hand to her head like a phone.

Before Jenny could take her seat, the double doors leading into the treatment area opened again and a man in green scrubs walked toward them.

"Mrs. Canary?" he asked.

"Yes, I'm Mrs. Canary," Allison's mother responded as she stood up.

"Please come with me."

The three cousins looked at each other for a few minutes without saying a word wondering if they should stay or to go home. Finally, Mac made the decision.

"Let's go," he said directing his words to Jenny. "They may be in there for a long time. Anyway, I'm hungry and if we don't hurry we're going to miss dinner. We'll find out how they are later."

Mac and Jenny got home just as their mother was putting a homemade pizza on the table.

"Hurry and wash up you two," she directed. "Dinner is on the table. I want to hear what happened to Joe and Allison."

The evening meal lasted longer than usual as the twins recounted every detail of their harrowing adventure at the old bridge. The meal would have lasted even longer had Jenny's cell phone not interrupted the conversation. She looked at the caller ID, stood up, and pushed her chair back under the table.

"Excuse me," she said, "I need to take this."

Jenny answered the call from Joe on the way upstairs to her room.

"What did they say? Are you okay?" she asked as she flopped down on her bed.

"Yeah, I think so. They took x-rays and stuff and nothing is broken. I don't have a **CONCUSSION** or anything, but the doctor did say that my ribs are bruised and I might be sore for a few days. I guess we'll have to see what happens."

"Oh, that's wonderful Joe!" Jenny said. "I was so afraid you were hurt."

"He said the average person probably would have been hurt very badly, but because I was in good shape from football conditioning, I made it just fine."

A profound sense of relief washed over Jenny as she listened to his words.

"I'll bet your dad was relieved. What did he say?"

She heard her friend exhale loudly before he spoke.

"He said just what I expected. I got a lecture on how dangerous it was to fool around on train tracks and that I was lucky to be alive."

"But you weren't fooling around on the train tracks, you were saving Allison!" Jenny protested.

"I know, but that didn't make any difference. Listen, Jen, I've got to go, but I wanted you to know that I'm okay. I'll call you tomorrow afternoon and we'll see if we can get the information on that car."

As soon as the call ended, Jenny went downstairs to

rejoin her family who was still sitting around the table.

"I just talked to Joe," she announced as she slid back into her chair. "The ER doctor checked him out and said that he seems to be okay, but that he might be a little sore for a day or two."

"That's good news!" Mac exclaimed. "I was afraid he wouldn't be able to play football this weekend. That would be terrible since we only have one more game after this one and he's our best wide receiver. I wish I could play too, but since my fingers are still too numb to throw a football I know that I won't get to play."

"Mac just told us what happened at that old railroad bridge. It frightens me to think what could have happened," Meghan said as she began to gather the dishes from the table.

"Do you have any idea how badly your friend was hurt?" her dad asked. "Mac told us that you called her mother to let her know that her daughter was in the ER. That was very thoughtful of you, Jen. Good for you!"

"I knew she needed to know," Jenny said. "Honestly, I'm not sure Allison was even breathing when the train crew pulled her out of the creek. It's just a good thing Louie knew what to do or I'm sure she wouldn't have made it."

Meghan had just finished loading the dishwasher when she turned back to the table.

"I think you should call Allison's mother tomorrow, Jen, and find out how she is doing. From what Mac told us, I think she might be hurt very badly. Don't be surprised if the news isn't good."

CHAPTER SIXTEEN

"Sunday morning dawned a lot brighter than Jenny's mood. Her mother's warning about Allison's possible condition deeply concerned her and she feared the worst. The teen had picked up her phone to call Mrs. Canary at least three times, but at the last minute couldn't bring herself to make the call.

Finally, she decided to call Louie hoping he would give her enough inspiration to make the call. As usual, he answered on the first ring.

"Hey," Jenny greeted her best friend.

"Hey, yourself. What's up?"

"Good news and bad news, and I'm depressed over the bad news. That's why I'm calling you."

"Gee thanks!" Louie said with mock sarcasm. "So you want me to be depressed, too, is that it?"

"No, I'm just worried about Allison, that's all. I'm

afraid she might not be doing very well. I've started to call her mother several times and I just can't go through with it," Jenny said as she rearranged the bright yellow throw pillows she had propped behind her back.

"The other thing that makes me sad is that all of the old bridge pictures she was so excited about taking with her cell phone are now at the bottom of the creek."

"Wait a minute!" Louie exclaimed. "I don't think so."

"What are you talking about?"

"I hadn't thought about it until now, but when Joe tackled Allison I saw her phone fly out of her hand. It went straight up into the air and then it must have come down onto the tracks because I don't remember seeing it go into the creek."

"Seriously? Are you telling me that there's a chance Allison's phone might be on the bridge? If it landed on the tracks, don't you think the train ran over it and smashed it?" Jenny asked clearly surprised.

"No, I think if it fell on the bridge, it's okay. I've got a little time this afternoon, want to go see if we can find it?"

"Absolutely! Can you be ready in 15 minutes?"

Jenny's mood was suddenly soaring as she raced down the stairs.

"I'm going over to Louie's," she shouted to her mother on her way out the door. "I'll be back in a little while."

Louie was equally excited about the possibility of finding Allison's phone when he climbed into Jenny's car.

"I've been playing that scene over and over in my mind," he told her. "I think I know where her phone might have landed."

As soon as Jenny parked by the side of the road, the

two friends hurried through the tall grass toward the railroad tracks.

"You go see if you can find it," Jenny told him as they reached the old bridge. "I'm going to stand here and watch for a train. It's hard to believe you can't hear a train coming until it's almost on you, but you can't. We found that out the hard way. I sure don't want a repeat of yesterday."

She watched as the boy made his way to the center of the bridge. Making sure there were no approaching trains, she took a close look at the old bridge. She hadn't noticed before, but there was about two feet of space on each side of the tracks which she decided must be a walkway.

For several minutes she watched as Louie slowly walked over the bridge carefully examining every possible place the phone might have landed. With each step he took, her hopes faded. Then just when it seemed as though he had examined every inch of the bridge, he stopped, bent down, picked up something, and waved it in the air.

"I found it!" he shrieked at the top of his voice. "I found Allison's phone. It was lying right up against the side support and it's not damaged at all! Let's get out of here before there's another train!"

As soon as they were safely back in the car and Jenny had examined the phone so that she, too was satisfied that it wasn't damaged, she felt brave enough to call Mrs. Canary. After a number of rings with no answer, Jenny was just about to end the call when the woman answered.

"Hello, Mrs. Canary? It's Jennifer Joulian. I'm calling to find out how Allison is feeling."

For a moment, it was obvious that the woman was at a loss as to who was calling.

"Oh, yes, Jennifer. You're the young woman I met at the hospital. Thank you so much for calling to ask about Allison. She sustained quite a few injuries including a broken arm, broken ribs, and a **PUNCTURED LUNG**, but we have every reason to believe that she will make a complete recovery. I want you to know that we're so grateful to everyone who helped her, especially the young man that pushed her out of harm's way."

"That's fantastic news, Mrs. Canary!" Jenny said. "Also, I wanted to let you know that my cousin, Louie just found Allison's cell phone on the old bridge. Please tell her for us. We'll be happy to bring it to her as soon as she's able to have visitors."

"Oh, that's wonderful! Please thank him for finding her phone. I know she will be thrilled to have it back. Right now she's heavily sedated and has a chest tube, so she probably won't be able to have visitors for several days, but do check back. I know she will be happy to see all of you."

As soon as the call ended, Louie, who had been eavesdropping, was nearly ecstatic.

"She's going to be all right!" he nearly yelled. "I was afraid that she wasn't going to make it when the train crew pulled her out of the creek, but she's going to get well. We've got to tell Joe! Let's call him right now!"

Jenny had started her car and was preparing to pull back onto the highway when she heard Louie mention calling Joe, so she stopped.

"We can't call him right now, Louie. When he called me last night to tell me that he was okay, he said that he was in trouble for "fooling around" on the bridge and that his dad had given him a major lecture. I'm afraid this might not be a good time to call. Anyway, he's supposed to call me back later this afternoon when he can talk."

A quick glance at Louie, who had just gone from great joy to slumping in his seat and frowning, told Jenny that he really wanted to tell Joe the good news about Allison himself.

"Listen, Louie, really I think you should be the one to tell Joe about Allison," she said. "As soon as he calls, I'll ask him to call you and I won't mention Allison, okay?"

She wasn't sure her offer did much to improve his attitude, but it was the best she could do for now.

"Remember me telling you this morning that I had good news and bad news?"

"Yeah, so isn't this the good news?" he asked.

"No, this was actually the bad news that just got turned into good news, thanks to you. The good news is that when Joe calls me this afternoon, we'll be able to find out who owns that black car we followed to the old shack.

"What? Joe knows who owns that car?"

"No, but Joe has a credit card that will get us into the report that shows the car's ownership. Then we will know who that girl is who is camping in the old shack."

"Seriously? Joe has a credit card? Awesome!"

Louie was bordering on becoming ecstatic at the prospect of solving the mystery at the old shack.

"What are we going to do when we find out who it is? Do we tell Mr. George?" he asked.

Jenny thought for a moment before answering.

"I don't know. If you'll remember we haven't even told him about the girl yet. Maybe when we find out who owns the car, we should just tell him everything. What do you think?"

"I don't know, either."

"Maybe we'll know what to do when we find out who owns the car," she suggested.

On the way home, the two continued to discuss the pros and cons of telling Mr. George about their discoveries.

"Do you want me to keep Allison's phone until we give it to her?" Jenny asked as she pulled into the circle drive in front of Louie's house. "I promise I won't give it to her without you."

"Yeah, might be best," he said handing over the phone.

Jenny had been home less than twenty minutes when Joe called.

"Hi, Jen, I've got my credit card out if you want to see if we can find the owner of that car," Joe said. "How do you want to do this? Do you want me to pull the site up on my computer or do you want to pull it up and I'll give you my number?"

"It might be easier for me to pull it up since I have it bookmarked," she said. "It will just take me a second to pull it up. This is one of those sites that you get the first record for $2.95 and then they sign you up for a subscription for $19.95 a month unless you cancel, which we will do as soon as we get the information. Okay, Joe, I'm ready, what is number on your credit card and when does it expire?"

As soon as she typed in the license tag number and Joe's credit card information, the name of the the car's owner appeared on the screen.

"Oh my gosh!" the boy heard her exclaim.

"What is it, Jen?"

"This is very interesting. It says the car is a 1996, 4-door, 4-cylinder Honda Accord and it even gives the VIN. I think that means Vehicle Identification Number. Wait until you hear the owner's name! This car isn't even registered to a woman. According to this site, the person who owns the car is Gorman Elliott George. Oh, wow! Have you ever heard of him?"

"No, never heard of him," Joe replied. "Do you think he's related to Mr. George at school? That would be something, wouldn't it? Maybe he's connected with all the drugs you all found at the old shack."

"That's a scary thought, Joe!" she said. "Let me try something real quick. I'm going to cancel our subscription and then I'm going to get on the public records site and see what I can find. Sometimes they even list relatives."

"Jen, what are you going to do if you find out they're related. Now that's scary!"

He could hear Jenny's keyboard clicking in the background as he put away his credit card and sat back down at his desk.

"Well, I was hoping I wouldn't find this," he heard her say after the keyboard clicks stopped. "Watson George shows up as a possible relative. I think I'm going to be sick. Whatever you do, don't tell Louie. He will be devastated," Jenny said.

"Well, wait a minute. Can you check out arrest records and stuff like that on the public records website? Maybe that will shed some light on this."

"Great idea! While I'm doing that, why don't you call Louie? I think he wants to talk to you, and then call me back. Maybe I'll know something by then."

For the next 30 minutes, Jenny poured over any online record that she could find that might shed some light on the mysterious Gorman George. By the time Joe called back, she had all the evidence she needed.

"What did you find out?" he asked. "Was there anything on Gorman George?"

"Oh, yeah!" Jenny said. "I don't know if Watson George fits into any of this, but it looks like Gorman George has been arrested numerous times on drug charges. I can't tell for sure, but it looks like he might even be in the county jail as we speak."

"Seriously? Did you find out anything about that woman you and Louie followed?"

"Not really. There were several female relatives associated with him on the public site, but it doesn't specify their relationship or their age. So there's no way to tell if the girl we saw is actually one of his relatives," she told him.

Jenny closed her laptop and sat back in her desk chair before continuing the conversation.

"Did you talk to Louie?" she asked. "I know that he was anxious to talk to you."

"I did. He wanted me to know that Allison Canary was in the hospital and that she's expected to make a full recovery. He told me at least three times how impressed he is that I saved her life and not to worry because I landed on top of her. I told him that if he hadn't known how to do first aid she would have died for sure, so we both saved her."

Jenny smiled to herself knowing how much it meant to Louie to tell Joe about Allison and to secretly congratulate herself for not saying anything about it to Joe.

"I'd better go, Jen. I've got some reading to do before class tomorrow."

"Thanks again for using your credit card to find out

who owned that car. We could have never found out otherwise. By the way, how are you feeling? Are you okay?"

"I think so. The doctor said that I might be a little stiff and sore for the next couple of days and that seems to be what's happening. Nothing serious, so don't worry."

Jenny was about to end the call when Joe suddenly had question.

"Hey, Jen, one more thing," he said. "Now that you know who owns that car, don't you think you should say something to somebody about all those drugs you guys found in the old shack?"

The instant Jenny's call with Joe ended, she immediately called Louie.

She opened her conversation with, "You'll never guess who owns that black Honda we saw at the Gas and Grub!"

"Who?" he asked clearly intrigued.

"When I put Joe's credit card number into the search site a little while ago and the tag number you copied, the owner's name and car description came right up. That car is a 4-cylinder, 1996 Honda Accord and it's registered to Gorman Elliott George."

"Gorman Elliott George? Seriously? Do you think he's related to Mr. George?"

Jenny could tell from the sound of Louie's questions that he was not only surprised by the information but also horrified at the possibility this man and maybe even the girl at the shack, could be related to his hero.

"Unfortunately, I think he might be," she said. "I also looked him up on some of the public records websites to see what else I could find out about this guy. The court records show that he's been arrested several times for drug possession and I wouldn't be surprised if he's not in jail right now. One section also listed people that might be related to him and Watson George's name was listed as well as some female names. However, it didn't specify how they were related to Gorman George or their ages."

The phone went silent for several seconds. The blonde teenager knew that there was no point in saying anything else until her best friend had processed the information that could be harmful to his Scout leader. Finally, he spoke.

"I don't care if that Gorman guy is a drug dealer, it doesn't mean that Mr. George is one, too!" he said angrily coming to his mentor's defense.

"No one is accusing Mr. George of dealing drugs, Louie. From what I know about him, I don't think anyone would ever accuse him of doing that."

"Well, they had better not!"

"I guess you realize that we've got to make a decision. Now that we know that a girl is living in the old shack and using drugs, her life could be in danger. I think we've got to tell Mr. George about it tomorrow, especially since we also know that one of his relatives might be involved."

"You're probably right, but I want to think about it. Can we talk about it again on the way to school tomorrow?"

"Oh, sure. That's all I had to tell you. I'll pick you up in the morning at the regular time."

CHAPTER SEVENTEEN

Her conversation with Louie had left her worried and a little depressed. It was too early to go to bed and she was in no mood to study, so she was at a loss as to what to do next when Mac knocked on her bedroom door.

"Hey, Jen, didn't you hear Mom a while ago? She said to tell you that she's getting ready to put the sandwich stuff away and if you're hungry, you'd better get down there."

"Okay, thanks, Mac. Oh, and guess what? Louie found Allison's cell phone on the bridge this afternoon, so I called Mrs. Canary to tell her and to ask about Allison. She said that Allison had several broken bones and a punctured lung, but she's expected to make a full recovery. And since Joe is okay, too, I guess you know what that means?"

"No idea. What are you talking about?" Mac asked obviously puzzled.

"It means that your theory about evil spirits or a curse

on that old bridge just got trashed. If there really had been an evil spirit there, neither one of them would have survived. Sorry bro, that old myth just got debunked!"

The next morning as Jenny pulled into the circle drive to pick up Louie, she noticed that he was frowning as he picked up his backpack and headed to the car.

"What's up with you?" she asked as he climbed into the car and closed the door. "Is everything all right?"

"Oh, I guess," he said with a total lack of enthusiasm. "Actually no it isn't all right. I don't think I slept much at all last night thinking about that Gorman guy."

Jenny started to chuckle but caught herself in time.

"You don't need to worry about him," she said trying to sound reassuring. "I think you're more worried about Mr. George being involved in this than anything."

The boy looked out the side window for a while before turning back to answer her.

"Yeah, you're probably right, Jen. I've decided that we need to tell Mr. George about everything and I'm really dreading it."

The girl turned her head to look at her best friend who was plainly miserable.

"I agree, Louie, I think you're absolutely right. We need to tell him everything. Do you want to meet me in his room after school and we'll tell him together?"

"Yeah, I guess so."

"I don't know about you," Jenny said as she pulled into the school's parking lot, "but I'm going to have a hard time concentrating on schoolwork today."

After a miserable day of classes, the two hurried to Mr. George's classroom as soon as the final bell rang. When

Louie arrived the last of the math students were leaving for the day. He simply walked to one of the student desks on the front row and sat down to wait for Jenny. Mr. George was helping one of the students with a math problem and didn't notice Louie until the student finished the problem and was walking toward the door.

"Louie!" he exclaimed. "When did you come in?"

"I just got here," the boy replied. "Jenny is going to be here in a minute. Do you have time to talk to us when she gets here?"

"Well, sure Louie, I always have time to talk to you," the tall ex-soldier said with a hint of suspicion in his voice. "What's all this about?"

Before the boy could respond, Jenny walked into the room and set her bright yellow backpack on the floor next to Louie's chair.

"Mr. George, could we talk to you for a minute?"

Without a word, the teacher walked over to the classroom door and closed it. Then as Jenny slid into a chair next to her best friend, the Boy Scout leader walked back to the front of his desk and leaned against it. Jenny decided to speak first.

"Mr. George," she began, "we really need some help because we don't know what to do and we knew that we could trust you to help us."

"I appreciate that, Jennifer. How can I help you?"

Jenny began with her signature rush of words.

"A few weeks ago, Louie asked Mac and me if we would go back to the old shack with him so that he could see what was inside. It was too dark for him to see anything when Danny Collie locked him in it. We knew we probably shouldn't go because you had warned us not to, but we went on Saturday anyway."

"We almost couldn't get in," Louie said as he picked up the story. "Somebody had nailed a huge brace on the door and it took a long time for Mac and me to pry it open. We even had to use the tire iron in Jenny's car.

"We kept the door open for light, but it was still very dark in there. I had a high-powered flashlight, but all Mac and Jenny had were their cell phone flashlights, which didn't help very much. Mac went to explore one corner where a lot of furniture was piled up. I was going back there, too when I saw that old desk where I found the coffee can with the deed to the ranch inside."

Jenny could feel her face beginning to flush and her heart race as she stared at Mr. George, who was grimly staring back at them.

"I had gone to the other corner," she said when Louie stopped talking. "The first thing I saw was a pair of jeans with rhinestones on the back pockets and a bright orange sweatshirt draped over a chair. When I looked around a little more closely it looked as if someone was actually living there. That's when I saw a box with what looked like a lot of illegal drugs and syringes and stuff inside. It scared me and I guess I screamed."

"Yeah, you did, real loud!" Louie said. "That's what scared us. We thought you were hurt. Mac had to jump over some stuff to get to you and that's when he dropped his phone and it went under a huge piece of furniture."

"Wait!" Mr. George interrupted. "You found drugs in that old shack? What kind of drugs? How do you know that what you saw in that box were illegal drugs?"

Mr. George's intense interest in the box of drugs they found in the shack unnerved Jenny. His questions struck her as very strange.

"I didn't have a chance to take a very good look, but from what I saw the box was full of little bags of stuff and all kinds of prescription bottles, and syringes. I couldn't tell you what kinds of drugs were in the box," Louie said, "but I'll bet they were worth a lot of money on the street."

"Mac was just about to take a look in the box when we heard a noise that sounded like someone was trying to open the boarded up window. That really scared us!" Jenny said. "We were afraid that whoever owned the drugs was coming back and we didn't want to be there when that happened, so we got out of there as fast as we could! I've never been that scared in my entire life!" Jenny said.

She quickly glanced at Louie to see if he was as uncomfortable with the conversation as she was, but she couldn't tell for sure.

"After we ran outside and the boys closed the door and put the brace back on it, Mac realized that his phone was still in there," Jenny continued. "I think he might have gone back inside if we would have let him, but we decided it was too dangerous for that. We just wanted to get away from there as fast as we could."

Mr. George scowled as he listened to the kids relate their adventure.

"Then what happened?" he asked. "Did you get a chance to see who was trying to get into the shack?"

"No, we didn't see anyone. We just ran to Jenny's car which was parked by the foundation of that old homestead and got out of there as fast as we could," Louie said.

"Then if that was on Saturday, you and Mac must have gone back the next day because you called me on Sunday," Mr. George said to Louie.

"Right," Louie said. "We hadn't planned to go on Sunday. Jenny and I had planned to go back on Monday after school to hide in the woods to see if we could see anyone come or go out of the side window. Mac couldn't go because he had football practice. He didn't like the idea of Jenny going out there and refused to let her go after school," the teenager explained.

"So that's when you and Mac decided to go on Sunday by yourselves?" Mr. George asked Louie.

"Yeah, he called me and said that he was desperate to get his phone and asked me if I would go back to the old shack with him to find it."

"Didn't you think that was a little dangerous?" the teacher asked.

"Well, yeah, but we had a plan, so we thought we could pull it off."

"A plan?"

As Jenny listened to Louie and Mr. George exchange comments, she was becoming more and more uncomfortable with the situation and began to regret telling him anything.

"After I agreed to go with him," Louie continued, "we decided to hide in the brush and the trees on the side of the house and watch the window for a while. If we didn't see anyone, then I would climb the tree on the other side of the house and try to look in through some of the missing shingles on the roof, which I did. It was very dark inside and I couldn't see any lights or anything, so we decided it was okay to go in."

During Louie's explanation, Watson George apparently became tired of leaning against his desk and decided to sit on the front edge of it instead. She could hear him audibly exhale when Louie mentioned climbing the tree.

"We went around to the front of the old shack and lifted the brace off the door. We looked inside but didn't see anyone, so we went back to the corner where Mac dropped his phone. We tried to lift that huge piece of furniture off it, but it fell and a piece tore off and jammed into Mac's hand. That's when we called you for help."

For a long moment, no one said anything after the boy finished his version of the events that lead to Mac's injury. Finally Jenny spoke up.

"You need to tell him about the body, Louie," she said quietly as she looked at her cousin sitting beside her.

"Body? Are you telling me that you saw a human body? Where? In the shack?"

Louie quickly glanced at Jenny before answering.

"We didn't know anyone was in there when we went inside to find his phone," the boy began. "After Mac got hurt, he was very wobbly, so I had my arm around his waist trying to help him walk. I had my cell phone in the other hand with the flashlight on. When Mac stumbled and threw his arms up to keep from falling, he knocked my cell phone out of my hand. It landed on the floor with the flashlight pointed toward the back corner and that's when I saw what looked like a body stretched out on the floor under some blankets. I couldn't tell for sure but that's what it looked like?"

"Then what did you do?" the teacher asked, his face drawn with concern.

"I grabbed my phone and got Mac outside the shack

as fast as I could. I helped him sit down on a fallen tree trunk while I went back to put the brace back on the door. Then I tried to get someone to come and take Mac to the hospital, but no one answered. That's when I called you."

"Louie, why didn't you say something to me about the body you saw when I came to get you?"

"I guess I was afraid. I was so worried about Mac that I didn't even think about mentioning it. When Jen and I talked about it later, I wasn't totally sure that what I saw was really a body anyway. I thought maybe I was just so worried about getting Mac out of there that I just made it up."

"I'm not sure it was a body, either," Jenny said trying to rescue Louie from an awkward moment. "I didn't see anything like that when I was there. I told Louie that it could have been just a blanket or a sleeping bag or something rolled up on the floor. Even if it was a person covered up with those blankets, we're positive nobody died because we actually saw the girl that's living in the old shack."

Jenny had deliberately fixed her eyes on Watson George's face as she tried to convince him that Louie had been mistaken about the body he thought he saw. Instead of relieving her anxiety about the Boy Scout leader's possible involvement with the drugs, it only intensified it as the concern on his face seemed to dissolve into anger.

"How could you possibly know that?" he said as he glared at Jenny.

Jenny and Louie looked at each other for a long minute realizing that they had probably said too much. The color had drained from Louie's face and he seemed to be nervous as he continually shifted in his chair. However, they both knew that they were committed now, so Jenny continued.

"I knew it was that girl because we saw her at the Gas and Grub and I recognized the clothes that I had seen draped over the chair at the old shack," Jenny said solemnly. "I'm absolutely positive that it was her because she was wearing the same ripped up jeans with the rhinestone pockets and a neon orange sweatshirt with a red heart embroidered on the front of it."

Jenny cautiously watched Mr. George's face as she described the girl. She couldn't decide if Louie's math teacher was angry, confused, or concerned as his emotions seemed to change with each word she spoke.

"Did you both get a good look at her?" he asked.

"Yes we did," the cousins said in unison.

"What did she look like?"

"I saw her first," Jenny said. "I was paying at the counter when this girl nearly bumped into me when she walked into the store. I would say that she's probably about 5'4". She's shorter than I am and very thin. I couldn't see her eyes, but she has dark, shaggy hair. My initial reaction was that she was a homeless person, but then I saw her clothes and I knew who she was. I watched her for a couple of minutes as she picked up a few food items before I went back to my car."

Mr. George got down off his desk and walked a few steps toward Jenny and Louie, but didn't say anything.

"I told Louie to watch for her so that we could see where she went. In a few minutes, she came out of the store carrying a couple of plastic bags and got into an older model black Honda. Louie wrote down the description of the car and the tag number and we followed her as she drove out of the parking lot."

"Yeah!" Louie said finally regaining his confidence

and ready to contribute to the story. "It was just like in the movies! We didn't want her to know that we were following her, so Jen had to be careful. The girl drove straight to the bridge on the highway, the one that's not very far from the old shack and parked her car on the side of the road. We watched her run across the highway, so Jen parked on the other end of the bridge and we ran after her. We got to the woods next to the old shack just in time to see her pull the board off the side window, climb inside, and then put it back on from the inside."

Watson George, without saying a word, began to pace back and forth in front of the first row of student desks. Jenny had made up her mind not to say anything else when Louie excitedly continued his monolog.

"Since we had a description of the car and the tag number, Jen thought maybe she could find out who owned the car on the Internet. It wasn't easy, but she found out!" Louie exclaimed happily.

As she listened to her best friend innocently tell their secrets, it was all she could do to keep from groaning and burying her head in her hands. Instead of being excited to share what she found on the Internet, Jenny instantly felt a knot forming in the pit of her stomach. She could feel her face getting hot and she knew that it was probably bright red. And she also knew that she was trapped.

Mr. George immediately stopped pacing, walked to a spot directly in front of Jenny's chair, and looked down at her.

"So who owns the car, Jennifer?" he asked in an unusually flat voice.

Jenny opened her mouth to respond and for an awful moment, no sound came out.

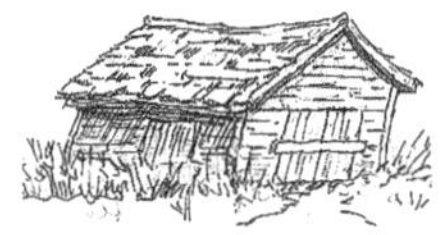

CHAPTER EIGHTEEN

"According to the Internet, the car is registered to Gorman Elliott George," Jenny finally said in a weak voice barely above a stage whisper.

She heard the ex-solder inhale sharply as she finished speaking. Then without a sound, he returned to his desk, picked up his book bag, and walked out of the room leaving Jenny and Louie sitting in stunned silence on the front row.

"I was afraid he might not take this very well," Jenny said when she finally felt like speaking again. "Maybe we shouldn't have we told him who owned the car."

Louie took his mentor's response personally and was all but in tears.

"I am so in trouble," the boy moaned. "Mr. George told me not to go back to the old shack in the first place and now I've really made him mad. What if he never speaks to me again? What if he throws me out of the Boy Scouts?"

"Oh, come on Louie you know he would never do that! It's obvious that he likes you; he'll speak to you again."

"I wasn't expecting him to react like that when he found out that Gorman George owned that car or I would have never said anything. My guess is that he's related to that guy. Who knows? Gorman George might even be his brother or something."

"I guess Gorman George could be his brother, but until Mr. George tells us what's going on, there's no way of knowing why he reacted like that. Obviously, it's something serious, but all we can do now is to wait until he tells us. One thing for sure, we won't be going back to the old shack!"

Louie was still troubled about the conversation with his Scout leader when Jenny picked him up for school the next morning.

"I hope you're not going to spend all day worrying about what happened with Mr. George yesterday," she told him. "I'm sure that whatever upset him is over by now. Would it make you feel any better if I met you in his room again after school? Then we'll both know for sure that everything is fine."

"Yeah, I guess," the boy said unenthusiastically.

Jenny didn't have time to give the previous day's episode a single thought. When the bell rang, she hurried to the math classroom and was surprised to find her best friend standing dejectedly beside the closed door.

"What's going on, Louie? Where's Mr. George?"

"I don't know, Jen. When I went to math class this afternoon, there was a substitute teacher and all she told us was that Mr. George was taking some personal time and that she didn't know when he would be back. That really doesn't sound good to me."

"Don't read too much into it," Jenny advised. "I'm sure we'll find out soon enough."

Mr. George was not at school the next day or the next.

By the end of the week, Louie was so worried over Mr. George's absence that he was ready to do anything to find his beloved mentor.

"Do you think he might have gone back to the shack to look for that girl?" he asked Jenny on the way home from school. "Do you think he knew her? Should we go back there one more time just to make sure something hasn't happened to Mr. George?"

"Absolutely not!" she told him as they stopped at a red light. "We're definitely not going back there ever again. I don't know where Mr. George went, but I did find out that he's going to be gone next week, too."

"Oh, yeah? How do you know that, Jen?"

"Because I stopped by the office over lunch hour to see my friend Maddie, who is one of the office assistants, and she told me that she would see what she could find out. She texted me 4th hour and told me he's taking some personal time, but we already knew that."

"Who's Maddie?"

"Madison Morgan. She's on my soccer team and if anyone can find out stuff like this it's Maddie."

For a few minutes, Mr. George's absence was the main topic of the Joulian's dinner conversation until Mac changed it to football.

"Are you guys going to the game tomorrow night?" he asked. "It's the last one before we play for the finals."

"Are you playing?" his dad asked. "I thought you were

out for the season."

Mac took a long sip of his iced tea before answering.

"No, I'm not playing, but Coach wants me to suit up and sit on the bench with the team. I haven't thrown a football since I hurt my hand weeks ago. It doesn't hurt, but I still don't have a lot of feeling in those two fingers, so I couldn't control the football very well. He doesn't want me to push it and maybe do permanent damage, but at least I get to work out with the team, so that's something."

"That's too bad, Mac," his mother sympathized. "I know how much football means to you. At least if you take care of your hand now, you'll get to play next year."

Mac frowned as he poured himself another glass of iced tea. Then he winked at his sister across the table and grinned mischeviuosly.

"Well, I know somebody that will definitely be at the game tomorrow night. In fact, I know somebody that hasn't missed a game for weeks, isn't that right, Jen?"

"I didn't know that you were such a football fan, Jen," her mother said obviously surprised.

"I wouldn't say that she's a fan of the game, just a certain player," Mac continued to tease. "Oh, yeah, she and her posse get to the stadium as soon as the gates open to get a good seat. Tell me again, Jen, which number are you watching these days? Is it 59, 27, 63?"

The tall blonde girl could feel her face getting hot and she knew that it was probably flaming bright red as she stared at her empty plate.

"Posse? What's your posse, Jen?' her father asked genuinely puzzled.

"I'd say it's about half of her soccer team," her brother

continued to tease. "I'd be shocked if all those girls together could come up with the rules of the game. I don't think they're all that interested in the game, only certain players! Right, Jen?"

Mac took another long sip of iced tea before continuing to grin and to torment his twin.

"Shall I tell you-know-who that you'll be at the game? He always asks me if you'll be there. Shall I find out what number jersey he's wearing tomorrow night so you won't be watching the wrong player?" the boy asked with a snicker.

"You are just horrible! Why don't you mind your own business for once!" his sister said as she jumped up from the table, glared at him, and hurried out of the kitchen before he could say anything else.

"Who is 'you-know-who'?" his mother asked.

"Can't tell," Mac said with a wink as he stood up and pushed in his chair. "You'll have to ask her."

Both Jenny and Mac were still asleep when Meghan and Carson left for the veterinary clinic early Saturday morning. At 9:15 a.m. Jenny's cell phone rang. Still too sleepy to retrieve her phone, the message went to voice mail.

"Hi, Honey," she heard her mother say. "I hope I didn't wake you, but I wanted to let you know that I'm helping your dad at the clinic today and also there is a pan of homemade pecan rolls in the oven to go with your breakfast. That's it. We should be home about the regular time. Bye."

Jenny was tempted to get up and go downstairs but decided that she wanted to sleep a while longer. A little over an hour later, she was awakened for the second time by her brother yelling from the foot of the stairs.

"Hey, Jen, you'd better get down here. Mom left some-pecan rolls in the oven and they are awesome. If you don't get down here soon, they just might be all gone."

Even though the warmth of her comforter on a chilly Saturday morning was tempting, Jenny finally managed to climb out of bed and make her way down to the kitchen.

"That was really a good game last night," she said to Mac as she helped herself to a couple of rolls and slid into her chair at the table. "I'm glad we finally won."

"We wouldn't have had a chance if Joe hadn't gotten loose and made those two touchdowns in the last quarter. He's so fast it's just unbelievable! If he keeps playing like that, he'll get a football scholarship for sure."

"That just makes me very sad," Jenny said before she took another bite of pecan roll.

"Why? You're sad because Joe's such an awesome player?" Mac asked obviously baffled.

"No, I'm sad because Joe's such a talented player and he makes all these incredible plays and his dad is never there to see them."

Mac pushed his chair back from the table and got to his feet.

"Yeah, you're right. That is sad. His dad never goes to anything."

As Jenny sat alone at the kitchen table finishing her breakfast, she couldn't get Mac's words out of her head. 'His dad never goes to anything.' As the words kept repeating in her mind, the sadness she felt for Joe suddenly began to manifest as anger.

"His dad never goes to anything, huh?" she heard herself say aloud. "Well, we'll see about that!"

Jenny received such good news late Sunday afternoon

that she couldn't wait to share it.

"Guess what?" she excitedly said to Louie the instant he answered her call. "Mrs. Canary just called me and said that Allison is doing so well that she's going to be released from the hospital tomorrow. "Isn't that great?"

"Yeah, it is! I really don't know Allison very well, so I didn't know that she was still in the hospital."

"I actually don't know her all that well, either. I've had a couple of classes with her and I see her around, but that's about it. I sent her pictures of the old shack because I knew that she was an artist and liked to paint old buildings and stuff."

"It would have been so bad if her phone with all her pictures had gone into the creek when Joe tackled her. It would have been lost forever," Louie said.

"Thanks to you, not only was her phone saved but so was her life!"

"Oh, come on, Jen, Joe saved her life. The only thing I did was a little first aid to keep her going until the ambulance got there," the teenager protested.

"I agree that Joe saved her from being hit by the train, but a little first aid? That's what saved her life! One of the train guys told Joe that she was hurt so badly that if you hadn't known how to do first aid, she would have died right there. So, own it; you saved her life."

Then Louie abruptly ended the conversation.

"Listen, Jen, I've got to go. I'm supposed to go somewhere with Mom this afternoon. I'll see you in the morning."

Jenny had planned to discuss several things with her best friend, so she was taken aback that the call ended so suddenly. She couldn't decide if he really had to go somewhere or if he just didn't want to talk about Allison. For whatever reason, it was obvious that the call was over for the day.

With nothing else to do, Jenny decided to study for a while before dinner but quickly realized that she couldn't concentrate on the material. Instead, she decided to stretch out on her bed and organize her thoughts but instead fell into a deep sleep.

The next morning, the first words out of Louie's mouth as he climbed into Jenny's car were about Mr. George.

"Do you think Mr. George will really be gone all week?" he asked obviously hoping that she would say no.

"I have no idea, Louie. All I know is what Maddie told me. If it would make you feel any better, I'll try to talk to her today to see if she's heard anything else. I'll meet you at Mr. George's room to tell you what I found out, okay?"

Jenny was already planning to talk to Maddie at lunch, but about something entirely different.

As soon as her lunch period began, instead of going to the cafeteria Jenny hurried to the office to talk to her friend.

"Will you do me a favor, Maddie?" she asked as soon as her friend was available. "Can you look up this man's phone number and text it to me?" she said slipping a small piece of folded paper into the girl's hand. "It's Joe Stillman's father and it's a surprise."

The girl clutched it in her hand and mumbled, "I'll see if I can find it."

"Thanks, Maddie, oh, and one other thing," Jenny said as she turned to go, "have you heard anything else about when Mr. George might be coming back?"

"Not since last week, but I'll let you know if I hear anything."

Jenny's cell phone chimed with a text message from Maddie immediately after the final bell rang.

Here's the phone number you wanted. 499-811-0120.
Nothing on Mr. George.

Jenny was so excited about getting Phillip Stillman's number that she was tempted to jog all the way to Mr. George's room. Just like before, Louie was dejectedly standing beside the closed classroom door.

"No Mr. George? she asked.

"No, and the sub didn't know anything about when he would return either."

Jenny was too elated to be depressed about the missing math instructor, but she also knew how much he meant to Louie, so she tried to tone down her enthusiasm.

"I know it's hard to wait especially since we don't know what's happening, but that's all we can do right now."

"Yeah, I know, but I'm really worried about him."

"Me, too, but there's nothing we can do. I'm sure if he wants us to know what he's been up to, he will tell us when he gets back."

As soon as Jenny got home she immediately went up to her room to finalize her grand plan. Phil Stillman was the crowning piece of the plan and now that she had his cell phone number, there was no reason to wait, or was there? She couldn't be sure.

Jenny decided that it might be better to actually put her plan down on paper with all of the times, dates, and contact numbers so she wouldn't forget anything. That accomplished, she decided that tomorrow might be better to call him after all. She was about to go downstairs when she heard Mac coming up the stairs to go to his room.

"Hey, Mac?" she called as she hurried out of her room, "Is Friday night the last football game of the season?"

"Well, actually last week would have been our last game of the season, but we won so Friday is for the championship. If we win that one, we will be the champions of our division. I think we have a pretty good chance of doing that, too since we're playing on our home field."

"So it's the same time and the same place as all the other games?" she asked.

"Yes, it is. Why are you asking? Are you and your posse going to be there?"

"Oh, yeah!" she said enthusiastically as she brushed past him and continued downstairs. He couldn't hear her last words, "You have no idea."

CHAPTER NINETEEN

Meghan was already in the kitchen getting ready to start supper when Jenny burst into the room.

"Hi Mom!" she said with more exuberance than usual. "What's for dinner, it sure smells good! Would you like for me to set the table?"

"We're having one of your favorites, chili and corn-bread, and yes, I would like for you to set the table with a small plate and a soup bowl."

"So what are you and Dad planning to do this week-end? Anything special," the teen asked as she began to put the silverware on the table.

"Goodness, Jenny, this is only Monday evening. I have no idea what your father has planned for this weekend. I'm sure we will be working at the clinic on Saturday, but other than that I have no idea. Why are you asking?"

"Oh, no reason, I was just wondering, that's all."

"So the answer to your question is, I don't know. I'll be happy to ask your father when he gets here if you really want to know."

"No, that's okay, I was just curious."

After the family sat down for dinner, Carson opened the conversation.

"Well, I hope you all had a better day than I did?"

"That doesn't sound good, dear," Meghan said as she retrieved a pan of cornbread from the oven and set it down in the middle of the table.

"What happened, Dad?" Mac asked.

His father took a large piece of cornbread and crumbled it into his chili bowl before he answered.

"Remember me telling you all about that yellow Lab that got hit by a truck? I think he's just about well and then something else happens to him. I just hate it because he's such a sweet dog, and he deserves so much better than this."

The veterinarian paused his story to take a bite of chili while everyone else stopped eating and looked at him expecting to hear the worst.

"That dog has a cast on both of his front legs, and he also has a lot of stitches on his belly and hindquarters, so he hasn't been able to move very much. Today, I took the cast off his right leg, and the instant I turned around to pick up some gauze, he jumped or rather fell off the table. I guess that he was so excited to be free of the cast that he wanted to jump up and play. Unfortunately, he hit the edge of the exam table on his way down and tore a few of the stitches loose on his belly. I was afraid for a minute that he had broken his leg again, but it seems to be okay."

"Oh, that poor dog!" Jenny said sadly. "Did the owner

ever call or come back to check on him?"

"No, and that's another thing," her father said. "When I gave that man a rough estimate of what it would cost to put his dog back together, I was afraid that he would bail, but he didn't seem to be too concerned about it."

The next morning, Louie was still inside when Jenny pulled into the circle drive in front of his house. When he didn't come out, she honked the horn once.

"Are you okay?" Jenny asked as he climbed in the front seat. "I was worried when I didn't see you on the porch. That's not like you."

"I'm okay. I just couldn't seem to get it together this morning."

"Because you're still worried about Mr. George?"

"Yeah, I guess."

"Listen, Louie, I may need your help with something. I won't know if I can do it until this evening, but if I can, will you help me?"

The excitement in his friend's voice prompted a quizzical grin.

"Sure, what do you need me to do?" he asked.

"I can't tell you until I know something. As soon as I do, I'll call you and we can make some plans, okay?"

Jenny couldn't concentrate in any of her classes, but instead went over and over in her mind what she was going to say to Phil Stillman. Instead of taking class notes, she wrote and rewrote what she had planned.

She was already waiting at the math classroom door when Louie finally came out.

"Is Mr. George back? she asked when she noticed a hint of a smile on his face.

"No, not yet, but the sub said that he would definitely be back on Monday."

"That's good news!"

"I guess. I wish he was back now, not Monday."

Jenny had decided to set her plan in motion as soon as she finished dinner. Back in her room, she opened her bright yellow backpack and retrieved the notes she had devised during class. Deciding they couldn't be improved, she sat down at her desk, took a few deep breaths to settle her nerves, and reached for her phone. The man answered on the second ring.

"Phil Stillman," she heard a deep male voice say.

"Mr. Stillman, this is Joe's friend Jenny Joulian. You met me at the Emergency Room the day Joe saved our friend Allison Canary from the train."

"Yes, I remember, you're the tall blonde girl. What can I do for you, Jenny?"

"You probably already know this, but our high school football team is playing for the state championship Friday night. My twin brother was the starting quarterback and Joe is the best wide receiver they've ever had. Since it's such an important game and the last one of the season, my whole family is going and we would like to invite you to sit with us to watch the big game."

When he didn't immediately respond, Jenny could feel anxiety beginning to surge through her body.

"Well, I don't know if I can make it, Jenny, but it's kind of you to call. What time does the game start and where are they playing?"

His last two questions gave the teen a shred of hope that he might actually be considering accepting her invitation to watch Joe play.

"The game is at the high school stadium right by the school. It actually starts at 7:00 p.m., but we'll probably get there about 6:30 to get a good seat. I could meet you at the front gate if that's too early for you and we can save a seat for you.

"I'm working in Dallas this week," he said. "I'm not sure I can get there in time, but you're welcome to call me about noon on Friday if you'd like and I will tell you then if I can make it to the game."

"Thank you, Mr. Stillman! I know it will mean a lot to Joe if you can be there. I think you would enjoy meeting my parents, and I know they would enjoy meeting you, too."

"I appreciate the invitation, Jenny. Call me Friday and I'll let you know."

Jenny realized that she was visibly shaking when the call ended. Part of her desperately wanted to believe that Phil Stillman was going to make an effort to get to the game and part of her suspected he had no interest in going to the game at all. But either way, she was committed and she had to put the rest of the plan together.

'Okay,' she told herself, 'Phase One is activated. What am I going to do if Phase Two doesn't fly?'

Thursday evening's dinner had been over for at least 15 minutes, but the family was still gathered around the table sipping iced tea when the Joulian's land line rang. Meghan was sitting closest to the portable phone on the kitchen cabinet, so she got up to answer it.

"Hi Katie, how are you?" the others heard her greet her sister.

"What? . . . We weren't planning to go to the game

since Mac isn't playing, . . . Why? . . . I didn't know you were a football fan . . . I don't know . . . I'm going to have to find that out. I'll call you back just as soon as I know what's going on. Thanks, Katie."

Meghan placed the phone back in its cradle on the counter and returned to her seat at the table.

"That was Katie," she said directing her remarks to her 16-year-old-daughter. "She said that she was calling to find out what time we were going to the game Friday night and where we were going to meet them. Apparently Louie told her that we were all going to the game, and he asked her to call me to find out where to meet. Is that true?"

"Yes, that's true," Jenny said. "I just thought it would be nice if we all went to show our support for Mac since it's the championship game. Louie said Uncle Juan and Aunt Katie had never been to a game, so he thought they might like to go, too."

Meghan pursed her lips and looked at her husband.

"Believe it or not, Katie actually sounded excited about going. I'm not too excited about going to the game since Mac isn't playing, but if she and Juan really want to go, maybe we should go. What do you think, Carson?"

"I think we should go. We haven't been to a game since Mac hurt his hand, so yes, I think we should go, especially since it is for the championship. Maybe they would like to meet us for an early dinner before we go to the game. Why don't you ask Katie if they would like to do that when you call her back?"

"Jenny, it would have been nice if you would have asked us if we had plans for Friday night before you set all this up," she said sternly.

"Well, I asked you Monday before dinner if you and Dad had any plans for Friday."

"Yes, and I told you that I didn't know!"

The conversation was plainly amusing to Mac as he sat back in his chair with a big grin on his face.

"So you guys are really going to the game! That's great! Even though I'll only be sitting on the bench, it still means a lot to know you're there," he said.

"Yes, we're really going," his mother confirmed.

Jenny was so excited that Phase Two of her plan was in place that she could barely contain herself. Nobody knew about Phase One and Phil Stillman except Louie, who had obviously done his part to make Phase Two happen.

"Mom, when you call Aunt Katie back, ask her if they would like to meet us at Chopsticks. I know it's her favorite place!" Jenny said as she pushed back from the table and hurried out of the kitchen.

'I can't believe he actually pulled that off!' Jenny thought as she bounded up the stairs to her room. 'I really didn't think there was any way Aunt Katie and Uncle Juan would ever go to a football game. They're really not sports fans at all.'

Grabbing her cell phone and flopping down onto her bed, the teenager called her best friend.

"It worked!" she nearly shouted into the phone. "When my parents found out that your parents wanted to go to the game, they were all in! They were trying to decide where to meet before the game so I suggested Chopsticks since I know it's one of your mother's favorites. Now if Phil Stillman will just show up, it will be perfect. I so want him to be there for Joe!"

"I really hope he does," Louie agreed. "I guess we won't know until tomorrow."

Jenny spent the next morning looking at her watch every five minutes and rehearsing in her mind what she was going to say to Phil Stillman as soon as her lunch period arrived. As soon as, the bell rang. She bolted out of the classroom and headed for her locker to grab her phone. Then she made her way to the front door to go outside away from other students to make the call. In a quiet spot near the corner of the building, she found Phil Stillman's number in her call log. Jenny was so nervous as she activated the call that she could barely breathe. Finally on the fourth ring, the same deep, male voice she heard before answered the call.

"Phil Stillman."

"Hello, Mr. Stillman?" the girl began in a slightly shaky voice. "This is Jenny Joulian. You asked me to call at noon to remind you about the football game tonight."

"Yes, I remember. What time did you say the game started?"

"The game starts at 7:00 o'clock, but my family and I are going to get there about 6:30 to reserve good seats."

"There's no way I could get there by 6:30!" the man declared.

Jenny could feel her hopes rapidly fade.

"I'm working in Dallas today," he continued. "Depending on the traffic and how things go, I might be able to get there around 7:00 at the earliest."

Suddenly her hopes began to soar.

"We'll save a seat for you and I'll wait for you at the front gate," she offered.

"That's fine, Jenny, but do me a favor. Please don't say

anything to Joe in case something comes up and I can't make it. Thank you for calling, goodbye."

Jenny felt as though she had just gotten off an emotional rollercoaster. She had no idea if the man was really planning to go to the game or not. With only fifteen minutes left in her lunch period, she had barely enough time to put her phone back in her locker and eat a granola bar from the vending machine on the way to her next class.

Louie was waiting by Mr. George's classroom door, but this time he seemed to be excited instead of depressed.

"So how did it go?" he asked while she was still several feet away. "Did you call Mr. Stillman? Is he going to meet us the game?"

"I talked to him, but really I don't know. Come on, I'll tell you what he said on the way home."

Meghan was in the kitchen when Jenny excitedly burst through the back door.

"Hi, Mom! Are we going to meet Aunt Katie and Uncle Juan for dinner before the game?" Jenny asked.

"Yes, we are," her mother answered. "If you want to go, you'd better get ready because we're meeting them at Chopsticks about 5:00 o'clock."

Both families arrived at the restaurant at about the same time. Jenny was so anxious about Phil Stillman that she could barely enjoy her meal. All she could think about was getting to the stadium as quickly as possible.

Finally, the meal was over and they all arrived at the game a little before 6:30 p.m. Jenny led them to her favorite section in the stands and they were early enough to select the best seats. Jenny sat with them for 15 minutes before she announced that she was possibly meeting someone else and that she would be back before the game started.

"Louie, can you save these two seats?" she asked pointing to the two seats beside him. "I'm going down to stand by the gate. Keep your fingers crossed."

As she hurried down to the stadium entrance, Jenny was afraid that Phil Stillman wouldn't show up, but at the same time she was also worried that he would show up. In any event, it really didn't matter since Joe had no idea any of this was happening. All she could do now was stand at the entrance and wait as excited football fans pushed their way into the stands.

CHAPTER TWENTY

At 7:00 o'clock there was still no sign of Phil Stillman. She knew that she was about to miss the kickoff, but decided to wait for a few minutes longer just in case. The roar from the crowd told her that the game was in progress. Just as she was ready to give up and return to her seat in the stands she heard Phil Stillman call her name.

"Jenny!" the man shouted as he rushed toward her. "Sorry I'm late, but the traffic was terrible! Thank you for waiting for me."

The girl turned to see the same nice-looking gentleman she had seen in the Emergency Room lobby striding rapidly toward her. It was obvious that he had not stopped to change as he was dressed more appropriately for a business meeting than a high school football game.

"I'm so glad you could make it!" Jenny said making no effort to conceal her excitement. "The game has already started, but my family is saving seats for us."

As the tall blonde teenager led the way, Joe's dad and Jenny made their way to their seats. Louie saw them coming and moved over so that Mr. Stillman could sit between Jenny and her dad. After hasty introductions, the focus returned to the game.

"Is our team wearing the blue jerseys?" Phil Stillman whispered to Jenny.

She was so shocked by his question that all she could do was nod.

The game started out to be a low-scoring defensive struggle. At the beginning of the second quarter, the opposing team scored a touchdown. Then just before halftime, the home team made a field goal. No other points were scored, so the half ended with the opposing team 7 and the home team 3.

Jenny spent the game with one eye on the field and the other on Phil Stillman. She couldn't decide if he was enjoying the game or not. It was soon apparent that he didn't know much about the game of football.

During halftime, Louie's dad, who seemed to be having a wonderful time, decided to treat everyone to a soft drink. He handed Louie some money and instructed him to take orders. Jenny volunteered to go to the concession stand with him to help carry the drinks. As the two friends were standing in line to order, the only thing they could talk about was Joe's dad.

"Were you surprised that he actually showed up?" Louie asked. "From what you told me, I really didn't think he would come."

Jenny thought for a minute before answering.

"Yeah, I guess in a way I was surprised, too. It's just that I wanted him to come so badly for Joe. It's funny, but I don't think he knows anything about football. He wasn't even sure which team was ours. Maybe he was embarrassed to go to the games. Maybe I'm wrong, but it sure seems like he just doesn't care."

The second half had just gotten under way when the teens returned with the soft drinks. Damien Venn, the back-up quarterback, had only completed a few passes and was nearly intercepted twice, so the coaches decided to abandon the passing game and concentrate on running the ball. However, by the end of the third quarter, that strategy fell short as well. The good news for the home team was that the opposing team hadn't scored any points either.

On the third down of the fourth quarter's opening play, Venn faked a hand-off to one of the running backs and instead tossed the ball to another player. The player wearing #59 twisted away from the only defender who had a chance to stop him and then out-ran the rest of the field to score a 45-yard touchdown.

The home team fans were on their feet cheering wildly as the play unfolded. Even Phil Stillman was caught up in the excitement.

"Look at that kid run!" he shouted. "There's no way they can catch him! He's too fast for all of them! That guy is by far the best player on the whole team!"

It suddenly occurred to Jenny that he had no idea who #59 was, nor did anyone else in her family. She decided not to say anything for the time being.

The score was now 10-7 in favor of the home team. The high school band was enthusiastically playing the school fight song while the cheerleaders were excitedly running along the sideline waving their pompoms.

With time running out, the hometown fans were beginning to smell victory when the opposing team suddenly ran a trick play and scored a touchdown. Then in an instant, the mood in the stands changed. Instead of winning, they were now behind 14-10. Fans on both sides of the field were screaming support for their teams.

The last series for the home team started with a touch back on the 25-yard line. With less than 52 seconds left in the game, Venn apparently realized he had to move the team fast. Ignoring his coaches' instructions to run the ball, he stepped back out of the pocket to pass and was immediately tackled so violently that his helmet flew off. A collective gasp arose from the stands as the young man lay motionless on the field.

Within seconds the team trainers and coaches were at the young player's side to determine if his condition warranted a stretcher or an ambulance. Hundreds of people in the stands fell silent, shocked at the severity of the hit and fearing the worst.

Finally, after several minutes, the boy was helped to his feet and able to walk back to the bench under his own power. The fans on both sides clapped and cheered loudly for the injured player. When the game resumed, the boys in blue had a new quarterback.

"It's Mac!" Jenny shrieked turning to Phil Stillman. "That's my twin brother! He's the starting quarterback, but he hasn't been able to play because he injured his hand. He's the best! He'll get a touchdown! You'll see!"

Visibly surprised to see Mac take the field, Carson and

Meghan simply looked at one another.

Mac's family watched as he quickly lined up the players. They could hear him barking numbers as the play began. The running play, probably designed by one of the coaches, netted the team four yards before their progress was stopped on the 29-yard line. Not enough for a first down let alone a touchdown.

With seconds ticking off the clock and facing a third down, the team hurried back to the line. This time, Mac lined up in a shotgun formation. As soon as the ball was snapped, he backed up a few steps and threw a short, wobbling pass to one of the receivers who was immediately forced out of bounds. The play was enough for a first down at the 36-yard line with 27 seconds left on the clock.

"I can't believe he's trying to pass!" Jenny whispered to Louie. "I don't think he has much feeling in his third and fourth fingers, so he probably can't grip the ball very well."

"That's your son?" Phil Stillman asked leaning over toward Carson. "I sure hope he can throw the ball better than that next time. They've got 27 seconds to make a touchdown or the game's over."

Jenny couldn't hear Phil Stillman's comments over of the crowd noise but she could see her father's reaction. He was obviously displeased about what he had heard the man say because he frowned and immediately shouted something back. The only words she could clearly hear were "Mac" and "quarterback."

She suspected that Mr. Stillman must have said something insulting about Mac. Her first impulse was to come to her brother's defense, but she managed to stop herself before she said something that she knew she would regret. Instead, she only glared at Joe's father for a second. As the play started, Jenny crossed her fingers and along with the rest of the home team's fans, literally held her breath.

Again Mac lined up in the shotgun formation. This time as soon as the ball was snapped, instead of passing he handed it off to a running back, who was standing behind him. The player darted past him, ran laterally for a few feet, and then pitched the ball back. The play confused the defense just long enough for #59 to break free and begin sprinting down the field. Mac stepped out of the pocket and let fly a long, arcing pass that literally landed in his favorite target's arms. None of the defensive players could catch the wide receiver as he ran untouched into the end zone.

The crowd was already on its feet and cheering wildly even before the two referees signaled a touchdown. With only 12 seconds left on the clock, the team lined up for the point-after attempt. The kicker, a smaller boy with a soccer-style delivery, sent the ball solidly through the uprights for the extra point.

With only enough time for one more play, the kicker booted the ball away and pinned the opposing team inside their 8-yard line. Their quarterback was stopped for a loss and the game was over. Final score: Home 17 – Visitors 14.

Jenny was still a little irritated with Phil Stillman but was so excited that Mac had thrown the winning touchdown that it didn't seem to matter.

"Great game!" she heard the former military officer shout to her dad. "That #59 is something else! Your son can really throw a football and if he hits #59 like he did today it's game over!"

"Like I told you, Mac is a tremendous athlete, so I'm

not surprised," Carson shouted back over the party atmosphere in the stadium.

Jenny wasn't sure how to tell Joe's father, but he needed to know that #59 wasn't just another player.

As the fans pushed their way out of the stadium, Jenny yelled above the noise and grabbed Phil Stillman's arm to get his attention.

"#59 is Joe, Mr. Stillman. Your son is the best wide receiver on the entire team!"

The man turned around and for a few seconds, looked at her but didn't say anything or even seem to hear what she had just said, so she loudly repeated her message.

Finally, she heard him mumble, "#59 is Joe? #59 is my son, Joe?"

The man was obviously stunned.

"That's right, Mr. Stillman. Now you know why I invited you to the game. I wanted you to have a chance to see what a fabulous player Joe is. I'm so glad you got to see them win the championship!"

"Thank you, Jenny, thank you," he said so softly that she could barely hear him over the noise. "I appreciate this more than you will ever know."

Then he was gone, swallowed up by the surging crowd. Jenny's family was almost to the exit when she caught up with them. A quick glance at her mother and she could see that the woman was almost as excited as she was over the outcome of the game.

"We've got to go celebrate!" she said excitedly. "Where can we go, Carson?"

"What about the Malt Shoppe?" her sister Katie volunteered. "I think it's still open. If not, I guess we could always go to the Wide Awake Grill. It's open 24-7."

Her last suggestion prompted a groan from her hand surgeon husband.

"Okay, then, let's meet at the Malt Shoppe," Carson said making the final decision.

After a full evening of football excitement topped off with an ice cream sundae, Jenny was ready to call it a night. She had just gone to bed when her cell phone rang. Curious as to who would be calling this late, she immediately got up, grabbed her phone, and crawled back under the covers.

"Hello?"

"Hi Jen, it's Joe. Sorry to be calling so late, but I wanted to talk to you tonight."

"Not a problem. What's up?"

"When I got home after the game, my dad was waiting for me. He told me that you had called him and invited him to the game. He said that when you called the first time, he had decided not to go, but when you called back at noon today and invited him to sit with your family, something made him change his mind. He told me that he didn't even know that it was me that made both touchdowns until you told him. I think he was really embarrassed about that.

"But, here's what I really wanted to tell you, Jen. After we discussed the game, he told me how proud he was of me. I couldn't believe it! He's never, ever said anything like that to me before, ever and it's all because of you. I don't know how to thank you! You called my dad and invited him to the game not once, but twice! That really means a lot to me, Jen. I know he would have never gone otherwise."

Jenny could hear the emotion coloring each of Joe's words and she honestly thought for a minute that he might burst into tears.

"Oh, Joe, you don't need to thank me. I'm just so glad he came to the game and got to see you play! But more than that, I'm happy that he told you how proud he is of you. You so deserve it!"

"Something about that game has definitely changed him, Jen. He even apologized for missing all my games in the past and he told me that next year he's going to go to every one of them! Can you believe that?"

Jenny was nearly in tears herself listening to the pain in her friend's voice. She was so grateful that Phil Stillman had accepted her invitation that she totally forgot how irritated she had been with him at the game.

"Oh, Joe, that's great! Please tell your dad that he's always welcome to sit with us."

"I will, thank you, I appreciate that," he said pausing for a moment before continuing. "There's something else I need to ask you, Jen."

"Oh yeah, what's that?"

"All season Coach promised us that if we won the championship, he and the rest of the staff would treat the entire team to a special dinner with the biggest steaks they could find. He also told us that we could each bring a date if we wanted to. Well, we won the championship, so I was wondering if you would be my date to the team dinner?"

If Jenny hadn't been lying down in bed when she heard his invitation, there would have been a strong possibility that her knees would have buckled and she would have been lying on the floor instead.

"Yes, of course, yes, I'd love to go," she finally managed to stammer.

"Great!" Joe said obviously delighted. "I'll get the details next week and let you know about the time and everything. And Jen, thanks again!"

Suddenly Jenny wasn't sleepy anymore. The girl couldn't have been more excited if she had just won the lottery. All she could do was lie awake for hours and think about Joe, his father, the game, and the big steak dinner.

CHAPTER TWENTY-ONE

Carson and Meghan had left for the vet clinic hours before the twins woke up and wandered downstairs for something to eat.

"So how did you like the game?" Mac asked as he fumbled around in the refrigerator for something to drink.

"I liked it a lot better when you got in the game," she said. "Do you realize that almost every single person in the stands was cheering when you walked onto the field? You and Joe were just spectacular!"

"Speaking of Joe . . . Oh, poor Joe. Did he call you? Do you want some orange juice?" he asked as he removed the large carton of juice from the refrigerator.

"Yes, he did. Why poor Joe? And yes, I want some orange juice."

Mac was snickering as he poured two glasses of juice.

"After the game when we were in the dressing room,

Coach announced that we had earned the big steak dinner he had promised if we won the championship and that we could even bring a date. I'll bet Joe asked me a dozen times if I thought you would be his date to the dinner. I told him definitely not and to forget about it. No way. When he figured out that I was teasing him, he threw his shoe at me. So you told him no, right?"

"Absolutely. I told him no way was I going to any steak dinner with him," she said as she bent down and removed one of her comfy slippers.

Then she sat up and hurled the slipper across the kitchen table catching her twin in mid sip, causing him to spill some of his orange juice.

"Jenny's got a boyfriend, Jenny's got a boyfriend," Mac taunted as he wiped up the spilled juice.

"You're just horrible! Too bad, because no girl will want to go to the dinner with you!" she said with a grin as she retrieved her slipper and headed back upstairs.

Both twins were at home when Carson and Meghan returned from the veterinary clinic later in the afternoon. Jenny was in her room talking on the phone and Mac was in his room playing computer games.

"Hey, Jen," her father called from the foot of the stairs. "Can you come down here for a minute? There's somebody here that would like to meet you."

"What?" she called back puzzled. "Okay, I'll be right down."

Both parents were sitting at the kitchen table when she walked in.

"Did I hear you say that someone here wanted to meet me? Who?"

"Well, he's a pretty big guy with blonde hair, just like you, and he has big brown eyes. He's got a few scars and he limps a little, but he's very sweet. His name is Cowboy. Does he sound like your type?" her father asked trying not to grin.

Jenny just stood and stared at him trying to decide if it was a joke or if it was for real.

"I have no idea what you're talking about," she said clearly mystified.

"Well then, let me introduce you," he said as he opened the back door and stepped outside.

When he walked back inside a few seconds later, he was leading a Labrador retriever that seemed to be smiling as he furiously wagged his tail.

"This is Cowboy. And if you want him, he's all yours."

A quick look at Jenny's face told her dad that Cowboy had just found a forever home.

"He's beautiful, Dad! Of course, I want him!" Jenny exclaimed as she walked over to pet her new furry friend. "Is this the dog that got hit by a truck?"

"That's him. His owner never came back and on top of that when he first brought the dog in for treatment, he gave us a stolen credit card. So this dog is all yours!"

"Oh, I can't believe it! This is just the best, thanks, Dad! I'm going to take him upstairs and show him my room if that's ok."

"He's your dog, Sweetheart."

Cowboy and Jenny bounded up the stairs but stopped at Mac's room first.

"Mac," she called lightly tapping on his door. "You've got to see who's here! Can we come in?"

"We?" he asked opening his door to reveal an excited

girl and her new dog.

"This is Cowboy," she said as the dog instantly pushed his way over to Mac and began to nuzzle his hand.

"Where did you get him? Who does he belong to?" Mac asked as he reached down to pet his inquisitive visitor.

"He's mine," Jenny said proudly. "This is the dog that Dad's been telling us about. His owner never came back, so Dad brought him home and gave him to me because he knows that I love dogs so much."

Cowboy's tail wagged vigorously as Mac continued to scratch his ears.

"He really likes you, Mac!" Jenny said watching the two bond.

""Yeah, well, I like dogs, too," her brother said softly.

One look at his face and Jenny realized that Mac's feelings were hurt that Cowboy had been given to her.

"Wow, he really likes you," Jenny said. "Since you like him, too, from now on, Cowboy will be our dog, okay? That means you can share the chores, too – feeding, exercising, and training."

"Yeah, okay," Mac said with a grin. "Sounds good."

"Come on, Cowboy," Jenny said pulling on his leash. "I want to show you our room."

As soon as they walked into Jenny's bedroom, Cowboy immediately began to explore every corner of her room while Jenny retrieved her cell phone from its charger. Then while the dog continued to investigate, Jenny propped herself up on her bed and called Louie to share her good news.

"You'll never guess what Dad brought home," she began excitedly. "He brought a dog that I'm sharing with Mac! He's a yellow Labrador retriever, his name is Cowboy, and he's just beautiful!"

Finally, after listening for several minutes to Jenny's excited comments about her new friend, Louie interrupted.

"That's great, Jen. Can't wait to see him, but right now I'm worried about Monday."

"Monday?" Jenny asked unsure of what he was asking. "What's Monday?"

"It's the day Mr. George is supposed to be back at school, Jen," the boy said carefully. "He's been gone for almost two weeks now. When we told him about that girl in the old shack, he left so fast that he didn't say goodbye or anything, remember? Why do you think he did that? Do you think she's related to him? I can't figure it out, can you?"

Jenny was so excited about her new dog and her upcoming date with Joe that she totally forgot about Mr. George coming back to school on Monday.

"I forgot about Mr. George, Louie!" she exclaimed. "Honestly, I don't know what to think. But, you're absolutely right. It must have something to do with that girl in the old shack because he bolted when we told him that we found out who owned the black car."

"That's the only thing that makes any sense to me," he said.

Cowboy had finished checking out Jenny's room and was now more interested in getting to know his new friend. Without any warning, the large yellow Lab jumped onto Jenny's bed and proceeded to step on her and poke his nose into her face.

"No! Get off! Get down!" she yelled at the dog trying to push him away.

"Listen, Louie, I've got to go," Jenny said into her

phone. "This dog is trying to eat me alive. I'll see you Monday, okay?"

Early Monday morning, as Jenny drove up to Louie's house to pick him up for school, she could see her best friend pacing nervously back and forth in front of the porch steps. As soon as the car stopped, he grabbed his backpack, threw it in the back, and climbed into the front seat.

"Are you nervous, Jen?" he asked as soon as he had fastened his seatbelt. "I sure am. In a way, I really dread seeing Mr. George today, which is totally stupid because I miss him and I really want to find out what's going on. But in another way, maybe I really don't want to know what's going on. That doesn't make any sense, does it?"

Before she started out of the circle drive, she took a good look at the boy sitting beside her. Instead of sitting quietly in the passenger seat or looking out the side window as he usually did on the way to school, he was shifting around in the seat and pulling on the seatbelt.

"No," Jenny said wrinkling her brow. "I don't think I'm nervous; it's more like I'm uncomfortable about seeing Mr. George or something. I really don't know what I feel."

Before she could shift gears and head for the highway, her cell phone chimed with an incoming text.

"I just got a text from Mr. George!" she exclaimed as she glanced at her phone.

Could you and Louie meet me in
my room after school today?

"What did he say, Jen?" Louie asked as he leaned over trying to see the message.

"He wants to know if you and I could meet him in his room after school. Shall I text him back and say that we can meet him?"

"Yeah, for sure! At least now we know that he's back and he wants to talk to us. Text him back and tell him that we'll be there!"

While the car was still stopped, Jenny hurriedly sent Mr. George a reply text promising that they would be there after school.

As soon as the final bell rang, Jenny raced to Mr. George's math classroom. Instead of going in as he usually did, Louie was waiting for her by the door pacing.

"What's wrong, Louie? You shouldn't be this uptight about seeing Mr. George."

"Yeah, I know. I guess I just feel guilty that we found that information about the girl, especially if he's related to her or something."

"Well, it's too late to worry about that now. Come on, let's go in," she said.

Watson George was sitting behind his desk rearranging papers when the two cousins walked into the classroom. As soon as he saw them, he stood up and walked around to the front of his desk to greet them.

"Jenny, Louie, thank you for agreeing to meet me this afternoon. This has been a very strange week and a half and I'm sure you've been wondering what's going on. I have a lot to tell you, so this may take a while," the Boy Scout leader said as he walked to the door and closed it.

"Have a seat," he said gesturing toward the front row of student desks.

As the two cousins set their backpacks down and took

a seat, Mr. George pulled one of the desks out and turned it around to face them. Then he walked back to his desk and opened one of the drawers. They watched in silence as he pulled out the old coffee can Louie had found at the old shack and walked back to where they were sitting.

"This has been quite a ride," he said as sat down in the chair he had turned to face them. "Louie, I think you're going to be surprised when you find out what happened just because you went back to the old shack and found this old coffee can."

Jenny and Louie glanced at each other before staring intently at the rusty old can which Mr. George was holding in his right hand.

"I'm going to give you a little background information first. When I was in elementary school, my two best friends were Danny Collie and my cousin, Gorman George."

Louie couldn't help inhaling sharply at the mention of the two names. Danny Collie had nearly killed him over the legend of the lost gold a few months before and now Gorman George was somehow connected to the mysterious girl and the stash of drugs they saw at the old shack.

Watson George didn't miss the boy's reaction at the mention of the two names and tried to stifle a smile.

"Because I'm related to Gorman, I knew him long before I met Danny at school. The names on the papers you found in this old coffee can are his great grandparents, Caleb and Matilda Schnickel. The old papers appear to be a copy of the original deed to the farm they settled in the late 1800s. They were German immigrants who came to Oklahoma to start a new life, but they both passed away long before Gorman and I were born."

"Mr. George, did they get their farm as part of one of the land runs?" Louie asked.

"I don't know for sure, Louie, but there's a good chance they might have. As you probably remember from your Oklahoma history class, there were actually seven land runs in Oklahoma. This area was considered part of the unassigned land.

"Weren't there lots of Indians here then?" Jenny asked.

"Yes, there were, Jennifer. This was their home and the government basically stole it from them, put them on reservations, and gave their land to anyone who wanted it," he said with a noticeable edge to his voice.

Mr. George paused when he saw his listeners' wide eyes and shocked faces.

"Sorry, I didn't mean to get on my soapbox, but as a Native American this whole land run thing is a bit of a sore spot with me."

"He's Cherokee," Jenny quietly whispered to Louie.

"That's right, Jennifer. I'm part Cherokee. But I don't want you to think that Gorman's great grandparents did anything wrong. It was a great opportunity for them and they took it. Good for them."

The tall math teacher set the coffee can down on the floor and stood up.

"Anyway, back to the farm. As far as I know, the Schnickel's lived there for probably fifty or sixty years. By the time I was born, that old shack had been built to store what was left of their belongings. The original house and barn were demolished, so all that was left of their homestead was that shack.

"Gorman and his parents lived less than a mile away from the old homestead. When I was old enough to go to grade school, I used to go home with him after school to play until my dad picked me up for supper. We spent lots of time playing in that shack. In fact, that's probably what saved you when Danny Collie kidnapped you, Louie. Since he had spent a lot of time playing with us, too, it wasn't hard to guess where you were."

Louie was beginning to get restless, so he stood up and began to pace back and forth in front of the chairs. Jenny had been sitting with her head propped in her hand staring at Mr. George.

"Mr. George?" she asked when he stopped speaking.

"Yes, Jennifer?"

"Louie and I are afraid that we offended you when we told you that we had traced the car to your cousin and you left the room so quickly. We didn't mean to offend you and if we did, we're sorry."

"No, no, no, Jennifer," the man protested. "You didn't offend me; far from it. As soon as you told me about the girl you saw at the Gas and Grub, the drugs, and Gorman's car, all of the pieces fell into place and I knew that I had to act fast. That's why I left school in such a hurry."

Louie had returned to his seat and he and Jenny were listening intently to every word Mr. George was saying.

"What you two don't know is that Gorman and I lost touch with each other when I enlisted. The last time I had heard anything about him was roughly eight years ago when I separated from the service. A friend told me that Gorman had been in and out of prison on drug charges for years and that his only daughter, Amanda, had run away from his ex-wife when she was only thirteen. When you told me that you had seen drugs and someone passed out at the shack, something told me that it had to be his daughter.

"When I left here, I immediately drove to the old homestead and walked to the old shack. Just like you said, there was a heavy brace on the door, but it wasn't nailed down, so I lifted it off and went inside. It was very dark and at first, I couldn't see anything, but I had my military-style flashlight with me. As soon as I switched it on, I could see someone lying on the floor in the corner. I aimed the beam all around the shack to make sure there wasn't anyone else in there with me, but there wasn't. I didn't know if the person I saw lying there was dead or alive, or if it was a man or a woman.

"All I could tell from where I was standing was that it appeared to be an adult body covered with an old blanket just like you saw, Louie. I walked over to it and gently nudged it with my toe. It didn't move, so I reached down and pulled the blanket back."

Jenny gasped so loudly that Mr. George stopped talking and looked to see if anything was wrong.

"I'm so sorry, Mr. George," she apologized. "It was that girl, wasn't it?"

The former soldier walked back to the chair he had pulled out and sat down facing the two teens.

"I don't know if it was the girl you saw, Jennifer, but it was definitely a young female. I reached down and shook her shoulder, but she didn't move. She didn't look dead, her eyes were about half open, and her cheek was lukewarm, so it was obvious that she had overdosed on something. I **TURNED THE UNCONSCIOUS** girl over to make sure that she was breathing. My first impulse was to call 911, but I knew an ambulance crew would never be able to find the old shack in time. The only option was to pick her up and carry her to my car. By the time I got her into the back seat she was beginning to stir, so that was encouraging."

Louie stood up and started to pace again, but thought better of it and sat back down. Jenny reached over and patted his arm without taking her eyes off Watson George.

"Was she about to die?" the girl asked.

"Maybe, but I had no way of knowing. She was barely conscious and I was positive that she had **OVERDOSED** on something, but I had no idea what. The only thing I could do was to get her to the Emergency Room and hope for the best.

"While they were working on her, I stepped outside to make a few calls to see if anyone knew if Gorman was in the area. No one seemed to know anything about him."

"So you thought she might be your cousin's runaway daughter?" Jenny asked.

"I didn't know. She had no identification, and I hadn't had time to go back to the shack and look around."

"What did she look like?" Jenny asked.

"About all I can tell you is that she had short, dark hair and was slightly built. I didn't see her standing, so I don't know how tall she was, but she is probably short."

"That's her!" Louie exclaimed jumping to his feet. "That's got to be her!"

"That young lady apparently has a history of **DRUG ABUSE** since she was in such horrible physical condition. If I hadn't found her when I did, they said she very likely wouldn't have made it. I hope you realize that you two saved her life."

Louie and Jenny looked at each other and then back at Watson George.

"No, it's true. I mean it. If you two and Mac had obeyed me and not gone back to explore the old shack, she would have died. It's that simple. It's going to take a while before she's strong enough to be released from the hospital. In the meantime, I've got to find the answers to a lot of questions starting with who this young woman is."

Louie's mentor stood up, returned his chair to the front row, and walked back to his desk.

Since it was obvious the meeting was over, Jenny and Louie retrieved their backpacks and started for the door.

"I still want to know where he's been for a week and a half," Jenny whispered to her friend as they closed the door and started to walk down the hall.

"Yeah, me, too," Louie whispered back. "Do you think he will ever tell us?"

"The mystery of the old shack just got deeper, didn't it?" Louie asked as he settled into the passenger seat of Jenny's white Ford Focus for the ride home.

"Yeah, but at least we found out about those papers in that old rusty coffee can you found," Jenny agreed as she started her car.

"We know a little bit about Gorman George, but we still don't know anything about the girl we saw or if she was the same one he found at the shack or why there was such a heavy brace on the door."

It took Jenny a few minutes to respond as the heavy traffic demanded her undivided attention.

"Can you believe that Mr. George's cousin and his best friend are both drug dealers and served time in prison?"

"I know. It's weird," Louie agreed.

"You do realize that Mr. George doesn't have to tell us anything else, don't you?" Jenny continued as she pulled into the circle drive in front of the Morales' home.

"I know," the boy said before he opened the car door. "But I don't think he would have told us anything if he wasn't going to tell us the rest of it."

"I hope you're right," Jenny said as she waved good-bye. "I'll see you tomorrow."

Cowboy was anxiously waiting for his new owner to return home. The instant Jenny opened the back door, the yellow Lab barked a happy greeting and excitedly ran in a circle in front of her furiously wagging his tail.

"Come on, Cowboy, let's go upstairs. I've got some thinking to do before we eat."

CHAPTER TWENTY-TWO

A few minutes before dinner was ready, Jenny went back downstairs to help her mother get the big pot of home-made beef stew on the table with Cowboy close behind her.

"Jen, you're going to have to do something with your dog," Meghan said sternly. "I can't have him running all over the kitchen. Does he know how to sit, or stay, or anything?"

"I don't know!" Jenny exclaimed. "Let's find out."

The large yellow dog obviously wanted to be with his new friend and appeared eager to please her.

"Cowboy, sit!" Jenny commanded.

The young canine tilted his head to the side, looked at her quizzically, and immediately sat down.

"Wow!" Jenny exclaimed. "He knows how to sit! Good boy, Cowboy!"

Forgetting that she was supposed to be helping with dinner, the girl walked into the living room and called her new dog. Cowboy leaped to his feet and raced to her side.

"Okay, Cowboy, down," she said pointing at the floor. "Do you know a down?"

Again, the Lab paused for a moment and then obediently laid down at her feet.

"He knows a down!" Jenny excitedly called to her mother. "I wonder what else he knows."

"I don't know, but you need to wash your hands and stop playing with the dog. Call your dad and your brother, Jen. Dinner is ready."

As the family took their seats at the table, Cowboy claimed his place beside Jenny's chair, where he remained quietly throughout dinner.

"Do you still like the dog, Jen, or do we need to find him a new home?" Carson teased as he reached for his second piece of cornbread.

"I love him and so does Mac! Cowboy is just wonderful and he deserves a new forever home!" she declared glancing down at the dog contentedly snoozing by her chair.

"I thought you might say that," her father said with a sly grin.

"Thanks, Dad, for giving him a chance to get well and for bringing him home."

"You're welcome," the kind-hearted veterinarian said. "He's such a nice dog; your mother and I also thought he deserved a second chance.

During dinner, Jenny had a sudden brainstorm that nearly caused her to abandon dinner and reach for her cell phone. However, she managed to control the impulse, finish dinner, and help her mother clear the table. Then she bolted for her room with Cowboy close behind.

"Louie," she said as soon as her best friend answered the phone, "I just discovered something really important! Are you near your computer?"

"I can be in a couple of minutes. What did you find?"

"I know what Amanda George looks like, and she's not the girl we saw at the Gas and Grub! Maybe we can find that girl, too."

"Seriously? How did you do that?"

"It occurred to me at dinner that Amanda George might have gone to school long enough to be in the school's yearbook. I found her in the sophomore section five years back. I just sent you a link to that page. When it comes up, you'll see that she has long hair, she wears glasses, and she doesn't look anything like the girl we saw."

"I've got it, and you're right, she doesn't look anything like the girl we saw at the Gas and Grub!" Louie exclaimed. "How are we going to find that girl?"

"I thought maybe you could help me and we could scan the yearbook pages back even further and maybe she might show up."

"Great idea!"

After searching for nearly thirty minutes with no sign of the other girl, Louie was ready to give up.

"No, don't give up yet," Jenny protested. "I just have a feeling she's in here somewhere. Let's look at the sophomore section again. Maybe we overlooked her."

Almost immediately, Jenny found a picture that she was sure was the girl they had seen at the Gas and Grub.

"I found her!" Jenny exclaimed. "I was looking for a girl with short hair. This girl has long hair, but I'm positive it's her! Look for Lezlee Pomporo and tell me what you think. Her picture is on the fourth row, second from the left. It's her, I just know it is."

"I found her, but she looks different from the girl we saw," Louie said sounding disappointed.

"The girl we saw was very thin and had short cropped hair," Jenny explained. "When this picture was taken, this girl had long hair and was at least 20 pounds heavier. If you imagine it that way, can you see the resemblance?"

"I just don't know, Jen. I'm not very good at imagining things like this."

"Don't worry about it, Louie. I'm going to print out both pictures and show them to Mr. George tomorrow and see what he thinks, okay?"

The next morning Louie was anxiously waiting for Jenny to pick him up. He started talking the minute he was in the car fastening his seat belt.

"I've been thinking about the picture of the girl you said we saw at the Gas and Grub and I think you're right. I think it is her. Before we take off, are you going to text Mr. George and see if we can show him the yearbook pictures after school today?"

"Yes, I'm going to text him right now," Jenny said as she picked up her phone.

Mr. George, Louie and I have something
interesting to show you. Do you have
time to meet with us after school today?

A one-word reply text arrived before Jenny could turn out of the circle drive.

Absolutely.

"That was fast!" Jenny exclaimed. "He just texted back one word, 'Absolutely' so we're on."

The instant the final bell rang, both Louie and Jenny hurried to Watson George's math classroom. As usual, the boy arrived first and was already seated at a desk on the front row when Jenny arrived. Watson George was still seated behind his desk.

Before she sat down next to Louie, she propped her bright yellow backpack on the chair, opened it, and extracted two sheets of paper containing photographs. Then she set it down on the floor and sat down next to her best friend.

"I can't say that I was completely surprised by your text, Jennifer. You and Louie have to be the most diligent detectives I've ever seen," Mr. George began. "You said that you had something interesting to show me."

"Yes, we do," she said walking over to his desk and handing him the papers. "Louie and I were under the impression that the girl we saw at the Gas and Grub driving Gorman George's car must be his daughter, but we were wrong. As it turns out, it wasn't his daughter at all. It was another girl named Lezlee Pomporo. We think she's the one you took to the hospital."

The tall ex-soldier stared intently at the papers in his hand studying each one carefully.

"The picture in your right hand is Amanda George when she was a sophomore in high school five years ago. We found it online in the school yearbook. We're positive the other picture is the girl we saw at the Gas and Grub. She was also a sophomore in Amanda's class when this picture was taken. Back then, she had long hair like Amanda's and was probably 20 pounds heavier. You'll have to use your imagination, but does this look like the girl you rescued?"

For a long moment, Watson George continued to study the pictures without speaking. Finally, he stood up, walked over to the front row of chairs, and handed the papers back to Jenny.

"I honestly don't know if that is the girl I took to the hospital or not, Jennifer. I just checked to see if she was alive before I carried her out, so you might be right. I've never met Amanda, so I don't know what she looks like either. Like you and Louie, I just assumed it was Gorman's daughter since I knew she was a runaway and you saw her driving his car. The girl I took to the hospital had no identification, so I have no idea who she is, but she's probably a runaway, too."

There was no mistaking the sadness in the man's voice as he turned around and walked back to his desk.

"This is really turning out to be confusing, isn't it?" Louie said. "You thought you were rescuing Amanda and instead it turned out to be someone else we don't know, right?"

"That's right."

Jenny was a little disappointed that Mr. George couldn't positively identify Lezlee Pomoro as the girl he rescued. She was also concerned that he wasn't going to tell them anything else about what he had done the week and a half that he was gone.

"Mr. George, what happened after you took the girl to the hospital? Did you go back to the shack to see if you could find her ID?" she asked hoping her question would provide more details.

The teacher didn't respond immediately, which made Jenny uncomfortable. Instead, he looked as if he was trying to decide if he should say anything else. Then he leaned forward and put his folded arms on his desk before he spoke.

"Because there were so many drugs out there, I didn't want to go back to the old shack by myself. As soon as I left the hospital, I called the county sheriff's office to see if I could get someone to go out there with me.

"I made an appointment to meet a deputy at 9:00 a.m. the next morning. Because I knew that it would be difficult to explain where we were going, I met him at the coffee shop downtown and he followed me to the old shack. I thought we were just going out there to confiscate illegal drugs, but it turned out to be much more than that.

"I remembered what you told me about that girl using the side window, so when we parked at the old homestead, I told the deputy that I was going to walk around to the side of the shack in the event anyone tried to escape. As it turned out, no one else was in the shack, so the deputy called for me to come inside.

"Even with the front door open, it was still very dark, so the only light we really had was from our flashlights. The deputy immediately spotted the cardboard box of drugs and asked me to help him look around to see if there were any more. We didn't see anything else although it was very obvious that people had been camping out there for probably quite some time judging from the trash left behind."

Jenny quickly glanced at Louie, who was sitting on the edge of his chair, obviously captivated by his Boy Scout leader's experience.

"When we didn't find any more drugs or drug paraphernalia, the deputy picked up the cardboard box and took it to his car. He told me the sheriff would probably watch the shack for a while to see if anyone else showed up. Before he left, he nailed the brace on the door. I told him that I had a toolbox in my truck and offered to secure the side window, which he thought was a good idea.

"After I finished nailing the window shut from the outside, I decided to check it from the inside to make sure that nobody could just push it open. I didn't think they could, but I added a few more nails just to make sure. I was about to step over the pile of blankets where the girl I rescued was sleeping when something white caught my eye. I pulled the blanket back and found a piece of notebook paper folded in half hidden in the folds. I thought it might be important, so I folded it again and put it in my pocket."

Mr. George sat back in his chair and observed his two listeners, who were concentrating intently on his every word. He knew full well curiosity would prompt one of them to speak before he continued.

Jenny couldn't stand the suspense.

"Was something written on it, Mr. George? Could you read it?"

"Yes, there was something written on it, Jennifer. It was hard to read by flashlight, but I could read enough of it to know that it was the key to the mystery of the old shack."

"Seriously!" Louie exclaimed obviously intrigued. "You found the key to the mystery of the old shack on that piece of paper? Awesome!"

Jenny was clearly as excited by Watson George's revelation as her cousin, but she wanted to know what was written on the notebook paper stuck under the blanket.

"What was written on the paper, Mr. George? Can you tell us?"

The tall math teacher slid his desk chair back, stood up, and walked to the front of his desk. Before he spoke, he leaned against the older metal desk and observed the two teenagers hanging on his every word.

"It was a personal letter Amanda had written to her friend, apparently the girl you saw at the convenience store. As soon as I saw what it was, I took the letter to the hospital with instructions to get it to her.

"Before I took it to her, I made a copy of it just in case," the ex-soldier said as he reached into his desk drawer to retrieve the letter. He unfolded it and began to read.

Dear Lezlee,

I'm sorry I won't have a chance to tell you goodbye. I hope one day to see you again. When I went to court, the judge said I could either go back to jail for six months on drug charges, or I could go to rehab. No-brainer. I hate jail, so I chose rehab because it was free. It's run by a religious group and it's located somewhere in Texas. That's all I know about it. Maybe I can get clean this time. I wish you, Caycee, and Sara could go with me

The judge allowed me to come out here one more time with a police officer to pick up any personal items before I went to rehab. That gave me a chance to hide this letter for you. He also told the cop to secure the door, so no one could get in, but he didn't know about the window, so I hope you and the others can still stay here as long as you need to.

Please be careful. I wish more than anything that you could get off the drugs. They're so dangerous.

You'll always be my best friend forever.

Love, Amanda."

Jenny and Louie sat in wide-eyed silence as they listened to Mr. George recite what he remembered about the content of Amanda's letter. For a few minutes, no one spoke. Finally, Jenny again broke the silence.

"Wow, how sad! She sounded like she was going off forever to die, didn't she?"

Mr. George couldn't resist a chuckle.

"Not only was she not going off to die, she was actually going off to live."

"Seriously?" Louie said repeating his favorite word.

"Yes, seriously!" Watson George teased.

The teacher walked back to his chair and sat down behind his desk.

"When I found out what happened to Amanda, my first thought was to try to find her parents. I tried everything I could think of, but I could find no trace of her mother. No one I talked to had seen her for a long time, so I'm sure she probably remarried and moved out of the area.

"I thought it might be easier to find Gorman since I was sure he was probably in jail, prison, or a half-way house somewhere. Unfortunately, I hit a dead end with that, too. I guess with all the privacy laws they've got in place, it's either impossible to find out very much about anyone incarcerated or I was looking in the wrong place."

"That's not fair!" Jenny protested.

"I know, but that's the way it is."

"So what did you do then?" Louie asked impatiently wanting the story to continue.

Watson George clasped his hands behind his head and leaned back in his chair before resuming his story.

"I went to the courthouse and started searching

through the public records and recent court cases. It didn't take very long to locate the one I was trying to find since it was less than two months old. According to the court documents, Amanda George had been arrested for drug possession on September 4th. She was sentenced to six months in the county jail but instead was released to the Backwoods Begin Again Recovery Center for Addicted Women.

"I knew from Amanda's letter, that it was somewhere in Texas. I finally found a listing for the "Backwoods Recovery Center" online and called the number. Fortunately, it was the right place. I introduced myself and explained to the lady who answered the phone that I was related to Amanda George, who was living at the recovery center and asked if it would be possible for me to visit her. At first, I was afraid the lady would not allow me to come because she hesitated for so long. Finally, she asked me what day I wanted to visit. I suggested the weekend since it would take me several hours to get there. She gave me permission to arrive at 10:00 a.m. on Saturday.

"As soon as I drove down the long driveway and through the gate of the facility, it was obvious why they named it "Backwoods." Located in far southeast Texas, it is a beautiful wooded area with tall trees and a lake. Also, it's too far from a town or highway for residents to try to escape on foot."

Watson George reached into his top desk drawer and retrieved an attractive trifold brochure describing the amenities of the "Backwoods Begin Again Center for Addicted Women" and walked over to Jenny.

"This is exactly what it looks like, too," he said as he handed it to her.

Jenny scooted her chair closer to Louie so that both of them could see the folder.

"Wow! It looks like a resort!" Jenny exclaimed. "The main building is a log cabin!"

"That's right, Jennifer. It's much nicer than almost any of the residents have experienced. If you'll notice, there are several log cabins that house six residents to a cabin. However, they spend most of their time in counseling, in classes or participating in an activity."

Louie was craning his neck to get a better look at the activities list.

"Do they really have horses, canoes, campfires, and stuff like that?" he asked.

"Oh yes, those things, and a lot more."

"Did you get to see Amanda?" Jenny asked as she handed the brochure to Louie.

Mr. George walked back to his desk and leaned against the front of it again.

"Yes, I did, and I'll have to admit that it was extremely awkward at first. Bear in mind that we had never seen each other before and she really had no idea who I was. After I explained that her dad and I had been best friends in grade school and that we were cousins, she seemed to relax and accept me a little more. She wanted to know why I would take the time to drive all the way down to southeast Texas to see her. That question caught me off guard because I honestly didn't know myself. The only thing I could think of was to tell her that we were family and that's what families do."

While Jenny was absorbed in what Mr. George was saying, Louie was barely listening and instead carefully studying the Backwoods information brochure. Watson George was so engrossed in telling his experience that he didn't notice.

"Amanda told me in no uncertain terms that she didn't have a family. She obviously disliked her mother and had no idea what had happened to her. Sadly, her father died in prison three or four years ago while she was still in high school. As far as she was concerned, she had no one to care about her except for her addicted friends and the other runaways who hung out with her at the old shack."

"Oh, that poor girl!" Jenny softly exclaimed.

"Before I left, I told Amanda that I was her family and from now on I would care for her and help her as much as I could. We promised to stay in touch and I challenged her to take advantage of the six-month recovery program to really make a break with her old life and start again without drugs. I can tell you one thing; it was hard to walk away."

Louie suddenly realized that Mr. George had stopped speaking. He got to his feet and walked over to his teacher's desk to return the brochure.

"I wish I could go somewhere like that," he mumbled. "Boy Scout camp isn't nearly this awesome!"

His Boy Scout leader only smiled as he watched the two students retrieve their backpacks and head for the door.

As soon as they were seated in Jenny's car ready for the drive home, Louie became animated.

"At least now we know who nailed that brace shut," he said. "It was that cop that took Amanda back to the old shack. Too bad that he missed the side window."

"Yes it is, and we also know that Lezlee is the girl we saw at the Gas and Grub and that she is Amanda's best friend. There's only one thing that we don't know right now."

"Yeah? What's that?"

Jenny looked at her friend and smiled.

"What do you suppose happened to Gorman George's black Honda?"

"If she parked it at the bridge and left it for very long, I'm sure they towed it away. If you're really concerned about it, we could always drive by the yard where they take all those cars and see if we can find it," Louie offered.

"No, that's okay. I'm sure you're right."

The boy suddenly changed the subject.

"I know it's still a week away, but I can't figure out what my parents are getting me for my birthday. Neither one of them have said a word about it and I haven't seen anything that might give it away."

"I can't believe you'll be turning 16, Louie! I'm sure Uncle Juan and Aunt Katie have something special in mind and I promise we're definitely going to celebrate. I'm just glad your birthday is not this weekend because I'm going to the football banquet with Joe Saturday night and that's all I've been thinking about lately."

"Yeah, I know," he said shaking his head and making a face as he got out of the car.

CHAPTER TWENTY-THREE

The minute Jenny got home she raced up to her room to make sure everything was still in order with the new dress and shoes she was going to wear to the football banquet the next night. Her mother had surprised her with a shopping trip a few days before and had helped her pick out the perfect outfit to wear to the banquet. The girl was tempted to try it on again but decided against it.

The big day dawned sunny and bright, perfect for a victory celebration. Jenny was so nervous and excited about her date that she had slept poorly and was awake even before sunrise. Joe had called the night before to tell her that he was planning to pick her up at 5:30 Saturday afternoon, which gave her the entire day to worry about the banquet, which is exactly what she did.

Jenny decided that she needed plenty of time to get ready, so at 3:00 o'clock she ran a hot bath and tried to calm her nerves by soaking in the tub. By 5:00 o'clock, she was dressed in her new outfit and was nervously pacing in her room waiting for her date to arrive.

At exactly 5:30 p.m. the doorbell rang. Jenny was tempted to sprint down the stairs and fling open the front door but decided that she didn't want to appear too anxious. Instead, she waited for someone else to answer the door.

"Jenny, Joe's here," she heard her mother call from the foot of the stairs. "Are you ready?"

Not taking the time to answer, the excited girl took a deep breath and hurried out of her bedroom. Although she wanted to race down the stairs, her new high-heel shoes prompted her to take each step carefully. On her way downstairs, she could hear her mother talking to her date.

"Congratulations on your team winning the championship, Joe. Jenny tells me that the coach promised the entire team a steak dinner if you won. And that's tonight, right?"

"Yes, Ma'am," Joe said as he nervously played with his car keys.

Her question prompted the boy to excitedly share what he knew about the dinner.

"Our football banquet is going to be at school in the gym. They are setting up long tables for the guys on the team and their dates. The cheerleaders are doing some kind of fancy decorations and the coaches are going to be the waiters. It's going to be awesome!"

Jenny couldn't help smiling as she listened.

"It is going to be awesome," she agreed as she walked over to join her mother and Joe. "I know all of the cheerleaders and I know what they've got planned. I think you and Mac and the rest of the team are going to be really surprised."

Jenny was suddenly aware that Joe was staring at her as if he had never seen her before and she knew that her face was turning beet red.

"You two had better get out of here," her mother said with a slight grin as she ushered them to the front door. "You don't want to be late. Have a good time!"

Jenny was still recovering from the excitement of the night before when Cowboy, her big yellow lab decided it was time to wake up. He got up from his place at the foot of her bed, walked over and proceeded to nuzzle her cheek.

"Quit it!" she complained pushing the dog away. "What time is it anyway?" she mumbled turning over to see the red numerals on her digital alarm clock. "It's only 8:30. Go away."

Cowboy was determined that she wake up and pay attention to him and refused to be deterred. Finally, after a few minutes of trying to discourage her new furry friend, she gave up and got out of bed.

Downstairs her parents were finishing a leisurely Sunday morning breakfast when she appeared at the kitchen doorway with the dog by her side.

"Well good morning," her mother said when she saw her daughter. "Did you have a good time last night?" noting Jenny's broad smile.

"It was amazing," she said as she poured a glass of orange juice. "The cheerleaders had the tables decorated like a fancy restaurant. The coaches wore black slacks, white shirts, and black bow ties. They looked like real waiters and they did a great job, too!"

"Was it really a steak dinner like they promised?" her dad asked.

"Absolutely. We had huge steaks, baked potatoes, a salad, and dessert. Just like a real steakhouse only better."

"So what made it better?" her mother asked with a sly grin. "The food or Joe?"

Jenny was still smiling as she slid into her usual place at the table.

"Oh, I don't know," she grinned as she reached for a piece of toast. "Hard to say. The food was great, but he did invite me to the movies next weekend, so I guess I'd have to say, Joe."

Shortly after she had returned to her room, Jenny's cell phone rang.

"Guess what!" she heard the excited male voice say. "Guess what I'm getting for my birthday next weekend? I found the box! Mom and Dad are giving me a metal detector and it's just like Joe's! Do you think he'll ask me to go with him again since I'll have a metal detector, too?"

Jenny caught herself before she groaned.

"I'm sure he will, Louie," she said trying her best to sound enthusiastic. "Next time I talk to him I'll tell him you're getting a metal detector just like his for your birthday."

"Awesome! Thanks! Did you have a good time at the football banquet?"

"Yeah, it was great! He even asked me if I'd like to go out next weekend."

"And you told him no, right?" the boy teased.

"Yeah, something like that," Jenny said with a laugh.

Six months later Jenny's cell phone chimed with an incoming text just as she pulled her car to a stop in front of Louie's house.

Could you and Louie stop by my room after school today? Mr. George.

"I just got a text from Mr. George asking if we could stop by his room after school and I just texted back that we would be there. I wonder what this is all about," Jenny said obviously puzzled.

Both teens hurried to Mr. George's room as soon as the final bell rang. This time they both got to the classroom door at about the same time. Rushing into the room, they found the math instructor calmly sitting behind his desk.

"Thanks for stopping by," the math teacher said as the two cousins instinctively walked to the front row of student desks and sat down.

"I've got some news that I think might interest you. I got a call from Amanda last night. She finished her recovery program and will be coming back here in a few days. I think she's turned the corner; she sounded great. She asked me to help her do one thing when she gets here, which I promised to do. We also wanted to give you two and Mac a chance to join us."

Jenny and Louie looked at each other clearly mystified as to why Mr. George would want Mac to join them.

"Sure," Louie replied. "Count us in. What are we going to do?"

"I don't have the details yet, so all I can tell you is this. Could you meet Amanda and me next Saturday afternoon about 2:00 o'clock at the old shack?"

"At the old shack?" Jenny repeated furrowing her brow. "Seriously? Yes, I'm sure we can. I'll ask Mac to come with us."

Watson George said nothing else as he walked them to the classroom door.

"What do you make of that?" Louie asked as they got into the car.

"Not a clue. We'll have to wait until Saturday. I'll pick you up about 1:30 if you can get off that early."

"I'll be ready, I promise you that."

Saturday morning dawned chilly but clear and bright. Louie, Mac, and Jenny had done their best to guess what Mr. George and Amanda might have planned at the old shack, but nothing seemed to make any sense. At noon, Jenny's cell phone chimed.

Meet us at the old homestead at 2:00 p.m.
and we will all walk to the old shack.

"Listen to this, Mac," Jenny said as she read Mr. George's text. "This is weird! I'll text him back that we will meet him there."

At 1:15 p.m., Mac and Jenny climbed into her car and drove to the Morales home to pick up Louie. They arrived at the turn off with enough time to make the rough drive to the old homestead and park by 2:00 p.m. Mr. George and Amanda were already there.

"Amanda George, I'd like you to meet Mac and Jennifer Joulian and their cousin Louie Morales. They are the teenagers I told you about on the way out here."

"I'm so sorry your hand was injured," she said to Mac. "It's really a good thing that you all look out for one another."

"Come on, let's go!" Watson George interrupted trying to hurry the group along. "We don't want to miss this!"

Jenny was suddenly aware of a loud noise that sounded like a large motor of some kind as the five onlookers walked toward the shack. Then out of the brush at the side of the shack, a huge yellow front-end loader appeared heading straight for the old dilapidated building.

The group watched silently as a dark sedan furously honking its horn pulled through the underbrush behind the giant machine and stopped behind it. A man in a business suit got out of the car, ran through the high weeds toward the machine waving his arms and yelling for the operator to stop. Then he turned his attention to the spectators and strode rapidly toward them. When he reached the group, he paused in front of Watson George.

"I'm Danford Ammon," the man said, holding out his business card. "I'm from the Bureau of Indian Affairs. We received word this morning that this building was scheduled to be demolished today and I'm here to prevent it or any of the surrounding area from being destroyed or damaged."

Amanda George was shocked. "What are you talking about? This shack belongs to me and it's on my land. It should have been torn down years ago. I ordered it to be torn down today because it's dangerous and you don't have any right to stop me," she said challenging the man.

"Oh, but I do," the man informed her. "This structure should have never been built here in the first place, but now that it's here, it can't be torn down or the land disturbed in any way. I just ordered that equipment operator to leave."

"You can't do this!" the woman insisted. "I'll take it to court if I have to, but this old shack is coming down today."

"I'm afraid not. You can go to court if you want to, but I guarantee that you'll lose. This property is not going to be disturbed—not now, not ever."

"What's the problem here?" Mr. George asked the man trying to defuse the situation.

"Unfortunately this woman doesn't know that this place is a sacred spiritual site to the Native Americans in this area and it can't be desecrated any further. That means the structure cannot be torn down by law."

Without another word, the man from the BIA turned and walked back to his car. Shortly thereafter, the giant yellow front-end loader backed away and disappeared.

"I can't believe this!" a distraught Amanda George said shaking her head. "How on earth did the BIA find out that I had scheduled this to be torn down today?"

"Amanda, did you tell anyone this was going to happen today?" Jenny asked trying to solve the mystery.

"No, I didn't tell anyone," she said. Then after a short pause, "Well, actually I did tell one person. I told my friend Lezlee Pomporo that I was going to have the old shack torn down when I visited her at the hospital yesterday and she seemed to be excited about it."

"Lezlee Pomporo?" Watson George and Jenny Joulian exclaimed at the same moment.

Amanda's revelation was so shocking that no one spoke for a moment. Then Louie found his voice.

"Why would she turn you into the BIA?" Louie asked. "Is she an Indian?"

"I really don't know. She's never mentioned to me that she was Native American."

"I'm sure she must be Native American or she wouldn't have known that the old shack was built on sacred ground," the tall teacher explained. "Sacred spiritual places are very important to them."

"So what happens now?" Jenny wanted to know. "If the shack is still here, will runaways and druggies still try to use it?"

"Not if I can help it," Amanda said adamantly. "I'm definitely going to keep an eye on it to keep that from happening. It's also very tightly boarded up, so I'm sure that will be a deterrent as well."

"A sacred spiritual place," Louie repeated quietly. "I'm not sure what that means, but it's got to be important."

Mac was obviously puzzled.

"What does 'spiritual' mean anyway?" Mac asked wrinkling his brow. "Is that like ghosts or something?"

At the mention of ghosts, Louie became animated.

"Wow! I'll bet you're right Mac. Maybe it might mean vampires, too!"

"That's enough, boys," Watson George said interrupting them. "A sacred spiritual site has nothing to do with ghosts or vampires. Just think of it as part of their religion. Come on, let's go and leave this old shack in peace."

As the five walked slowly back to the old homestead where the cars were parked, Louie wasn't ready to leave the subject of ghosts and vampires.

"Mr. George?" he asked as he slowly walked beside his mentor. "Are ghosts and vampires real, or are they just a myth or something?"

The man couldn't help smiling as he answered the boy's question.

"I don't know anything about vampires, Louie, but I'm pretty sure there's a good chance ghosts might be real. In fact, there are all kinds of ghost stories around here. If you're really interested, why don't you kids stop by my room one of these days after school? I'll be happy to tell you some of the scariest ghost stories I know. You can check them out and decide for yourself if they're real or not, that is if you're brave enough.

DR. JORDAN'S SCIENCE NOTES

DUST-BORNE DISEASES
(SEE PAGES 34, 54, 56, 57, 76)

There are many problems that you can get from inhaling dust from dirty environments like the old shack. Mold can cause asthma-like symptoms which, while aggravating and disconcerting, are usually not a major problem. Notice I included that word "usually" because occasionally they can cause very severe problems. Molds are generally fungi (the plural of fungus) and are able to remain alive for long periods of time and the spores can be difficult to kill.

Another fairly common problem from areas where bird droppings have been located is histoplasmosis. It is

Special thanks to Clifford Wlodaver, MD who is an infectious disease specialist in practice in Midwest City, Oklahoma.

another fungus disease. It is probably more commonly encountered in dirt but if there have been birds roosting in the area you are trying to clean up, that is a definite possibility. That does include backyard chickens and if you are cleaning out a chicken coop wearing a mask is a very good idea. Most cases of histoplasmosis do not cause any symptoms and it is not uncommon on a routine chest x-ray done for some other reason to see small areas in the lungs that are result of a previous histoplasmosis infection. It can occasionally cause eye problems known has ocular histoplasmosis syndrome which fortunately can be treated although the vision loss does not come back. The goal is to prevent it from getting worse. It can however, in other cases, cause seizures, and rarely death. Most of the people who get serious problems from histoplasmosis have some other major health problem that keeps their immune system from fighting this fungal infection. As I stated, this fungus grows in the feces of birds.

Also in dust is the Hantavirus which comes from rodent droppings. This is a much more serious problem than histoplasmosis and some reports say that 30% to 40% of people who get sick from the Hantavirus infection will die. It is not contagious between humans, but it is more common in environments where you are exposed to mouse droppings. Sweeping out the garage or the storage shed or in the case of our story, the old shack, are all places where mice or rats have been likely to make a nest. When their urine or feces dries out it can get into the dust and into your lungs. Early on, the symptoms can seem like a bad case of flu with fever, headaches, and muscle aches along with vomiting or diarrhea and cramping pain. It, however, progresses from that to fluid accumulating in the lungs which will then cause shortness of breath. Once shortness of breath starts, the mortality rate starts to climb quickly. It is not something to mess around with. If you are going to be in a place that is at risk, you should wear a mask that is at least an N95 mask. Most importantly, try not to sweep or vacuum these areas which kick dust up in the air. Rather, wet down the floor or whatever you are trying to clean up and clean it with a mop and a disinfectant like Clorox. The filter on the vacuum is not good enough to catch the virus and the air coming out of the back of the vacuum will just spread the virus all over.

THE RULE OF BERRIES

(SEE PAGE 60)

In the wild, there are frequently berries that are encountered. The question is whether they are edible or not. The general rule of berries is that blue or black berries are almost always edible, red berries are sometimes edible, and white berries are almost never edible. This is also true in the grocery store. I cannot remember seeing white berries for sale in the grocery store.

SPIDER BITES

(SEE PAGE 76)

There are thousands of species of spiders but a very small percentage of them are venomous. These spiders are present throughout the world. In the United States and Canada, of the approximately 3500 species of spiders, only 21 are venomous to humans and have the potential to cause any significant problems. All spiders kill their prey by injecting venom but for the most part it does not affect humans. Three of those 21 are not considered serious risks. There are 13 species of recluse spiders and five species of widow spiders, the most famous of which is the black widow. They occur throughout the United States but not every species is in every part. In the area where the story is set in Central Oklahoma, there are three widow species, two black widows and one brown widow and only one recluse species that being the brown recluse.

Identification of these species is problematic. The pictures you always see of the red hourglass sign on the black widow is in fact on the bottom of the black widow, i.e. its stomach side to use the human analogy and so when they are walking along, what you see is the back side and you cannot see that right red hourglass pattern. Obviously, if you see a black spider, you are not going to pick it up to look on its underside. The brown recluse spider is said to have a dark violin shape on the top of the part that is close to the head of the spider known as the cephalothorax. Unfortunately, not all brown recluses are brown. They come in multiple shades and the supposed violin-shaped area is quite small. The widow spiders build very scraggly spider webs and it looks almost like strands of spider webs. They are outdoor spiders are quite shy, and will tend to move away from you. The same cannot be said for the recluse spiders.

Those are indoor spiders and would likely be in some place like the old shack. There is a possibility there is black widow there because it is full of good hiding places but it is more likely that the type of spider that would bite you in that sort of building would be a brown recluse.

Recluse spiders have short fangs and cannot penetrate

human skin unless they are being pressed up against the skin. Most bites therefore occur when you try to put on shoes or a glove or use a towel that has a spider in it. It makes sense therefore when putting on shoes or some clothes that had not been worn in a while to shake them to make sure that there are no spiders. Clothes that have been left in a pile on the floor are a good habitat for these spiders. That is one more reason to pick up and straighten up your clothes if you are in a habit of just throwing them on the floor. I am sure your parents would appreciate it, so now there are two reasons to not leave your clothes lying around on the floor.

About 50% of spider bites do not result in necrosis or any other symptoms. The bite usually is painless when you receive it and then it starts to itch in a few hours. It then becomes painful and the skin necrosis will occur over the course of several days. This can be full-thickness necrosis all the way through the skin into the tissue underneath the skin.

There are no good treatments for the necrosis that results from a brown recluse spider other than general wound care to keep the area clean. Many things had been tried but most of them had not been shown conclusively to work.

Black widow bites tend to be something you feel at the time you get bitten. It typically causes more redness and inflammation and not as much necrosis as the recluse spider bites. They also typically cause more systemic symptoms with abdominal pain, chest pain, headache, nausea, and a fever. It is only the female black widow who actually will bite. She is the one with that hourglass deformity on her ventral side which while it is always shown in the pictures, it is not something you will be able to see. She also is quite a bit bigger than the male.

The treatment for a black widow spider bite is what is known as supportive treatment, which is to treat the symptoms. Applying an ice pack to the area and elevating the limb to decrease swelling are examples of supportive treatment. If there are problems with breathing, swallowing, abdominal or chest pain, you should immediately go to the hospital.

TICK-BORNE DISEASES
(SEE PAGES 76, 130)

A common tick-borne disease in the United States is Lyme disease which was named after the town of Lyme, Connecticut where the first cluster of cases was identified. This requires the tick to be in place for several hours and some reports say 24 hours before you would get infected. This disease is transmitted by deer ticks. The disease itself starts first with a rash which is characterized by its large size of at least 5 cm and a clear area in the middle so it looks like a bull's eye. If untreated, it can cause joint pain. Since this is from inflammation in the joint, it is an itis and so technically it is arthritis. Not all arthritis is caused by old age. There are some forms of arthritis that are caused by infections and Lyme disease is on that list. Lyme disease would be unlikely for anybody to catch in Oklahoma where the story is based.

The most common tick-borne disease in Oklahoma is Rocky Mountain spotted fever. It is called Rocky Mountain spotted fever but in fact it is much more common elsewhere. Rocky Mountain spotted fever is transmitted by dog ticks and so it is much more likely that you will come in contact with these types of ticks rather than those that transmit Lyme disease.

Rocky Mountain spotted fever is caused by a weird species of bacteria known as Rickettsia. It causes inflammation of the blood vessels. That inflammation can cause a very high fever. The fever will usually occur prior to the rash, which starts at the tick bite and travels from there. It goes up the leg if bitten on the foot or ankle, or up the arm if bitten on the hand or lower arm. The rash itself starts with red spots, and while noticeable and aggravating, is not the dangerous part of the disease.

The inflammation causes damage to the blood vessels which then causes them to be blocked and all those microscopic blockages decrease blood flow. This can cause significant problems wherever that occurs. While about 50% of patients who get Rocky Mountain spotted fever do not have any significant problems, those who develop the full-blown disease need to be treated. Fortunately, there is an easy treatment with the antibiotic Doxycycline. Untreated, however, the full-blown disease has had a reported 75% mortality so it is not something to take chances with.

All tick-borne diseases require the tick to be in contact with your skin for hours. That suggests some easy prevention techniques. Mosquito and tick repellant are very helpful if you are going to be in tall grass or in the woods. Treating your dog for ticks is also important. Wearing light-colored clothing so that the dark ticks are easier to spot is helpful. Tucking your pants into your socks so that ticks cannot crawl up your leg is also effective although it may make you look like a nerd. Seventy-five percent of Lyme disease occurs in June, July, and August when only one-third of the ticks are infected. Later fifty percentof the ticks are infected but fewer cases occur. That is probably because people wear shorts in the hot weather and long pants in the cooler fall.

Finally, check yourself for ticks after you have been in those environments. The scariest problem with ticks is tick paralysis. This is a result of neurotoxin injected from the salivary glands into you. For this to occur, the tick has to be on the person at least two days. The paralysis is progressive and the greatest amount of toxin is not produced until the fifth or sixth day of tick attachment. If untreated, theoretically, it can cause respiratory paralysis and death although that is quite rare. It is usually in children that this occurs.

If the tick is removed, then no further toxin is injected and the patient quickly recovers. This is part of the reason why you should check for ticks when you come in from outside. Since ticks like to hide in the hair, if there are no obvious ticks elsewhere, then you should check the scalp because that is usually where the tick will be found. If tick paralysis is occurring and you can't find the tick, shave the head.

PENETRATING INJURIES

(SEE PAGE 92)

In the story, Mac gets a very large splinter into the palm of his hand. This is a penetrating injury and like all of them, the two issues are infection and associated injuries. Gunshot wounds technically are penetrating injuries but are usually considered a separate category. They were discussed in depth in the Mystery of the Old Skull.

Any penetrating injury from an object is considered contaminated unless it is a sterile needle. Whether or not it results in an obvious infection depends upon how contaminated the object was, the amount of foreign material inside, the blood supply to the area of injury and the effectiveness of your own immune system.

The question is should you immediately remove something that has penetrated the body. The instinctive thing to do is to remove it as quickly as possible. In general, if that is easily accomplished, that should be done. The exceptions are rare but there can be a traumatic situation where some sort of a long metal rod penetrates through the body so half of it is out the front and half of it is out the back.

The other exception would be stab wounds or other penetrating injuries in the chest area. There are cases where a blood vessel has been damaged or the heart itself but whatever went in is actually closing off the hole in the blood vessel and when it is removed it, the patient immediately starts to bleed and will then bleed out. (Bleeding out is also discussed in the Mystery of the Old Skull.) Those cases obviously are extreme emergencies. They will sometimes require very dramatic treatment such as opening up somebody's chest in the emergency room and doing internal cardiac massage while the damaged heart muscle is sutured shut. I once listened to a talk by a vascular surgeon who said that 10% of those arriving at LA County Hospital with penetrating injuries to the heart were in fact able to be saved and could walk out of the door of the hospital. Ten percent is not a very high percentage but it is better than 0%.

Except for those dramatic cases, it is generally okay to remove the penetrating nail or splinter or whatever quickly to limit the amount of contamination. If a blood vessel in an arm or leg has been damaged, that is something that can usually be managed with compression. Arteries are surprisingly tough and will get pushed out of the way by relatively blunt objects such as nails or splinters. Obviously, they can be cut by knives. Once the object is out, then the question is how the is wound cleaned.

Today that would usually be done in an emergency room or in an operating room depending on the extent of the contamination. The basic principle is that all dirt or grass or other foreign material should be removed. Tiny splinters in the fingers or feet can be removed and if they cannot be removed, they can frequently be left where they are and the body will usually push them out. In the unusual instance where that does not happen, the body will wall them off and form what is called an inclusion cyst. Anything bigger than a small splinter, however, requires cleansing. If emergency care is not available, then the basic principle is copious irrigation with whatever is available. Sterile water is best but if it is not available then ordinary tap water is generally quite clean and would be the next best choice. The main thing to do is to use a lot of it. There is a saying in surgery that the solution to pollution is dilution which simply means to use a lot of fluid to wash out the contaminants. In the operating room, we will use battery-operated power irrigators and will generally put some antiseptic in the irrigating fluid, usually Betadine solution (make sure it is not Betadine scrub, which has soap in it which can damage the tissues). The scientific literature in the case of total joint replacements suggests that the Betadine in the irrigating solution lowers the infection rate. The data is not as clear for contaminated wounds but that is what we would generally do. The main thing is just to use a lot of fluid. In the operating room, we would also physically remove any visible contaminants and then remove any muscle that does not look red and fresh like raw beef. You do not want to leave behind any gross contamination or any obviously devitalized tissue which will harbor bacteria. One of my friends had a saying that dead tissue is supposed to be contaminated by bacteria and it does not matter if it is a dead zebra in Africa or dead tissue in you.

The other lesson that has been learned repeatedly in the military is that contaminated or possibly contaminated wounds are not closed even after cleaning out the tissue if there was any significant amount of trauma. For blast injuries and gunshot wounds, surgeons will clean them out, leave them open, and then re-operate frequently until they are sure that there is no dead contaminated tissue being left behind. Small low-energy type injuries such as a skin laceration from nail or a sharp metal object will be cleaned and usually closed but when in doubt; it is safer to not suture it closed. That can always be done at a later date.

In the story, the splinter that went deep into Mac's hand is obviously not sterile and will cause significant contamination. That sort of injury would typically be taken to surgery for an irrigation and debridement which means open it up, wash it out, and clean it up. The radial artery and ulnar artery which are the main blood supplies to the hand cross the palm and could be damaged. Since there are two of them, you can get by with just one although that is not ideal and an obviously lacerated artery would be repaired. More important are the nerves which go through the palm down to the fingers. If a nerve is lacerated then wherever it was going would be numb and that can cause significant problems because if you cannot feel your finger, you cannot use it properly. Lacerated nerves would be repaired.

CONCUSSIONS

(SEE PAGES 94, 175)

A concussion is a bruise on the brain. Just like bruises on your arm and leg, they come in all grades of severity. Some bruises are very minor and of no consequence and some are major and will leave lifetime complications. The reason the brain gets bruised is because the brain is slightly smaller than the inside size of the skull. There are several layers around the brain that hold the cerebrospinal fluid, and this provides some cushioning, though not enough. It, however, does not provide enough. When the skull starts or stops moving very suddenly, the brain will hit the inside of the skull and that is what causes the bruising. So for example, if you fall and hit your head on the floor, the skull stops moving, but the brain keeps moving until it hits the inside of the skull and stops. That sudden stop where the brain itself bangs into the skull is what causes the concussion. The other mechanism is when the skull starts moving suddenly such as when a boxer hits his opponent. The bone of the skull moves faster than the brain and bangs into the brain, again causing the bruising, i.e., concussion. Sometimes also, when a brain hits the inside of the skull, it bounces off one side and hits the other side of the skull and can cause a second injury to the brain on the opposite side which is known as countrecoup injury. Whatever the mechanism, the brain hitting the skull or the skull hitting the brain, the result is damage to the brain cells.

The symptoms of the concussion may be as mild as a few-second disorientation or as severe as being unconscious and in a coma and never waking up. In between are all the grades of injury.

The symptoms of the less severe injury usually are being dazed which shows up as the person staring into space, acting like they are confused or out of it. They can also get ringing in their ears which is a common symptom of a mild concussion and gave rise to the term "getting their bell rung." The other symptoms of a concussion include, headache, nausea, vomiting, loss of memory for the event, disorientation as to where they are or what is going on, progressing on to loss of consciousness for varying periods of time.

The assessment of a person who has had his "bell rung" which is a common event on the football sideline is to check his orientation and awareness of what is going on by looking for any signs of being confused or dazed. This would include asking the athlete what team they are playing, what the score is, if he has any ringing in his ears, is he nauseated, does he have any double vision, etc., and then checking his balance, coordination, and neurological function.

The prognosis (outcome) depends on the severity of injury, but a number of things are important to remember. When formal testing to check thinking abilities, such as doing math problems and the like, is assessed, keep in mind that the effect of a concussion can cause difficulties for weeks. This is not something that goes away in a few minutes. That is true even if the athlete looks like they are normal.

A second lesson that has been learned is if while the athlete or patient has any symptoms of the concussion persisting a second injury occurs, that injury is usually much worse. That is why for instance a boxer that is knocked unconscious is not allowed to box for at least three months and new evidence suggests that that is probably too soon.

What has also been recognized is that the effect of minor concussions is cumulative and can cause a permanent loss of thinking ability so that the athlete or patient acts like they have Alzheimer's even though they are very young. They have difficulty with all thinking functions. This is known as chronic traumatic encephalopathy (CTE). In the past, it has been called being punch drunk which was the term applied to boxers who had the chronic traumatic encephalopathy. A recent brain autopsy study on professional football showed the vast majority had some evidence of CTE.

PHYSICAL CONDITIONING, FOOTBALL OR ANY SPORT TRAINING

(SEE PAGE 143)

One of the most basic rules of sports conditioning and training is that the closer your training program mimics the demands of the sport, the more useful it will be. It is therefore helpful to think about what the demands of your particular sport would be. Some sports are very one dimensional such as distance running or swimming, but even with these sports there are training things that need to be considered which we will discuss shortly. You will also need to know what muscles are being used in the particular activity. Running is obviously a leg exercise. In swimming, 90% of the propulsion comes from the arms and therefore a strength conditioning program for swimmers would be different than it would be for runners or sprinters. Swimmers also need strong core muscles. Other sports have a preponderance of demands on one part of the body or the other. Football is mainly a game of legs while wrestling primarily depends upon upper body strength. Obviously, football players also use their arms especially on the defensive side and wrestlers do a lot of pushing with their legs. The demands of other sports are more evenly distributed such as tennis or basketball. In addition to strength or endurance, some sports require balance, quickness, and eye-hand coordination; some sports depend of those skills more than others. I have read the claim that basketball has the highest demands on endurance, strength, quickness, and eye-hand coordination. Athletes in other sports might dispute that claim.

Since training that mimics the sport is critical for whatever sport you are playing, ask yourself what actually is needed and work on that.

In the story, Mac plays football. He is the quarterback and training programs in team sports often need to be position specific. The quarterback would need an arm strengthening program to strengthen the muscles used in throwing where an offensive lineman who is never going to be throwing would not need the same conditioning program. Defensive linemen need to be able to move their feet very quickly to shift positions while pass blocking and they might need some extra training in that area. In general, however, football is a game of legs and 75% of the strength program for football should focus on the legs.

Strength Training

Strength training is critical for many sports. The basic principle of strength training is that it is necessary to overload the muscle a reasonable amount which will cause microscopic tearing of the muscle fibers. The body in the process of healing that tearing will put in extra protein, making the muscle bigger and stronger. The tendons that attach the muscle to bone also will become stronger but that is a much slower process. In a rat study, the muscles grew measurably larger in six weeks but the tendons did not become measurably bigger until six months of an exercise program.

Because we are causing damage and then allowing the body to heal, it is very critical that after a strength training workout, there are two or perhaps three days of rest. If the body does not have time to recover and do the actual rebuilding required, the muscles will become smaller and weaker. This is known as overtraining and occasionally you will hear of an athlete who says, "I am working out harder than I ever did and I am getting weaker." Almost invariably, that is an overtraining issue because the body has not been given enough time to recover after a vigorous workout.

If after exercise you have any pain known as post-exertion muscle soreness, it means you went from microscopic muscle fiber damage to something more severe. Now there is actual inflammation as the body tries to clean up the damaged tissue. That means that the degree of damage is greater than normal and it is an important principle to never work a sore muscle. It may take five or seven days for the soreness to go away completely depending on how badly the muscle was damaged.

Running Training

There are two things that determine how fast you can run. One of them is your leg length. The bigger steps you take, the faster you can run. Carl Lewis is a famous Olympic sprinter who had very long legs and was usually not leading at 40 meters. However, once he got his legs moving, he took such long steps that he would pass everybody and he won a number of gold medals. The present sprint champion, Usain Bolt is also tall and has long legs. That is a genetic gift and many of us are not so blessed.

The second factor that determines running speed then is how fast you move your legs, how fast you can take steps, or what is sometimes called the turnover rate. That is partly genetic and partly we have some control over it. The genetic part depends on the type of muscle fibers. There are fast twitch fibers, which as the name implies, contract very quickly and provides improved jumping ability or sprinting ability but have limited endurance. There are also slow twitch fibers, which are the kind used for lower speed, long-distance activities. How much of each you have is again genetic. That is easy to test by measuring your ability to jump vertically and see how high you can reach. You have read or heard of athletes who will have a 30-inch vertical which really means a 30-inch vertical jumping ability. If you have a high vertical leaping ability, you have been blessed with a large amount of fast twitch fibers in your legs and sports that require sprinting would be ones you are genetically gifted for. If you have a minimal leaping ability, you can still improve your sprint speed but you are obviously more genetically gifted for endurance activities.

The part you can control is how you train your muscles to respond quickly and which muscles you work. Weightlifting typically works on your fast twitch fibers so to improve your sprint speed you need to do some weight work with your legs. Every elite sprinter does that, which is quite obvious when you look at their muscles while they are running. To improve your turnover, there are two sets of muscles that are critical. The first of these will probably surprise you; it is your hamstrings. If you have ever looked at a helicopter, you know that that big blade spins around and goes "wop, wop, wop" and the little blade spins very quickly. If you stand up with your knees straight and try to swing your leg back and forth as fast as you can, then do the same thing with your knee bent, it is much easier for your hip flexor muscles to move the leg if the knee is bent. The faster the hamstrings can shorten your leg by bending your knee, the faster the hip flexors can pull your femur from behind your body to in front of your body. From there, all that has to happen is for your knee has to straighten out and your foot automatically lands on the ground. So the two muscle groups that you need to work on with weight training for sprinting are your hamstrings and your hip flexors. Your goal is to get your leg from behind you to in front of you as quickly as possible. When you see sprinters sprint and they "pull up," they never grab their quadriceps, they always grab their hamstrings because their brain is trying to fire those hamstrings as fast as possible and sometimes the muscles will tear.

Football is a game of short sprints. The farthest the player would ever have to run is 100 yards. In a high school football game, people have measured how much time players are actually running. When they add up all the stops and starts from the beginning of the play until the end of the play, it is only 8 minutes out of the 48-minute football game. The rest of the time they are in the huddle or waiting on the sidelines. Soccer is usually thought to be more of a running sport, but in a 60-minute game, players are only running for 20 minutes. For twenty minutes they are basically standing waiting for the ball to come to them and the other 20 minutes they are jogging to the area where the ball is but not actually sprinting. Therefore, the ideal sprint program for football or soccer would focus on muscle strength in the hamstrings and hip flexors.

The other part of increasing your leg speed is training your brain and nerves to fire the muscles more quickly. An easy way to do that is overspeed training where you take advantage of your protective reflexes and help train your muscles to respond more quickly. Overspeed training can be as simple as running downhill which forces your legs to move faster and faster to keep from falling on your face. Sometimes you will see people tie a long bungee cord around their waists, back up and then it slingshots them forward, which is another way to do the same thing. You either move your legs faster or fall or your face.

Lastly, it has been shown that we can only maintain an endurance pace that is 90% of our sprint pace, so elite distance runners also work on their sprint speed. By increasing that, they can then increase their endurance speed.

DROWNING

(SEE PAGE 161)

Drowning is a tragedy that is usually avoidable. The greatest cause of death in natural disasters most years in the United States is from flash floods. This is much more likely to happen in a desert-like environment such as Arizona or Southern California. It may be a clear sunny day without a cloud in the sky but if 20 miles away it is pouring rain, that water will come rushing down a dry stream bed and if you happen to be walking in it you will likely be swept away and drown. It is never good when hiking to walk on the bottom of stream beds just for that reason. In this day and age with improved weather maps, it is easier to find out if there is any rain somewhere near where you are hiking but it is better to be safe than sorry.

There are sad cases where an infant will fall into a bucket but does not have the strength to get out of it and then drowns. Some buckets in fact have warnings on the side about that exact tragedy. Drowning in swimming pools is usually a result of trying to swim alone and then something happens, the person cannot get out of the pool and ends up drowning.

As discussed in the Mystery of the Old Skull in the section on survival kits, the most critical problem for survival is a loss of oxygen or the ability to breath from any number of causes. Not all drownings are fatal. How much damage the person sustains depends on a number of factors including their age, how long they were without oxygen, and whether they fell into warm or cold water. The brain damage from lack of oxygen is known as an anoxic encephalopathy and it can leave a person permanently comatose or only mildly impaired.

The reason that the water temperature matters is an amazing feature that we have known as the mammalian dive reflex. There have been documented cases of young children trapped under the ice for amazing amounts of time and being entirely normal once they were rescued. This reflex is triggered when cold water hits the face. It slows down the heart. It causes blood vessels in the arms and legs to constrict, forcing blood back into the center of the body where there is more available for the brain.

The treatment for drowning depends on what kind of drowning it is. Not all drowning victims have the lungs full of water. There is a phenomenon known as dry drowning. It occurs when water hits the larynx and causes such a violent spasm of the larynx that it actually squeezes shut and there is no air moving. The result is the same of course, no oxygen causes death.

If you look up dry drowning on the Internet you will find a discussion of dry drowning that it really is near drowning with a delayed response. In this case, the person will appear to be in trouble and may even be unconscious briefly but will then recover and seem to be okay. They will usually be coughing violently because in fact there is some water in the lungs. Sometime later they will be in trouble again from an inflammatory reaction in the lungs which brings more fluid from their body into the lungs which prevents oxygen exchange. They are drowning in their own fluids. This is a real emergency and a delay in treatment can cause death. If you see someone who appears to have had a near drowning they need to be carefully watched. If they don't go to the emergency room at the time of the incident at least they should stay somewhere they can get to one quickly.

The other kind of drowning is what you would expect, wet drowning, where there in fact is water in the lungs.

The treatment for drowning is largely common sense. The lungs need to be emptied and the breathing restarted. Emptying the lungs requires rolling the patient over. In the case of a small child, it may be possible to pick them up by their feet and just drain the water out of their lungs. Then start CPR to get the air moving again. Obviously you should call 911 and get help.

PNEUMOTHORAX (PUNCTURED LUNG)
(SEE PAGE 180)

In the story, when Allison fell off the railroad trestle, she had a fractured rib and a punctured lung. This officially is called a pneumothorax if it is only air between the lung tissue and the lining of the lung called pleura. It could also be called a hemothorax if it is blood that is causing the collapsed lung and it is not uncommon that it is a little bit of both. That would be known as a hemopneumothorax.

Lung tissue is very thin and flimsy which you would expect since you have to bring the blood in close contact with the air so the oxygen can diffuse from the air in your lungs into the blood, and carbon dioxide in the blood can diffuse out into the air in your lungs to get exhaled. The lung tissue is basically plastered up against the lining known as the pleura. A pneumothorax occurs when air gets between the lung tissue and the pleura, allowing the lung to collapse. This can occur in a number of ways. People with chronic obstructive pulmonary disease will sometimes cough violently and rupture one of the alveoli in the lungs. That allows air to leak out and get in the space between the lung tissue and the pleura, causing the lung to collapse. In the story, the broken rib could get pushed inward and rip the pleura which would allow blood to collect between the lung and the pleura causing a hemothorax. If the rib went all the way through the lung tissue, you would get a hemopneumothorax.

This obviously means that one part of the lung, or not uncommonly a whole lung is so collapsed that it is not working. This will cause significant shortness of breath.

The only good treatment for this is a chest tube which is something that puts a suction tube in between the lung and the pleura, which sucks out all the blood and air and allows the lung to re-expand.

Related to a pneumothorax from a broken rib are penetrating injuries to the lungs. This will cause what is known as a sucking chest wound. When the person tries to inhale, air will get sucked into the wound and get in the space between the pleura and the lungs, promoting a pneumothorax. The emergency treatment for this is to cover the hole with an occlusive dressing that is airtight. Saran wrap or something like that would work as would anything else sort of rubbery that would seal the hole. This will not treat the pneumothorax but it will keep it from getting worse.

How We Breathe

There is a common idea that we are able to suck air into our lungs. In fact, that is not the case. What we do is create a vacuum and the atmospheric pressure pushes the air into our lungs. The way we create that vacuum is twofold. One is by tightening the diaphragm. In a relaxed state, the diaphragm is curved. Imagine a curved string and when the ends of the string are pulled, the string straightens out. That is what happens with the diaphragm. When the muscles contract, it straightens out which gets rid of the curve and pulls it lower.

Since the lungs are attached to the pleura which is attached to the diaphragm, the whole lower portion of the lung gets pulled down which then creates the vacuum allowing the air to come in. That is important because when you are vertical, gravity is pulling your liver and all of your abdominal contents down and it makes it easier for the diaphragm to do its job. When you are lying down, all of those things push up on the diaphragm making it work harder.

Because it is harder to work if you are sick and you do not breathe completely, it is easier to get pneumonia. One of the complications of hip fractures for instance is pneumonia and it is one of the reasons why we always try to get the patients' hips fixed quickly so we can get them sitting up or out of the bed standing which helps to improve their lung function and decrease the risk of pneumonia. Pneumonia is just an infection in the lung. It is quite obvious that when you take a deep breath, the diaphragm pushes on your abdomen because you can see the abdomen rising and falling as you breathe.

The second thing that helps create the vacuum is the motion of the ribs. If you imagine a bucket handle sitting next to the bucket and then as you swing the handle around it gets further away from the side of the bucket; the ribs work like that. They angle downward and the muscles between the ribs, when they contract, will twist the ribs slightly pulling them a little farther away, expanding the chest and creating the vacuum. Again, when you take a deep breath, you can see your chest expand. Those muscles are very critical for breathing. Also, although it may seem gross, when you eat barbequed ribs, what you are actually eating is the muscles that the animal used to breathe.

DRUG ABUSE
(SEE PAGE 106, 237-238)

All drugs are chemicals that our body metabolizes one way or another. This includes drugs for hypertension or diabetes or anything else. There are also a great many chemicals in food or plants that have the potential to either help us or harm us. It does not matter if the drug is synthetic or "natural" or "organic." Socrates was killed by eating the root of hemlock which would certainly be considered organic or natural. Arsenic is an element in the periodic table so it too would be a "natural" poison.

When we are discussing drug abuse as we use it in this day and age, we are discussing drugs that are known as psychotropic drugs which mean their action is on the brain and they somehow change our perceptions. The mescaline that comes from the Peyote cactus is natural or organic but it causes hallucinations the same as LSD which is synthetic.

Heroin comes from the sap that comes out of the opium poppy. Its effects have been known for a very long time and in fact the name of that poppy is Papaver somniferum from the Latin word that means to make you sleepy. The powerful painkiller morphine is a derivative of that but it is a liquid. Some clever chemists figured out that if you hydroxylate the morphine it will become heroin which is a powder. The advantage of that of course is that it is much easier to transport. In the past, opium was more commonly used and abused. In fact, there is in the history of China what are known as the Opium Wars which are a significant sore spot between the Chinese and Westerners. There is an entire class of prescription drugs that are known as the opioid painkillers.

In the story, we are not told exactly what kind of drugs were in the old shack but based on the description of the drug paraphernalia and the fact that Lezlee was not moving and unresponsive when Louie first saw her, we can presume that she had overdosed on heroin. Unfortunately, in the United States right now, there is an increasing heroin epidemic. This is brought about by two things. One is the fact that physicians are now much more careful about prescribing prescription opioids. As physicians have become more careful, the patients have trouble getting those drugs and so now they are switching to heroin which they can buy on the street. The second factor in the increasing heroin abuse is the fact the drug is now considerably cheaper than it has been in the past.

TURNING UNCONSCIOUS PATIENTS
(SEE PAGE 237)

In the story, when Allison fell off the railroad trestle landing in the water and knocking herself unconscious, she was given first aid by Louie and Joe. Before they could do that, they had to turn her over so that she was face up. There is a right way and a wrong way to do that and it can make a huge difference. Because the person is unconscious, they cannot tell you if they have feeling in their hands and feet or to guide you as you roll them over. Every unconscious person who needs to be rolled over should be assumed to have a neck injury until proven otherwise. If in fact they do have a neck injury and you just grab them by their shoulders and turn them over, that can twist their neck and can then cause spinal cord injury leaving them a quadriplegic.

The right way to do it is what is called log-rolling the patient. This is not something that you can do with just one person. It is a two-person job. One person holds the head and puts a little bit of pull on it in the line of the spine. The other person rolls the patient over and the critical step is that as the body is turned over, the person holding the head turns the head at the same time so that there is no twisting of the neck. This will prevent any spinal cord injury if there is not one already. There is no way of knowing if an unconscious patient already has a spinal cord injury and log-rolling them will not correct it. Even with a conscious patient who is able to feel their fingers and toes, it is still a good idea to support the head as the patient is rolled face up.

The question then becomes, what do you do with an unconscious person who is face down and you are the only one there? If the patient is breathing and has a normal pulse, that takes some of the urgency out of the situation and you can wait until help arrives. If, however, the person is not breathing, it is obviously critical to get them face up so that you can start CPR. In that case, you have to use one hand to support the head as best you can by putting your hand essentially under their ear. Use your other hand to roll the patient and try and roll their head up on your wrist as you are bringing them to the face up position. It's not ideal but better than letting them die because they were not breathing.

MATH TRICKS
(BONUS)

Squaring any number that ends in 5 is very easy and can be done in your head. The last two numbers of the answer is always 25. To figure out the first part of the answer, you take the first number of the number that you are squaring, add 1 to one of those numbers and multiply them together. That will be the first part of the answer to the squared number. For example 15 x 15, it ends in 25, you make one of the 1s a 2, multiply them together which gives you 2, and the answer is 225. 25 x 25, it ends in 25, you make one of the 2s a 3, and multiply them and that becomes a 6, so the answer to the 25 x 25 is 625. 45 x 45, ends in 25, make one of the 4s a 5, multiply them together and comes out to 20 so the answer is 2025.

That is pretty cool but the rest of this is even cooler. If you take the number above and below the one you are squaring and multiply them together, the answer will be one number less than the squared number ending in 5, so that 24 x 26 is 624 or 44 x 46 would be 2024 and so on.

If you go down by 2, for instance, 23 x 27, that will be four less than the 625 and will be 621 (obviously any problem with 3 multiplied by 7 will have to end in 1). It turns out that when you go down 2, if you square the amount that you are down, that is how much less the answer will be than the original number ending in 25. To again use 25 x 25, if the 23 x 27 is two down, and so the answer would be four less or 621. 22 x 28, that is three down which squared equals 9, so the answer will be 616, four down would be 609, and five down, i.e., 20 x 30 will be 600. Personally, I think it is just as easy to remember that 3 x 7 has to end in 1 and 2 x 8 has to end in 6 and 1 x 9 has to end in a 9.

ABOUT THE AUTHORS

Marilyn Ratzlaff

Marilyn is a professional writer with over 18 years' experience in the publishing industry. She holds a Bachelor of Science degree in Radio/TV from Oklahoma State University and a Master of Arts degree in English with emphasis in Creative Writing from the University of Central Oklahoma.

Christopher Jordan, MD

Dr. Christopher Jordan is an orthopedic surgeon in Midwest City, Oklahoma. He received his medical degree from Loyola University Chicago Stritch School of Medicine and did his orthopedic residency training at Northwestern in Chicago. He was on the part-time clinical teaching faculty at USC for 19 years and moved his practice to Oklahoma in 2001.

Special thanks to Clifford Wlodaver, MD who is an infectious disease specialist in practice in Midwest City, Oklahoma.

ABOUT THE ARTIST

Steve Boaldin

A professional western artist, he is best known for traveling to working cattle ranches and capturing the cowboys and the ranchers on canvas and on film. His "Art of a Cowboy," is featured online, in local and regional galleries, and most recently as a PBS documentary.

www.ingramcontent.com/pod-product-compliance
Lightning Source LLC
Chambersburg PA
CBHW071308200626
46813CB00015B/589

* 9 7 8 0 9 9 7 3 4 3 7 2 4 *